# PERFECT YOU

## ELIZABETH SCOTT

**Simon Pulse**

New York   London   Toronto   Sydney

Also by Elizabeth Scott

*bloom*

〰

SIMON PULSE
An imprint of Simon & Schuster
Children's Publishing Division
1230 Avenue of the Americas, New York, NY 10020
Copyright © 2008 by Elizabeth Spencer
All rights reserved, including the right
of reproduction in whole or in part in any form.
SIMON PULSE and colophon are trademarks
of Simon & Schuster, Inc.
Designed by Tom Daly
The text of this book was set in Berkeley.
Manufactured in the United States of America
First Simon Pulse edition March 2008
6 8 10 9 7
Library of Congress Control Number 2007929324
ISBN-13: 978-1-4169-5355-5
ISBN-10: 1-4169-5355-8

Thanks to Jennifer Klonsky for her infectious enthusiasm and belief in my work; Michael del Rosario for making sure I get everything promptly and not minding when I call and leave one-word ("Yay!") messages; Lucille Rettino, Orly Sigal, Kelly Stocks, and Paul Crichton for all they do; Victor Iannone and Hector Martinez for their amazing kindness; and, of course, Robin Rue, who continually proves why she's the best agent around.

Thanks also go to Katharine Beutner, Diana Fox, Clara Jaeckel, Susie LeBlanc, Donna Randa-Gomez, and Janel Winter for reading drafts and providing encouragement. I am so lucky to know all of you!

As always, thanks to my husband for his love and support.

This book never would have happened without two people: Jessica Brearton and Amy Pascale. Amy, you told me what I didn't want to hear, but yes, you were right, and I'm glad I kept going! Jess, you listened to me worry—and then worry some more— and still cheered me on every step of the way. Thank you both for reminding me what true friendship is.

# one

**Vitamins had ruined my life.**

Not that there was much left to ruin, but still.

I know blaming vitamins for my horrible life sounds strange. After all, vitamins are supposed to keep people healthy. Also, they're inanimate objects. But thanks to them I was stuck in the Jackson Center Mall watching my father run around in a bee costume.

I sank into the chair by our cash register as Dad walked up to two women. They looked around when he started talking, searching for a way out. They wouldn't find one. In our section of the mall, there wasn't much around, which was how we could afford our booth.

I watched the women smile and step away, an almost dance

I'd seen plenty over the few days I'd worked here. After they left, Dad came over to me, grinning, and said, "Kate, I think I made a sale! Those two women I just talked to said they'd tell their husbands about the reformulated B Buzz! tablets. Isn't that great? Now I think I'll fly—get it?—down to the department store and see if I can give samples to people as they walk out."

I handed over the samples—small plastic bags stamped with the Perfect You logo—and watched him lurch down the hallway, off balance because of his costume. As soon as he was gone, I got out my history homework.

This was not how I'd pictured my sophomore year. Not that the first half had been wonderful so far, but this was definitely an all-time low.

Four hours and one history chapter later, the mall closed. Dad and I boxed up the extra vitamins he'd been so sure we'd sell, and then I waited while he ran the box back to the storage space we rented from the mall.

"Pretty good day, right?" he said when he got back. The antennae he was wearing bobbed up and down as he talked. "Todd and I sold one bottle of B Buzz! in the morning, and I bet those two women come back tomorrow. Don't you think they will?"

I shrugged, because it was much easier than telling Dad I was sure they wouldn't. It was also easier than mentioning that we owed eighty bucks for the rented bee costume, and that was far more than the amount we'd taken in from the one bottle of vitamins it supposedly sold.

When we got home, Mom was sitting at the kitchen table

flipping through the checkbook and frowning. She'd been doing that a lot lately.

"How did it go?" she asked, putting the checkbook down.

I left before she could say anything else, heading back to my room. I took a second to stop in the living room and stand in front of the television though, watching as my brother, Todd, lifted himself up off the sofa long enough to say, "Kate, you freak, move. I'm watching something important."

Last week Todd decided he wanted to be an actor. So far all it meant was that he spent even more time than usual watching television. For a college graduate, he sure was on the fast track to nowhere.

"You can't learn to act watching basketball."

"You can't. I can. Now move."

I started singing and kept it up until he lunged at me.

I have a terrible singing voice, and not in the "I'm saying it's terrible to be modest" kind of way. Last week, when I quit the school choir, the director tried to keep the joy off his face but couldn't quite contain it.

I hadn't cared about that, though. I knew my voice sucked, and quitting was a relief. The only reason I'd stayed as long as I had was because of Anna. All fall I'd suffered through practices, hoping she'd come back. That she'd want to be in choir again. That she'd want to be my friend again.

That maybe she'd at least talk to me again.

In the fall, I thought there was no way life could get any worse.

I was wrong. So very, very wrong.

3

Almost a month ago, my father got up and went to work at Corpus Software like always, running late because he'd gotten caught up in his latest video game, forgetting about his job in favor of slaying dragons or driving cars or whatever it was that had him obsessed that week.

But then, when he got to work, his desk was broken. Really broken.

It had split right down the middle, and everything breakable—picture frames with photos of all of us, his coffee mug, and the clay thing my brother made during the two weeks he wanted to be a potter—was broken.

The one thing that hadn't broken was a small brown glass jar of vitamins. Perfect You vitamins. Dad had bought them from a secretary who was moving out of town and spent her last day at work selling them. He'd only bought them to be nice.

But, long story short, Dad decided that the whole desk-breaking thing was a sign he needed to change his life, and that the unbroken vitamin bottle meant something.

So he quit his job to sell Perfect You vitamins.

Yes, really.

He cashed in his retirement fund, bought box after box of vitamins, and then rented a tiny freestanding booth in the mall. He even hired someone to work with him, but Gary quit last week, after Dad told him he couldn't pay him. That's when I had to quit choir and start working with Dad after school.

So now I had no best friend, and I had a job at the mall selling vitamins with my father.

Life had definitely gotten much worse.

# two

I saw Anna as soon as I got to school the next morning. When Dad dropped me off, she was standing on the sidewalk holding hands with her boyfriend, Sam. She waved in my direction as I walked toward her, and for a second I hoped she was waving at me even though I knew she wasn't. I hated how easy it was for her to act like she'd never known me.

I hated how I still hoped she would notice me.

No one ever asked me why Anna and I weren't friends anymore. I guess everyone automatically understood that when Anna became popular, there was no way she had room in her life for me. Even the Jennifers, three girls I'd tried to be friends with in the fall until I realized they drove me crazy, never asked what happened.

Actually, one person had asked about Anna. Will Miller said, "So what's up with you and Anna?" about a week after school started, but I knew he was just being an ass. Will was like that, one of those guys who was cute and knew it. He'd hooked up with at least half the girls in school, and last year, I swear that every week he made out with a different girl before class. I hadn't liked him since the day I met him.

I tried to avoid him, in fact, but this year he was in my first-period class. It was bad enough I had to start every morning with biology, and Will just made things worse.

For instance, when class was over, we ended up walking into the hall at the same time, and he said, "Hey, what did your frog ever do to you? I saw you hack its legs off."

I sighed. Will always seemed to take some sort of perverse delight in talking to me, but lately he'd been even more annoying about it than usual. "I didn't hack its legs off. My scalpel slipped."

"Wow, promise me you aren't going into medicine."

I glared at him and he grinned, unleashing his dimples. I looked away and saw Anna coming down the hall, walking in the middle of a group of girls we used to make fun of. Two of them waved at Will, and one said, "Any chance we can get you to go shirtless for the next pep rally?"

He shrugged, still grinning, and Anna said, "Think about it, will you?" Her gaze moved over me like I wasn't even there.

I walked away, telling myself I didn't care and wishing I could forget her like she'd forgotten me.

Of course Will caught up to me. "What do you think? Should I do it? I know you've secretly been dying to check me out."

"Right, because if I see your scrawny chest I can die a happy woman." Will actually had a very nice chest. The thing was, he knew that too, because he was always willing to run around shirtless with JHS RULES! painted on him during stupid pep rallies.

"I like that a glimpse of my chest could provide you with the equivalent of a rich and full life."

"The key words in my sentence were 'see your chest' and 'die.' The 'happy' part was me trying to be nice."

"So you say." He unleashed the dimples again, smiling like he knew something, and I felt my face heat up because Will really was cute and I wasn't as immune to him as I wanted to be.

I didn't want him to guess that, though, so I forced myself to look at him. Or at least look at his forehead.

"All right, you caught me. I'm secretly obsessed with you and spend all my free time writing about you in my journal. 'Dear Diary, today Will was an ass for the 467th day in a row. He's so dreamy.'"

He laughed and then leaned in toward me, touching the tip of my nose with his index finger. For some reason, I felt a little breathless. "Are you okay?"

"Aside from you, yes."

Okay, here's the truth. I knew exactly why I felt breathless. I had, let's say, "thoughts" about Will, and not the kind of thoughts I wanted to have, where I was able to forget he existed and also meet an amazing guy who really liked me. No, I had thoughts like me and Will somehow getting trapped in a classroom and Will realizing he wanted me, and I . . . well, let's just say I had a vivid imagination and leave it at that.

The problem was, I had these thoughts a lot. A LOT.

Will put a hand on my arm. It was very warm, and I stared at his fingers resting against my skin, cursing my overactive brain and reminding myself to breathe.

"Seriously, I'm sorry about everything with Anna."

That snapped me out of any "thoughts" I might have been thinking, and I shoved his hand off and walked away. I hated the way I felt around him, the way I wanted him. I hated that he was the only person who'd ever asked me what happened when Anna and I stopped being friends.

I hated that he was the only person who'd acted like her forgetting me meant something.

# three

**Dad picked me up when school was over, leaving**
Todd "in charge" at the mall. We went home, so I could change and
pack myself some dinner, and he sat on the sofa and played the
video game he and Todd had bought and started a few days ago.

I thought it was weird and pathetic that Dad sometimes
acted like he was Todd's age or worse, my age, but Mom didn't
seem to care and always thought it was funny when he used to
call in sick to stay home and finish whatever game he was playing. She said Dad was young at heart, and that he reminded her
it was important to have fun.

I would have settled for his kind of fun being less about
quitting his job to sell infomercial vitamins, but then I hadn't gotten a say in any of that.

"You want me to pack you something to eat?" I asked him.

He shook his head. "I'll eat when we get home so I can catch up with your mother. She said she'll make pancakes." He grinned at me. "You and me can split a stack. Get it?"

"Funny. And I can't. Homework." I smeared peanut butter on a piece of bread and looked in the fridge for jelly.

"You almost ready to go?"

"Almost." All I could find was orange marmalade. Ick. I finished making my sandwich anyway. With all my homework, plus the fact that I had first lunch block at school, which meant eating before eleven each morning, I needed to eat dinner before I got home from work.

"You look a little stressed," Dad said when we got to the mall. "You want to close up early tonight and go the movies? I want to see the one about the guy who moves into the cursed house."

"I really do have a lot of homework. Besides, Mom's making pancakes, remember?"

"Oh, right, I forgot." He looked disappointed, but then he spotted Todd talking to two girls and darted off in the direction of our booth, waving his arms to try and signal something. I slowed down and hoped no one had seen me come in with him. Sometimes being around Dad was like being with a little kid.

Todd left about ten seconds after I got to the booth, as usual, and when the mall finally closed, the register had twenty dollars less than it had the night before. ("Todd and I forgot to eat breakfast before we came in, so we had to get food and stuff," was Dad's explanation.)

We also hadn't sold a thing.

"Hey, maybe we should take some samples down to Sports Shack and catch people leaving," Dad said. "It's a potential customer base with a built-in interest in staying healthy, plus they always let people shop late."

"Homework," I reminded him again.

"Just for a few minutes? You can even pull the car around while I do it. Okay?"

A chance to drive wasn't something I would pass up, and Dad knew it. I'd gotten my license when I turned sixteen, but Mom refused to let me drive unless she or Dad were in the car until I was seventeen because Todd had driven our car into the garage door two weeks after he'd gotten his license.

And because I'd failed my driving test the first time I took it. But driving over all those cones could have happened to anyone, really.

I went and got the car, then drove over to the parking lot by Sports Shack. Dad was standing by the exit to the parking lot, trying to talk to everyone who came out. I drove around the mall twice, enjoying the feel of being in the car by myself, and when I got back, Dad was talking to an older guy in a Sports Shack uniform, holding his hands out like he did whenever he was sorry about something, and all the employees were standing by the huge floor-to-ceiling windows, watching.

Great. As if the bee costume wasn't enough of an embarrassment. I drove to an unlit portion of the parking lot and waited, hoping no one could see the car. Or me.

"Wow, was that guy uptight," Dad said when he finally got to the car. "I explained that I worked in the mall too, but he didn't care.

11

Hey, how come you parked way out here? And how come you're sitting all hunched over? Are you sick?"

"Just tired," I said, and was careful to keep my head down as we drove away.

The house smelled like pancakes when we got home, and Mom was on the phone with Grandma. I could tell because she kept rubbing her fingers down the space between her eyebrows like she had a headache.

"No, things are fine," she said, and waved at me, then blew Dad a kiss. "Look, can I call you tomorrow? Great. No, really, please forget what I said before. We'll get by."

She hung up and blew out a frustrated breath. "I think I might have burned some of the pancakes. Sorry." She looked at Dad. "You know how my mother is."

Dad went over and gave her a big hug, lifting her up off the ground. She laughed, and on that almost happy note, I left before she could ask him how sales were. Or before she could really start talking about Grandma.

# four

**Todd took me to school in the morning because**
Dad had spent all night working on a Perfect You project and
wanted to catch a few hours of sleep before the mall opened.

"Project?" I said. "What kind of project?"

"I don't know, Kate," Todd said, frowning at the dashboard
and tapping the gas gauge with one finger. "I was kind of asleep
when he told me. It's inhuman to be up this early, you know."

"You think? I only have to do it five days a week."

"Yeah, but you're in high school. I'm not, and I didn't sign
up to be your chauffeur. I mean, it's bad enough that now I
have to get up before ten so I can be at the stupid mall when
it opens."

"Oh, poor freeloading baby who has to get up and work for

a few hours. Maybe if you didn't stay up all night talking on the phone you'd be more rested."

"You want to walk to school?"

"Please. Mom would kill you."

Todd grunted, because we both knew I was right, and then slammed on the brakes as the light up ahead turned red. While we waited for it to change, he ran his fingers through his hair, grinning when he noticed a girl in the car next to us watching him.

Aside from having the same hair color, a dark reddish-blond, Todd and I don't look very much alike. This is because I'm average-looking and he's so good-looking that girls in cars next to us at traffic lights see him and give him their phone numbers. He gets more calls in a day (and at night) than I get . . . well, ever.

When we stopped at the next light, the girl in the car next to us asked Todd if he wanted to get coffee.

"I don't have a lot of time later today, but how about now, before work?" she said.

I snorted, thinking about Todd's definition of work.

Todd elbowed me and said, "I'd love to." Then he drove to school like he was in a race.

"Great, now I'm here early," I said as he dropped me off. "What am I supposed to do before first period starts?"

"I don't care what you do as long as you get out of the car."

"You suck."

"I'll be sure to think about that when I'm drinking coffee with . . . um . . ."

"Sarah."

"I knew that. Anyway, I'll be sure to worry about it while I'm with her and you're stuck in school."

I slammed the car door as hard as I could when I got out, but he didn't even notice. Figured.

I went to the library and finished the English reading I hadn't done last night, and then went to first period.

Jennifer M., who sat across from me, grabbed my arm as soon as I sat down. "I'm freaking out!"

I sighed. This was one of the many reasons I had stopped hanging out with the Jennifers. They were all constantly freaking out about something. "What's wrong?"

"The PSATs. I'm taking them again, I think, but what if I do worse than last time?"

"You'll do fine," I said, and Jennifer T. leaned toward us and said, "See, I told you."

That made the third Jennifer, Jennifer S., look nervous. Jennifer M. was Jennifer S.'s best friend, or at least she had been in the fall. Now she was spending a lot of time with Jennifer T.

I looked down at my desk and wondered if I could get away with putting my head down and taking a nap.

"What about you, Will?" Jennifer M. said, letting go of my arm in order to grab his. He sat across from her too, one desk in front of me. "Oh, wait, you did really good, didn't you?"

"Yeah, but I was just trying to keep up with certain people." Will looked back at me and grinned.

"Kate, I thought you said you just did okay," Jennifer M. said.

"I did," I said through clenched teeth. "Will's trying to be funny. Laugh so he'll shut up."

Jennifer M. said, "Kate, you're funny," in the same tone of voice she always used whenever she didn't understand why I'd said something, and then started talking to Jennifer T. as Jennifer S. watched, still looking nervous.

Will looked at them for a second and then turned back around again, whispering, "Kate, don't be like that. You know I only did so well because I yearn—see, SAT word—to follow you to college and steal your heart."

"Uh-huh. Too bad for you I don't plan on attending clown college."

He grinned. "Only you would ignore the incredibly sweet thing I just said."

"Only you would describe one of your asinine comments as incredibly sweet."

"Asinine? Now there's an SAT word. In fact—"

"Mr. Miller, do you mind?" Our teacher, Mr. Clark, had come in, reeking of cigarettes like always.

"Nope," Will said, and then shook his head in apology when Mr. Clark glared at him.

"Don't worry," I whispered as Will turned back around. "You can always look up what asinine means in the dictionary. It'll be easy to find because your picture will be next to the definition." And then I grinned, because I'd gotten the last word in, and that hadn't happened in our last three conversations.

I knew it was pathetic to be happy about something like that. And to actually keep track of who got the last word in. But hey, I had to take what I could get.

Especially because when I went to lunch, I saw Anna.

Since lunch periods at Jackson High are only twenty minutes long, I always get in line for soup or salad. It's the busiest line, and the slowest, and by the time I get my cup of lukewarm soup and pay for it, I have just enough time to drink it before I go to class. Today the line moved a little faster than usual, though, and by the time I paid there was enough time to grab a seat and eat my soup before the bell rang.

That's when I saw her. Anna was a cheerleader now, even though she'd always made fun of them before, and cheerleaders ate during first lunch block when there was a basketball game. I'd seen her a few times before, always surrounded by her new friends, always sitting right next to Diane.

Today, Anna was sitting with Tara.

Tara was a senior, and she was so popular that she could do anything. She ate when she wanted, went to classes when she wanted, and when she got a bad dye job and her hair turned orange, a bunch of girls dyed their hair orange too. If an actual world leader had that much power, we'd all be living under one big dictatorship. Scary thought.

I watched Anna laugh, grinning the way she did when she was happy but embarrassed. The last time she'd smiled at me like that was last year, when she was complaining about her eleventh birthday party and I'd reminded her it was ancient history and that she'd just gotten a solo in choir.

Last year, Anna would have been sitting with me, and we'd have been talking about whoever was in her seat now.

The bell rang, and I chugged my soup. It was lukewarm and salty, and as I threw the cup away I saw Tara and Anna get up.

They hugged, and I saw Anna smile for real, radiant and wide, as Diane caught her eye. Anna used to smile like that at me.

Anna had treated me like crap and I knew it, but I couldn't bring myself to hate her. In fact, looking at Diane, I wished I were her so much I felt sick with it.

I walked by them both on my way out of the cafeteria. Diane didn't even see me, but Anna did. She saw me, and something flashed across her eyes, something that looked like sadness. I stopped, hoping she'd smile at me, but she turned away.

Just like she had the day I finally realized we weren't friends anymore.

# five

**I can't remember a time when I didn't know Anna.**
One of my first memories is building a tower of blocks with her
in day care, holding one and waiting for her to tell me where to
put it.

We did everything together. We both learned to swim in the
same class at the community center. We both got bikes for our
fifth birthdays, and learned to ride wobbling around the cul-de-
sac at the end of her street. We both got our ears pierced when we
were in fifth grade. We even bought our first bras together,
although, to be totally honest, I didn't really need one at the time.

Up until the middle of ninth grade, Anna was about eighty
pounds overweight, had braces, and wore glasses, the kind with
heavy, thick lenses. People made fun of her but she never cared,

would just look at me and roll her eyes. Anna always walked and talked and acted like she knew exactly who she was and no one could tell her otherwise. She was as brave as I wanted to be.

Then, last March, Sam bumped into Anna in the hallway after second period and said, "Watch it, wide load."

Anna had liked Sam since middle school, and her crush only got worse during our first year of high school. She was crazy about him, and seeing her face after he said that made me want to cry.

She did cry, although not until she'd made it to the girls' room. I followed her and said everything would be okay as I handed her paper towels to use as tissues.

She made a face at me and said, "How can you say that?"

"Because it will be," I said.

And it was, because Sam came up to her at the end of the day and apologized for yelling.

"See?" I said after he'd left. "I told you he didn't mean it. You wanna come over for dinner after choir practice?"

She tugged the bottom of her shirt down over her stomach. "I'm fat, aren't I?"

"Anna!"

"Kate, I am."

"Come on, you look fine."

"Liar," she said, her voice curiously flat, and then the choir director came out and told us practice was starting and could we please hurry up and come inside?

At lunch the next day, Anna wanted to buy salad, not pizza.

"Why?" I said. "I mean, I can understand skipping sausage

pizza, with those weird seed things in the meat. But this is pepperoni!"

"I want to eat better."

"I just said it isn't sausage."

She gave me a look.

"Okay, fine, we'll get salad. But Anna . . . is this because of yesterday? Because Sam said he was sorry."

"He said he was sorry he yelled. He didn't say he didn't mean what he said, and I—I'm fat. I'm fat and wear glasses and I'm tired of it. I'm sick of being the ugly girl. I want to be pretty."

"But I know Sam didn't mean it," I said, stunned by how angry she'd sounded. Anna always seemed so sure of herself, so proud of who she was.

"Of course he did," she said, and stared at me so hard I had to look away.

For the rest of the school year we ate salads for lunch. Anna lost about twenty pounds. We had a lot of fun shopping for new jeans for her to wear, and on the last day of school, I asked her if she wanted to join the community center and use the pool.

"I can't," she said.

"Come on, I hear Sam is lifeguarding."

"I can't, okay? I have to go to my stupid aunt's house in stupid Maine."

"What?"

"I know. What am I going to do in Maine all summer? I'll probably freeze to death my first day there."

"All summer?"

She nodded.

"When are you leaving?"

She looked at the floor. "Don't be mad, Kate, but . . . the day after tomorrow."

"The day after tomorrow?"

"I wanted to tell you before, but I was afraid you'd hate me because I'm going to be gone so long."

"Hate you?" I said, even though I sort of did because now I was going to be stuck in Jackson without her. "I'm going to miss you."

She knew what I was thinking because she said, "I'll call all the time and e-mail every day. You'll get sick of hearing from me, I swear."

I went with her and her mom to the airport, which was kind of scary because her mom cried a lot, and Anna called me from Maine that night. She said it was cold but pretty. "Everything is really, really green," she said.

It was the only time she called. I called her once, about a week after she did, but all I had to talk about was Todd and how annoying he was, plus her aunt had to use the phone. And then Mom freaked out when she got the bill.

I e-mailed her every day for a while but, again, I didn't have much to talk about, and whenever she wrote back she was always tired from doing stuff with her aunt and was never sure when she was coming home. I wondered why we didn't talk more, but Anna said she had to beg to use the computer, and her phone situation was like mine. It seemed like we were both having pretty boring summers, and I figured things would get back to normal as soon as she got home.

Then my mom saw her mom at the supermarket a couple of

days before school started, and I found out Anna had come home. I called her right away.

"You didn't tell me you were back! How come you didn't call me when you got home?"

"Kate, I've been home for two days and I've slept the whole time. My aunt made me get up at six every morning. How crazy is that?"

We made plans to meet at her house that night. I didn't recognize her when she opened the door. She was tan, and her hair was longer and dyed the color of corn silk, so pale it was almost white. Her glasses were gone, and her braces had come off. She also weighed about seventy pounds less than when she'd left.

"Wow, you look different," I said. She did. She looked like a model.

I was a little jealous. Okay, a lot jealous.

"I know," she said, and when she grinned at me I didn't even recognize her smile. It looked brighter and shinier somehow, different.

I should have guessed what was coming. Girls who looked like Anna didn't hang out with girls who looked like me. It's one of those laws of high school no one talks about but everyone knows. But she was my best friend, and she said she'd missed me, and when she talked about Maine she sounded just like she always had. ("So cold! But the ocean was gorgeous, Kate. I even went swimming a couple of times. Almost died from the cold, but I did it!")

That was the last time we talked. She didn't call me the night before school started to discuss what we should wear, and when I got to school she wasn't waiting outside for me like she always did. She wasn't in any of my classes or my lunch block, and whenever I saw her in the hall she was always walking away from me.

It was weird, and by the time she didn't show up for choir practice I knew something was wrong. I called her that night and her mother said she couldn't come to the phone.

"Is she sick?" I asked, and Anna's mother just said, "I'll tell her you called."

When Anna didn't talk to me again the next day, and didn't even seem to notice me when I waved at her, I figured she was mad at me. She didn't get mad often, but when she did she got really mad. I knew I should have called her more over the summer. I should have e-mailed more. I should have told her she looked amazing instead of being jealous and stupid and only saying she looked "different." I should have called her the night before school started instead of waiting for her to call me.

I knew I needed to say I was sorry and make things right, so the next day I went to the bathroom by the cafeteria before last period. Anna always went in there to check her hair and makeup.

She was there when I walked in, standing in front of the mirror like always, and I grinned at her reflection. "Hey."

Next to Anna, Diane Mullins was putting on lip gloss. She glanced at me in the mirror like I was some sort of weird bug and then turned toward Anna, dismissing me. "What do you think? Is this too red?"

Anna didn't say anything to me. She just looked at me in the mirror like she'd never seen me before, and then she turned to Diane and said, "It's perfect."

That's when I finally understood what was going on. Anna hadn't stopped talking to me because she was mad at me. Anna had stopped talking to me because I was still me and she'd become someone else. She'd become somebody.

She wasn't my best friend anymore. She wasn't even my friend.

But I wanted her to be.

I wanted our friendship back. I wanted it enough to keep hoping even though I hated myself for it. I hated how she made me wish we could go back to the way things were.

I hated how I knew, deep down, that I would do anything to be her friend again.

# six

**When school ended, I walked out to Dad's car, but** Dad wasn't in it.

"Todd, what are you doing here?"

"Hi to you too," he said, and motioned for me to get in. I did.

"Where's Dad?"

"At the mall. I said I'd pick you up."

"Why?"

Todd was silent for a second, acting like he was concentrating on pulling out of the parking lot. "Just felt like it."

"Sure you did. What are you avoiding?"

"Handing out flyers inviting people to the house for a Perfect You party tonight."

"That's not funny, Todd."

He glanced over at me, and then back at the road. "I'm not kidding. Dad's so-called project is a Perfect You house party. He stayed up last night reading about a woman who had one and made a ton of money."

"And so now he's inviting random people over to the house?"

"Oh no, it's better than that. He's called everyone he used to work with and then decided hey, why not invite total strangers, too? It seems a little—"

"Weird? Stupid? Insane?"

"All of them, which is why I'm going to see my friend Andy for a few days. You'll have to work by yourself tonight, but I'll leave a note for Mom to come pick you up, okay?" He dug around in the front pocket of his jeans, and the car swung into the other lane for a second.

"Todd!"

"Kate!" he replied, mocking me, and tossed a ten-dollar bill into my lap. "That's for food. I know I'm supposed to take you home so you can do whatever it is you do before work, but I want to get to Andy's place."

"You're kidding, right?"

He sighed. "Kate, I'm sorry you can't leave too, all right? Just go get something to eat and then show up at your regular time. Dad had me make flyers for the party, but I didn't make as many as he wanted, and when you get there he'll probably have handed them all out. So at least you won't have to worry about that." He gave me one of his aren't-I-great smiles, and pulled into the mall parking lot.

"That's really nice of you," I said tightly, getting out of the car. I wished I could run away like Todd.

"Hey," he said, and I turned back toward him.

"What?"

"Tell Dad I'm going to Andy's, will you? I forgot to mention it to him before."

I glared at him, because we both knew he hadn't forgotten. He just hadn't wanted to deal with Dad when he got upset. Neither of us did.

And sure enough, when I got to the booth after hanging around the food court for a while, the first thing Dad said was, "Where's Todd?"

I took a deep breath. "He's gone to see Andy."

"When? Wait, now?"

I nodded.

"Did he at least clean up the house while you were getting ready for work like he said he would?"

Todd hadn't even mentioned that request to me. Not that it was a surprise.

"He didn't—" I started to say, but Dad was looking at me with the big fake grin he wore when he was upset, so I just said, "He didn't do any cleaning when I was with him."

"Oh. Well, that's . . ." Dad sighed, still smiling his big fake smile. Then it got brighter, became a little more real. "Hey, I have an idea. What if I drive you home real fast right now? Then you can clean and have your mother bring you back to work until closing when she gets home."

Oh no. No no no. Dad was not sticking me with getting the house ready for his stupid party. I grabbed some of the sample bags he'd put out for today, Perfect You's Awesome Kids!

Chocolate Chew Vitamins, and walked off, heading toward the main mall hallway.

Dad didn't call after me or anything, of course. He would do anything to avoid an argument, just smiled that stupid fake smile whenever he was upset and acted like everything was fine until it was. When Mom got upset over his plan to quit his job for Perfect You, Dad had fake smiled for days until she'd given in.

Still, I couldn't believe he wanted me to go home and clean the house. It was his party, not mine, just like the whole Perfect You thing was supposed to be his dream job and not my forced after-school employment.

But then, avoiding things he didn't want to do was Dad's specialty. Whenever he didn't like something or didn't want to do it, he just wouldn't do it. And if you got upset, he'd just smile and say he was sorry and still not do it.

I sighed, totally frustrated, and turned the corner into the main part of the mall. As I did, I felt something slam into my legs. I looked down and saw it was a little kid. He was staring up at me, mouth open, clearly ready to scream or cry or both.

Then he saw the Chocolate Chews in my hand and yelled, "Is that candy? I want some!"

"Derek, please wait a moment," a woman said, walking quickly toward me, weighed down by shopping bags. I waited for her to say something else to the kid (like "Please don't yell") but instead she noticed me—and the Chocolate Chews—and her eyes brightened when I said, "Would you like a free sample?"

"Yes," she said, as Derek tried to grab one of the bags out of my hand, yelling his head off the whole time. "But only one piece, though. I don't like Derek to have too much candy."

"It's actually kids' vitamins."

"Oh, then it's healthy," the woman said, beaming. "Can he have the whole bag?"

"Sure, but there's only one vitamin in it," I said, a little taken aback by her and Derek, but opened the bag and gave the chew to Derek before passing it on to her.

Derek, I was pleased to note, had stopped yelling and was now grinning at me around a mouthful of Perfect You vitamin. It was probably the closest thing to a miracle I'd ever seen.

Derek's mom clearly thought so too because she said, "What's in these?" just as Will, of all people, came in through one of the mall corridor doors and Derek finished chewing, swallowed, and motioned for me to lean toward him.

Distracted by the sight of Will, I did, and Derek yelled, "More!" spraying Chocolate Chew on my face.

"Hey, Kate, what's up?" Will said. He was wearing a Sports Shack uniform and a name tag that said MY NAME IS TRAINEE.

Great. Just great. Of course I would see Will now. At least he didn't know where I worked.

I stood up and wiped my face off with the back of one hand, glaring at him.

"Go away," I muttered, as Derek screamed, "I WANT MORE CANDY NOW!"

"Is your store nearby?" Derek's mom said, as if her demon spawn hadn't just screamed at the top of his lungs. "Oh, wait. Is this bag right? Are these made by Perfect You? Don't they run those horrible infomercials?"

"I've never seen one," I said, which was technically true, because I left the room whenever Dad started watching one.

"Wait, you work at the Perfect You store?" Will said, and from the look on his face I could tell he'd already heard all about the vitamin guy who dressed up like a bee. And who'd hung around Sports Shack trying to hand out free samples until the manager made him leave.

"I do," I said, hoping I didn't sound as humiliated as I felt, and gave him a go-away-and-drop-dead look just as Derek yelled, "MORE!" one last time and then started to cry.

"Your mommy can buy you lots more if she wants," I told him. I knew it was a completely manipulative thing to say, but we needed the sale and besides, the kid had spit on me.

"Mommy," Derek said, voice quivering, and his mother said, "All right, we'll get some," shooting me a look as she motioned for me to start walking.

As I led them back to the booth, watching out for both Derek and his mother's shopping bags, Will said, "Later, Kate," and I heard laughter in his voice. I didn't know if it was at me or for the situation he'd seen me stuck in.

Knowing him, it was probably both. I looked back over my shoulder and glared at him again. He waved.

Jerk.

"I'm sorry if we chased that boy off," Derek's mother said as I bagged the box of chews she'd bought. "He was yummy looking."

Ewww. No one needed to hear someone that old say something like that, especially when my father was around and could say things like, "Who's yummy looking?"

31

"No one," I said, before he or anyone else could say another word. "I just ran into someone I know from school." I handed Derek's mom her Perfect You bag and credit card slip and tried not to glare as I said, "Have a nice day."

"So, this yummy guy," Dad said as soon as she'd left. "Do I know him? Is he an athlete?"

"Dad, please don't say yummy like that. And who cares if he plays sports?"

"Perfect You says sponsoring a local athlete is a great way to build buzz."

Unbelievable. Not that I wanted Dad to be interested in my nonexistent love life or anything, but did everything have to be about Perfect You? "Yes, Dad, he's an athlete. He runs triathlons and climbs mountains and is a professional ice carver. I'm sure he'd love to do it all covered with Perfect You ads."

He gave me a bright, fake smile and didn't say anything. Why couldn't he just get mad like a normal person? Why? I forced myself to take a deep breath. "Look, here's what happened. I ran into someone I go to school with and he found out I work here and—well, I'm going to get so much crap at school tomorrow I should just quit now."

"Why would anyone care that you work here?"

"Because I work selling overpriced vitamins with a guy who dresses up in insane costumes. Oh, and the guy in question happens to be my father. Can you see where that might cause problems, Dad?"

He turned away from me for a second, fiddling with a display he'd set up. When he looked back, he was still smiling his big fake grin, and when he spoke it was clear he was pretending our conversation hadn't happened. "I'm going to head home and get ready for the party now. I'll have Mom pick you up when the mall closes."

"Dad—"

He kissed my cheek and walked off before I could say anything else.

Unlike him, I didn't have the option of walking away, and had to stay in the booth all night. That made me mad, but then I thought about how upset Dad had been and felt sort of guilty, which then made me mad again because I hadn't done anything wrong. He was the one who'd wanted me to do everything for his stupid party.

And, on top of everything else, I had to worry about what Will was going to tell people.

I was thoroughly depressed by closing, but then Mom came in as I was shutting down the register.

"Hey," I said, glad to see her.

"Hi, Kate." She looked exhausted, and my stomach knotted.

"Is Dad still having his party?"

"No." Her voice was brittle, unhappy. This couldn't be good. "What happened?"

She told me the whole story on the way home. Twelve people showed up for the party. Ten of them were from Dad's old job, and the last two were a couple he'd talked to at the mall. The couple had shown up late and started trying to interest people in time-shares. Mom had to threaten to call the police before they would leave.

"The good news is, your father did sell a few things after they'd gone," she said, but she sure didn't sound like she thought it was good news.

"Why don't you tell him to quit this Perfect You crap and get a real job again?"

She sighed. "Kate, this is your dad's dream."

"So?"

"So it means something to him."

"Well then, I'm never going to school again. Why? Because it's my dream."

"Kate Louise Brown, don't you dare talk to me like that." Unlike Dad, Mom had no problem getting mad and yelling. "You're sixteen, and you have no idea what it's like to be an adult and have to deal with adult things."

Right. I just had to deal with a father who'd rather buy vitamins and play video games than do anything else. I just had to deal with having my best friend act like I didn't exist. I just had to deal with having my whole life fall apart.

And to top it all off, tomorrow I was going to have to deal with Will—and probably everyone else—knowing I worked for the crazy vitamin guy.

I would have liked to see an adult deal with all my problems.

# seven

**My world ended at 7:23 a.m., when I realized**
that something a lot worse than Will had happened.

I'd gotten to school, and as I walked inside I heard
snatches of conversations, stuff like "Perfect You? Isn't that,
like, sold in infomercials?" and "No, she sells it too. Her whole
family does."

Will, you jackass, I thought in silent fury and then, just
before I got to my locker, I heard someone say, "Diane Mullins
said her mom said it was the most pathetic thing she'd ever seen.
I mean, the guy invited people he used to work with to his house,
tried to sell them stuff, and then had totally random people show
up and try to sell stuff too?"

Yes, that's right. Diane Mullins, Anna's new best friend,

found out about my dad and his vitamins. And his so-called party. And then told people.

I don't mean to make it sound like I was all people were talking about. After all, I was still me, and news that a nobody sophomore had a father who sold crap infomercial vitamins was funny, but not huge gossip. In fact, I was pretty sure the only reason people were talking about it as much as they were was because it sort of involved Diane, who was way more popular than me.

Not that it didn't still suck, though.

I made it through first period by staring at my desk the whole time, but the second the bell rang, Jennifer T. cornered me.

"Is it true Diane Mullins was at your house last night?" she asked.

"What? No." I edged past her into the hall, but of course she followed me.

"Oh. Because I heard her and her mom came to a party your dad threw because he lost his job, only it wasn't a party and he tried to sell infomercial vitamins."

"He quit his job, Jennifer."

Her eyes widened. "So he's really selling infomercial vitamins? And at your house?"

"Yes. We also have a brothel in our garage. Are you looking for a job?"

"God, I was just asking. You don't have to be a bitch about it."

"Right, stupid me," I said, and walked off.

Then things got worse, because I saw Anna. She was walking with Diane, and when Diane saw me she laughed, and Anna . . . Anna laughed too.

She laughed at me.

I should have been furious, and part of me was—part of me actually hated her then—but after she walked by I just stood there, trying not to cry.

I didn't, even though I wanted to, and somehow made it through my next few classes. I hid out in the guidance office looking at college brochures during lunch, though, wanting a break from acting like I was okay.

Naturally, this meant that when the bell rang and I went out into the hallway, Will was there.

"There you are," he said, like he'd been looking for me. "Heard you ran off crying into the bathroom."

I gritted my teeth. "Well, now that you're here, I might."

He grinned. "I knew you were too tough to hide in the bathroom, much less cry."

"Right."

His smile faded. "What? I was just saying—"

"Look, what do you want? Yes, I work for the vitamin nut at the mall. Yes, as I'm sure you've already figured out, he also happens to be my father. Yes, apparently Diane's mother was at my house and I'm sure she suffered terribly, but you know what? I just don't feel that sorry for her right now."

"I figured your heart wouldn't be breaking over that," he said. "And I think it takes a certain amount of courage to wear a bee costume."

"Wow, thanks. Now I feel loads better. Don't you have a girl you should find and feel up before class starts or something?"

"Monica and I stopped hanging out last week. I'll try not to take it personally that you didn't notice."

"Who can keep track with you?"

"Nice to know you're trying," he said, grinning again, and then headed off down the hall.

# eight

**On Saturday night, Dad told me he needed me to** work at the mall on Sunday.

"Why?" I said. "I'm not supposed to work weekends, remember?"

I was sitting in the living room, trying to figure out what was going on with Mom, who was sitting at the kitchen table, staring off into space. She'd been on and off the phone all day, always taking the calls in her bedroom, and she'd been upset, like she was trying to solve a problem she already knew the answer to, only the answer wasn't one she liked.

"It's important," Dad said, and Mom looked at me and Dad then, staring at him for a moment before abruptly getting up and saying, "I'm going to bed."

"Kate, can you hold on for one sec?" Dad said.

"Sure." I watched him head after her, and when he came back a few minutes later, he was smiling his big fake smile again.

"So, can you work tomorrow?"

"Is Mom okay?"

"She's fine, just tired," he said, and his false smile slipped into something almost like a grimace for a moment. "I know you haven't worked weekends before, but it would really help me out if you could pitch in. I've got something big planned."

I didn't like the sound of that. "Like what?"

"I'm going to hold an information session at the library." He grinned at me, a real, happy smile. "Isn't that great?"

"Is the library going to let you sell stuff?"

"Well . . . no," he said. "But, see, I'm going to offer all our products outside afterward, in the parking lot across the street. I checked, and that's okay."

His big plan was selling vitamins in a parking lot? How could he not see how stupid that was?

I resisted the urge to speak until I'd calmed down, and then said, "What about my homework?"

I'd actually done most of it already—having no social life left plenty of time for homework—but I didn't want to give up my Sunday so Dad could hang out in the library parking lot trying to sell vitamins. I mean, my life had sunk low enough already.

"Oh." Dad's smile went fake again, the expression in his eyes shifting from happy to devastated. "I didn't think about that. I'm sorry, Kate. I'll do it another time."

"Dad, it's just—"

"I understand." He sighed. "I think maybe I'll go for a walk."

Dad never went for a walk unless he was so upset he couldn't stay in the house and keep acting like everything was fine. The last time he'd done it was when Grandma visited.

"I'll do it," I said, hating myself for making him as upset as Grandma did, and hating him for his stupid plan and obsessive love for Perfect You vitamins.

"Really?"

I nodded, and he looked so happy I almost wasn't sorry I'd agreed to help him.

"You are one amazing kid, you know that? Thank you for believing in me. It really means a lot."

I left the room before he could say anything else, because I wasn't amazing, and I didn't believe in him. I just hated it when he got upset.

I thought Sundays at the mall would be a little busier, but work was slow, as always, even though the mall was crowded. I spent most of the day stacking bottles of vitamins into small pyramids on top of our display case, bored and trying to avoid being seen by anyone I knew.

It worked for the most part, although in the afternoon Jennifer S. stopped by. She was alone and looked frustrated.

"Hey," she said. "I'm trying to buy a birthday present for my sister. What do you get a ten-year-old who thinks she knows everything?"

"A sign that says 'middle school will destroy you.'"

She laughed. "It really did suck, didn't it? I hated seventh grade."

"Me too." Anna and I had spent hours on the phone then, both of us miserable over everything. Until this year, I'd been sure I'd never have a worse one.

"It must be nice, working by yourself. No boss around or anything."

"Well, it's sitting in the mall trying to sell infomercial crap, but yeah, my dad isn't here today."

I heard how bitchy I sounded, and she didn't look like she was trying to make fun of me, but I really didn't want to go over the whole yes-my-father-is-a-freak thing again.

"Right. I guess I'd better let you get back to work, then," she said, her voice tight, and left.

I thought about calling after her, but what would I say after I told her I was sorry? I had no idea. Plus, if I did say something, what if it was the wrong thing and made her mad?

Besides, I never felt like I could be myself with her or any of the Jennifers. No one else was Anna, and even if I did become best friends with someone, it wouldn't be the same. I wouldn't have tried to learn how to skateboard with them, and they wouldn't have been there the first time I went out on a weekend without my parents around. I still remembered how cool I felt to be thirteen, an adult ticket holder at the movies with my best friend on a Friday night.

I stared down at the counter. How come it was so easy for Anna to forget all that? How could she forget all about me?

Maybe she hadn't, because when I looked up, she was looking at me.

I thought I was seeing things, but I wasn't. Anna was there, really there, standing at the edge of our section of the mall. I held my breath, hoping, but she turned around, like she was going to walk away. A wave of anger and sadness washed over me. Why did I still care about her at all? Why didn't she miss me like I missed her?

And then Sam and Will came up behind her, and she turned back toward me.

As the three of them walked in my direction, I felt my heart speed up, but Anna stopped in front of a store window just inside our section of the mall, staring inside. Sam stopped with her, wrapping his arms around her.

Will was the only one who came to the booth. He was still wearing a name tag that said his name was TRAINEE, and he tapped his fingers against the top of the counter, looking into the case.

"So, do you take any of this stuff?"

"Yes. All of it. Stop smudging the glass." Back behind him Anna was still looking in the store window.

"Wow, great salesmanship. No wonder you've got a line of customers."

"Will, what do you want?" Sam said something to Anna and she grinned, turning in his arms for a kiss and then pushing a lock of hair off his forehead. I thought of all the times she'd described how she'd do just that if she ever got to kiss him. What was it like to have that kind of dream come true? I bet it was the most amazing feeling in the world.

"Just saying hey to a fellow wage slave."

"Right, which is why you're over here all the time talking to me. Oh, wait."

"You should have told me you were feeling neglected. I would have come by before. The second I got hired, even."

"Shut up, Will." Anna and Sam turned away from the store window, walking toward the booth. Toward me. Time seemed to slow down as they got closer, and then I saw Sam glance at me and then Will, then look away.

Anna didn't look at me at all. She walked right by me like I wasn't even there.

I stared after her, furious—but also wishing she'd turn around, even if it was just for a second.

She didn't turn around, though, and Will tapped the counter again.

When I looked at him, he was leaning over it a little, staring at me. "Kate, do you like me at all? Say, enough to not run me over if I was lying mostly dead in the middle of the road?"

For a second I thought he was serious because he looked so intense, like he really wanted to know, but then some girl walking by said, "Hey, Will," and he turned and waved at her.

Yeah, I was keeping him up nights.

"Please. If you were mostly dead in the middle of the road I'd obviously stop. And then I'd watch you die."

"Kate—" he said, but I didn't get to hear whatever else he was going to say because a woman actually came up to the booth and said, "I need some help."

I started talking about vitamins right away, yammering about the ones I'd put on the counter, careful not to look at Will anymore. I still noticed when he walked away.

"Look," the woman said, interrupting me, "I just want to know where the bathrooms are."

"Oh. Section C, end of the hall."

I didn't see Anna again, but I wondered what she was doing. I wondered why she'd looked at me for that brief second, and wished it meant something even though I knew it didn't. I didn't see Will, either, but I didn't think about him at all.

Well, maybe I thought about him a little, but only for a few seconds.

Ten minutes, tops.

Mom was waiting outside for me when the mall closed. She didn't look happy.

"How was work?" she said.

"Slow. How was Dad's library thing?"

"I don't know. I haven't seen him. I left him a note telling him I'd come get you and I've been driving around for a while." Her voice was clipped, and her hands knotted together. "Kate, do you remember your father saying he was supposed to get one last check for all his vacation time?"

Oh no. This couldn't be good. "Sort of. What happened?"

"Nothing. It came yesterday. It's just that he thought he had more vacation time than he actually did and so the check was . . . smaller."

"How much smaller?"

She sighed. "A lot smaller. I've been talking to your grandmother and . . . well, she's offered to come help out."

"Grandma? Really?" Grandma and help didn't go together in

a sentence unless it was 'Help, Grandma is driving me crazy.' "Is that why you were so upset last night?"

She nodded.

"Was she mad when you said no?"

Mom looked at me, and then I knew exactly why she'd been so upset last night.

"You said yes," I said, incredulous. She'd told Grandma she could come visit?

She nodded.

"How long is she staying?"

"I don't know."

"A week? Two months? Five years? Come on, you must have some idea of how long she's—"

"Kate, stop it," she said, her voice sharp. "This wasn't easy for me, but it was the only choice I had."

I stared at her until she looked away. Grandma was her only choice? Grandma was going to help us?

It was official. There was absolutely, positively no way my life could get any worse.

# nine

**I hid out in my room all night, only leaving to make** myself a sandwich. I ended up throwing half of it away because Mom and Dad were sitting in the living room watching television.

I know that doesn't sound bad, but trust me, seeing them was like watching a car crash. Mom was curled up on the sofa, her expression a weird mix of sadness and anger, and Dad was sitting in the recliner, smiling so fixedly at the television screen I knew he had no idea what he was watching. They each asked me how I was, and both of their voices were so intense, Mom's filled with frustration and Dad's with fake cheer, that I didn't want to be around either one of them.

When I went to brush my teeth before bed, Todd was

standing in the bathroom with a plastic shower cap on his head, staring at a box in the sink.

"When did you get home?"

"Little while ago," he said.

"Do I want to know what happened to your hair?" I said, and reached for my toothbrush. "And, hey, did you hear about Grandma?"

"Grandma?" Todd looked at me. "What about—oh, shit, is that why Mom and Dad were acting so weird when I came in? Never mind, of course it was. What's she done now?"

"Shh," I whispered, pointing toward the still too-quiet living room, and shut the bathroom door, turning on the fan so the smell from Todd's head wouldn't kill me. "She's coming to visit. Mom wouldn't tell me for how long. She just said Grandma will be helping out, whatever that means."

"When?"

"I don't know. Soon. Guess you'll have to give up your room for her like always."

He made a face. "Great."

"Yeah," I said, and we both sighed.

"So, what happened?" I said, pointing at his hair.

"I went to a party, I met a girl who's a hairdresser, we got to talking, and she said I'd look great with red hair—"

"Ha! Let me see," I said, and reached for the cap.

"No way," he said, blocking my arm. "Anyway, afterward she said I could get rid of the color by stripping it or something. Whatever's in this box." He pointed at it, and I looked at its picture of an extremely blond woman and started laughing.

"Is your hair going to look like that? Because wow, will that be a really lovely look for you."

"Shut up, Grandma."

"I don't sound like her!"

"Sure you don't."

"I don't!"

"Okay. Grandma."

I elbowed him, and he grunted, frowning at his plastic-capped hair in the mirror. "So, Mom and Dad—"

"Acting weird since yesterday," I said.

"How did Dad's party go?"

"How do you think?"

"That bad?" he said.

I brushed, and then spit. "Worse. Some of the people he used to work with actually showed up, and one of them—"

"Has a kid you go to school with."

I nodded.

"How bad? Pointing and laughing bad?"

"I'm not popular enough for that. Just some laughing." I thought about Diane laughing at me, and how Anna had too, and felt my eyes burn. I blinked hard, then rinsed off my toothbrush and put it away. "Hey, how bad do you think things are, money-wise?"

Todd poked at his plastic cap, frowning. "Let's put it this way. Grandma's coming out to help."

I laughed, but only so I wouldn't cry. Todd must have seen that, because he tapped my shoulder instead of shoving me and said, "Look, I gotta rinse my head off. This stuff is starting to burn."

I went back to my room. When I got in bed, I could barely hear the television in the living room. I listened for a while, but never heard more than its low murmur. Mom and Dad still weren't speaking to each other.

When I woke up, Mom had already left for work and Dad had left a note saying he'd gone to the mall early and that Todd would drive me to school.

I woke Todd up. "Your hair turned out okay."

"Go away," he mumbled, and pulled the covers up over his head.

I tugged at them. "I need a ride to school."

He tugged them back. "Take the bus."

"I can't take the bus. No one takes the bus. I might as well wear a sign that says, 'I'm a loser.'"

"I'm sure you wouldn't need a sign."

I poked his side. "I'll tell Mom."

He sat up, rubbing his eyes and then glaring at me. "You suck."

"You do too. Now will you please take me to school?"

He did, but he drove really slowly, and I ended up getting there late, which meant I had to go to the main office and get a tardy slip. The secretary working at the front counter asked for my name, stared at me blankly when I said it, and then told me to sit down and wait.

A few minutes later Anna came in, carrying a stack of papers. "Permission forms for cheer regionals," she told the secretary. "Ms. Walters said I needed to bring them up here."

"Thank you, Anna," the secretary said.

Last year, she wouldn't have known who Anna was.

"Can I have a late pass to class? Ms. Walters forgot to give me one."

"Sure, just hold on a second."

Of course Anna would get her pass right away, and of course it wouldn't be a tardy. She wasn't even going to have to wait. That was the power of being someone. Even the adults who supposedly ran the school weren't immune to it.

"Thanks," Anna said, and looked around the office. When she saw me, she froze for a second and then turned away, looking back at the counter. I stared at the floor and wished her head would explode.

I wished that she'd say something to me.

When the secretary finally finished filling out Anna's slip and gave it to her, I had to remind her I was there. And tell her my name again.

I passed Anna in the halls later, and she didn't see me at all.

I thought about that for the rest of the day, how Anna could see me and turn away, or worse, not see me at all—and how, in spite of that, I still wished we were friends. I knew I should be angry and strong or whatever, but I missed her. And worse than her not looking at me, or even looking at me and then turning away, was her not being in my life at all. Losing her hurt more than anything.

I was still thinking about it when I got home from work and tried to do my homework, even though tomorrow was a teacher workday.

Teacher workdays used to mean a day off. They used to mean fun. Anna and I would spend all day at my house or hers, eating ice cream and watching movies, or planning our future in New York. Anna was going to be a famous singer and I was going to be her assistant, go with her to photo shoots and video shoots and fabulous parties.

The last teacher workday, I'd sat around watching television and arguing over the remote with Todd. And tomorrow I'd have to go to work. I almost wished I had to go to school instead.

I gave up on my homework and pushed my books away, tossing my pencil on top of them. Why did I have to learn more than I ever wanted to know about geometry but never got taught important stuff, like what to do when your best friend decides to act like she never knew you at all?

Or how come I hadn't learned ways to stop having locked-in-a-classroom fantasies about a guy who, back when I met him last year, heard me say he was cute and then came up to me and said sorry, I wasn't his type but, by the way, did I have a pen he could borrow?

Yes, that really happened.

The first week of ninth grade I made the mistake of nodding when some senior guys asked me if I thought Will was cute. Ever since, I've told myself I only nodded because I was a stupid, scared freshman, but that isn't entirely true, and that's what makes the story so humiliating.

Because, of course, as soon as I'd admitted he was cute, Will appeared, red-faced, and said thanks, but I wasn't his type, and could he borrow a pen?

AND I ACTUALLY GAVE HIM ONE.

That's the worst part. In spite of what he said, I gave him a pen. I was so mad at him. And at myself, for being so stupid, which probably explains why, when he finally spoke to me again (exactly three days later), this was what happened:

"Hey," he said.

"Give me back my pen," I said.

"I don't have it anymore," he said. (I would never tell him this, but it was cool he didn't pretend not to know what I was talking about.)

"You don't have it? Why? Did you freak out when someone asked you to write your name?"

"And do what?"

"What?" I said, and then immediately wished I'd said something else. Something smarter. Or at least more than one word.

"What did I do after I freaked out about having to write my name? Eat the pen?" He grinned. (This was when I first saw the dimples.)

"I don't know what you did," I snapped. "I'm not an illiterate jackass. And you owe me a pen."

He flushed, then laughed. I walked off. And later, as I was telling Anna everything, I thought about him nudging me into a corner and kissing me as I was in the middle of a much cleverer speech about my missing pen. Thus began the madness.

And somehow learning how to calculate triangle angles was more important than figuring out how to deal with this?

Please.

# ten

**We had a sale at work. It didn't go well. Dad hauled** a big box of vitamins out of storage and taped a handwritten SALE! sign on it.

"I don't know why we aren't drawing more customers," he said after a few hours. "I'm really surprised."

I wasn't surprised that people didn't want to dig through a big cardboard box of vitamins labeled with a ratty handmade sign, but then I was sixteen and rational, and he was old and had quit his job because his desk broke.

The whole time I was there, we only sold three bottles, and two of them were to a guy who argued over the price with me and then Dad until Dad caved in and sold them for half off because the labels were peeling back on one corner. Todd, who'd spent most of the day off doing whatever it was he did when he was supposed to be working (probably flirting), sold the other bottle and then asked Dad if he could take off.

Dad said yes, of course, and I slumped into the chair by our cash register, wishing I had a car and could take off. Or that I was at least allowed to drive on my own.

When the mall finally closed, Dad picked up the sale box and started reorganizing it, adding in bottles from the overflow he'd recently started to store in the tiny cabinet below our cash register.

"Things are a little cramped here, aren't they?" he said. "You know, I think I'll take some of these extras home now, and once we have a little more money coming in I'll rent more storage space from the mall."

And that's when I knew exactly why Grandma was coming. She had money. A lot of money, and things must be really bad for Mom to be willing to take it, because for as long as I could remember, Grandma would always drop hints about Mom not living the way she could, and Mom would always say, "I'm living the way I want to," and then leave the room if Grandma kept talking.

I looked at Dad's vitamins and added up the cost of all the bottles I could see on the counter—and in the box.

Yes, they were definitely why Grandma was coming.

"You want some help?"

Dad shook his head. "I've got a system. See? I'm going by type of supplement, not name."

"Okay, Dad." He was so weird.

"I'm going to need another box, though," he said. "Will you go out to the trash bins and find one?"

"Sure." Because nothing beat working at the mall selling vitamins with your dad except all that plus an end-of-the-day trip to the trash.

The trash bins were just outside our section of the mall, hidden behind a low brick wall and the loading dock. The only way to get to them was through the mall corridor, a long passage that snaked behind every store and was filled with storage lockers like the one Dad rented.

When I got outside, a guy wearing what looked like a coffee-place shirt was tossing trash. He nodded at me. "Vitamin place, right?"

"Right," I said cautiously. He wasn't gorgeous or anything, but he was cute in an "I-have-floppy-hair-and-sell-coffee-and-probably-play-the-guitar" kind of way. "You work at the coffee place, don't you?"

"Yep. Hey, can you tell your boss to stop talking about vitamins when he's in the store? My boss hates it, but I don't want to say anything because . . . ." He trailed off and mimed dropping money in a tip jar.

"Yeah, I'll get right on that."

"Thanks," he said, oblivious to my sarcasm. "I'll see you around, I guess."

"Great," I said, adding, "Moron," as he went back into the mall.

Then I heard someone laugh.

I wished I didn't know whose laugh it was, but I knew Will's laugh just like I knew he had a small scar right above his left elbow. You couldn't be reluctantly lust-ridden for someone without noticing stuff about them.

"It must be a convention," I said.

"I don't even get a 'Hey, Will' before you start insulting me?" He was standing by the loading dock, leaning against a pallet of plastic-wrapped shoeboxes.

"Nope. Bye."

"Hey, hold on," he said, and hopped down from the loading dock. I watched him walk toward me with a mixture of annoyance because he was Will, and, well, more annoyance because I liked watching him walk toward me. "Check it out. I got a new name tag today." He unclipped it and held it out toward me.

I looked at it. "A. GUY."

He grinned. "Someone actually asked me what the A stood for," he said, his hand brushing mine as he took the tag back, sliding it into his pocket. "I said Larry."

I laughed and he smiled at me again, dimples flashing. It was the closest thing to a nice moment I'd had with anyone in ages. Or ever with a guy.

So, naturally, Will ruined it, saying, "So, what's the deal with your dad? We have a notice up in the back saying we're supposed to get a manager right away if he comes in."

"Like you don't know," I said. "Am I supposed to tell you stories about my dad and his wacky vitamin-selling adventures now?"

"Hey, I was just—"

"Oh, I can't wait to hear this."

He blinked at me. "I was just trying to talk to you."

I hated how hot he was and hated myself more for noticing. For always noticing, even now. "Sure you were. Because you said so much when you were listening to the coffee guy complain about him. Oh, no, wait. You just laughed."

"Not at you. I wouldn't—"

"Make fun of me? Please."

He stared at me for a moment, and then said, "Look, Kate, I'm sorry."

For some reason, that made me furious. I didn't want his pity. I was sick of the mall, of vitamins, of everything. I lifted one hand, to either shove him or slap him, and he caught it. Caught me.

I froze. It wasn't that I wasn't angry anymore, because I was. I just felt so much other stuff too, stuff I didn't even have a name for, and it hit me so hard I couldn't move.

He didn't either, and as we stared at each other I felt a weird prickling heat, like a blush but stronger, shiver though me, and I knew something was going to happen.

And then it did, and he kissed me.

My very first kiss. With Will. It was like something out a dream.

Except that I was standing by a trash bin outside the mall. And I was with Will, who had kissed just about every girl in school, and who I didn't want to like.

"You jackass," I said, pulling away and trying to ignore how I was shaking all over.

He stared at me like he'd never seen me before.

"Jackass? You just shoved your tongue down my throat and now you're calling me names?"

"I didn't do that!"

"Did."

"Did not."

"Did," he said, and leaned in toward me.

"Did not," I said again, and then I—oh, this is the embarrassing part—I kissed him. I couldn't help it. The look on his face was so intense and the whole thing was so intense that I had to. I couldn't help myself.

And I didn't want to. At least not until the mall door opened and I heard someone say, "Oh."

Then I bolted, grabbing a box and taking off like I was being chased.

Which I wasn't. Will didn't come after me. Not that I wanted him to, or anything.

Besides, when I got home, I forgot all about the kiss, at least for a while, because when Dad and I walked in, Grandma was there.

# eleven

**"Darling,"** she said as soon as I saw her standing in our front hallway, and swooped in for a hug, moving past Dad like he wasn't there.

"Hi, Grandma," I said, feeling as small and plain as I always did around her. Grandma was close to six feet tall, and had modeled when she was younger. She had pictures of herself up all over her house to prove it, and even though she was old now, she still had the kind of face that made people stop and stare.

"I should take you to a proper salon and get your eyebrows shaped," she said. "There must be one around here somewhere. You have my eyebrows, darling, and they must be tamed!"

"Mother, Kate doesn't need anything done to her eyebrows." Mom gave my arm a soft, reassuring squeeze, letting me untangle myself from Grandma. "Besides, remember what happened when you had yours done right before my sixteenth birthday party?"

Grandma sighed. "I can't believe you remember that, Sharon."

"Mother, you wouldn't get out of bed for a week. I had to have Mrs. Glick next door drive me back to school because Daddy was in Switzerland."

Grandma waved one hand, as if shooing Mom's words away, and Mom frowned before turning to Dad, who'd sidestepped Grandma and taken Mom in his arms.

"You guys, no one needs to see that," Todd said, clipping me with an elbow as he walked up behind me, his version of a greeting. "Dad, I got up to the last level of our game. Want to see it?"

Dad did, of course, so we all ended up in the living room, me and Mom and Grandma sitting on the sofa while Dad and Todd sat on the floor blowing up imaginary bad guys.

"I see Steve still has his little hobby," Grandma said to Mom, and from the huge, fixed—and fake—smile on Dad's face, I could tell he was imagining that everyone on screen was Grandma.

"It helps me relax," he said without turning away from the game. "Sharon, are there any sandwiches?"

"Roast beef or ham?" Mom said, starting to get up, but Grandma put a hand on her knee.

"You were just saying how you wanted to sit and rest, darling."

Mom froze, then said, "Excuse me, Mother," her voice icy, and got up.

When she'd gone into the kitchen, Grandma looked at me. "You look tired, darling. Did you have a long day?"

Long and weird. I thought about Will, and the kiss, and felt a little shiver race through me. "Sort of. But at least I didn't have to go to school."

"No school? So you spent the day with your friends?" She smiled at me. "What did you buy?"

Grandma had friends, or at least said she did, and only ever did one thing with them: shop. Every closet in her house was filled with clothes and shoes and purses, all color-coordinated and numbered according to some system she'd set up. Mom once told me her first memory was sitting in a store watching Grandma look at shoes. I don't mind shopping, but Grandma treated it like it was a religion.

"I worked with Dad," I said. He glanced back at me, a real smile on his face, and I grinned back.

"Working? But darling, you're only sixteen."

"She knows how old she is, Mother," Mom called from the kitchen. "Steve's business is a family business. That means every-one pitches in. I told you that earlier."

"But poor Todd and Kate, working so hard—"

"It's not so bad, Grandma," Todd said, looking over his shoulder at her and then glancing back at Dad, who was staring at the television screen with his fake smile burned across his face again. "Besides, didn't our grandfather work all the time?"

"He was a very important man," Grandma said. "And creat-ing medicines isn't the sort of thing one takes a vacation from. But he never would have made me work, and your mother—oh, when she was a girl, she never wanted for anything. He took care of us and certainly wouldn't have quit his job to sell—"

"Mother," Mom said, coming back in and handing Dad a sandwich, "he was addicted to the painkillers he developed, and never noticed anything or anyone when he was at home, which wasn't often. Let's not make him into a saint, shall we?"

Grandma cleared her throat, looking upset. Dad squeezed Mom's hand, smiling a tense and very fake smile. Mom looked mad.

Todd glanced at them and then shot me a look, saying, "Hey, Grandma, Kate and I didn't give you your birthday presents the last time you were here."

"Right," I said, realizing what he was doing. Distracting Grandma was a good idea, and luckily, it was easy. "Do you want your gifts now?"

Grandma grinned, and the tension in the room, so strong a second ago, lessened. Still, I didn't know how were we going to survive living with her, especially when it took her about a minute to rip open all her presents and say, "Well, those were unusual!" before looking at us like she was waiting for more.

"I just remembered I have to . . . bake a cake for tomorrow," Mom said, disappearing back into the kitchen. "There's a birthday at work."

Me and Dad and Todd all stared after her, and then Dad said, "Ice!"

He turned to Grandma. "I know you like lots of ice when you have a drink, and our freezer still only makes cubed ice, not crushed. I'd better go get you some."

"I'll go with—" I said at the same time Todd said, "I'll grab my keys, Dad, and we can take my car."

So I ended up sitting in the living room with Grandma, who

smiled and then touched one perfectly manicured hand to the umbrella I'd given her.

"This is a very charming umbrella, darling," she said. "But this gift from your brother—what is it, and why does he think I want to read about trees crying?"

"It's a poem, Grandma." Before he wanted to be an actor, Todd was going to be a poet.

"Weep, deep, seek—ah, rhyming. I see." She sighed. "I don't suppose you got the picture of the Tiffany bracelet I sent?"

"We did." Grandma was always sending us ads for things we could get her as gifts. Usually they cost more than Todd's braces had, and Mom said we'd be paying for those until Todd had kids and they needed braces.

"Oh. Well, then, never mind," Grandma said, and looked around our living room, frowning at the stack of video games Dad had piled on the floor by the television. "I don't know how your mother's mind works. What kind of husband just sits around—?"

"Mother, stop," Mom called from the kitchen. "Why don't you come help me with this cake?"

"Darling, I'm fine out here. Did you ever get that nice book I sent about decorating on a budget?"

Mom came out of the kitchen, a cake mix box in one hand. "Yes, mother, but sadly, Steve and I don't have a spare twenty grand lying around to install specially textured walls in the living room. We'd rather send Kate to college."

"Oh darling, you could never change the walls in here. It would make the rest of the house look like even more of a disaster."

Mom rolled her eyes at me and went back into the kitchen.

I wondered how Grandma and my grandfather had produced my mother, who was always so sensible, and got up, telling Grandma I'd get her a drink. She always drank diet soda with a slice of lime and lots of ice. The ice would be wrong now, of course, which she wouldn't like, but at least I'd be able to get away from her for a minute or two.

Mom hugged me as soon as I came into the kitchen. "Grandma means well. She just doesn't always think before she speaks. Or acts."

I made a face. "I can tell. And I don't like the stuff she says about Dad. Plus she hated my gift."

"She didn't hate it. She . . . she believes everyone is just like her, Kate, and thinks only about clothing and jewelry and makeup. Buying useful gifts is not something my mother understands."

"You'd think she'd understand what an umbrella is for," I said, and got the glass Grandma always used out of the cabinet. "And how come she always says mean stuff about Dad?"

Mom sighed. "She doesn't understand him. My father was a workaholic, and when he was home . . . well, let's just say he wasn't happy. Your father, on the other hand, loves being home. He loves me and you kids. He likes to relax and have fun."

I opened the fridge and got out a lime, slicing off a piece and sticking it on the rim of the glass just like Grandma liked. "But your dad made lots of money, right?"

"He did," Mom said. "But it didn't do him or your grandmother or me much good." She handed me a diet soda, not meeting my eyes.

Maybe it hadn't done her much good then, but I was pretty sure money was the only reason why Grandma was here now. I didn't say that though, because something in the way Mom wouldn't look at me stopped me.

I took Grandma her drink and then sat next to her when she patted the sofa. "I want to hear all about you, darling," she said, jiggling her glass and frowning briefly at the ice. "How's school? Are there any boys in the picture?"

Great. I'd found something worse than working with Dad. "Um . . . is that outfit new?"

"It is, darling. I caught a plane to New York last week and spent four days shopping. Sometime you and I will have to go together. We'll make a little vacation out of it and—"

"No shopping vacations with Kate, Mother," Mom said, coming out of the kitchen. "The last thing she needs is to spend day after day trying on clothes and listening to you tell her how pretty she'd be if only she'd do this or that."

"Sharon, I'd never—"

"I haven't forgotten how we celebrated my eighteenth birthday, Mother."

"I haven't either," Grandma said, "A whole day together, and at the end of it you tell me you're going to college in California, never mind that you hadn't ever said a word about wanting to go there before."

"Yes, well, that's where Berkeley was," Mom said, her voice sharp. "And you managed well enough without me, didn't you?"

"We all do what we have to," Grandma said, her voice equally sharp, and I said I was tired and escaped to my room.

I closed my door, resting one hand against it. I'd had a picture of me and Anna at the Jackson Jamboree taped there once. I used to see it every night before I fell asleep. I kept it in my desk drawer now.

I turned, looking around my room. On my bed was an empty space where the stuffed monkey she'd given me when I was eight used to be.

I wished I could call Anna now and tell her about Grandma, about everything, but I couldn't.

I got the monkey out of the back of my closet and looked at it until my eyes burned. When I put it away, I told myself I wasn't crying, and ignored the wet spots that fell from my face onto the monkey's, closing the door before I could see it sitting there all alone.

Left behind and forgotten, just like me.

# twelve

**The next morning I was so nervous about seeing**
Will that when I got to school, I didn't even look for Anna.

I had no idea what was going to happen, other than that I'd
hoped things would be okay but was pretty sure they wouldn't be.
I mean, in my heart it was all happy endings, but even then I was
fuzzy on how to get there. And then there was the fact that I'd
kissed Will, who'd been with so many girls—and who so clearly
knew what he was doing—that he was basically a professional
kisser. Plus I'd run away after the kiss, and I was positive that
wasn't something your normal, well-adjusted sixteen-year-old girl
would do.

I saw Will as soon as I walked into first period. That was
normal, although the way my heart started pounding as soon as I

saw him wasn't. He was looking at the door, like he was waiting for someone, and as I came in he looked right at me and smiled.

"Hey," he said. That wasn't normal either. Will didn't notice me when I came into class. At least not like this.

I felt shaky, and my palms were wet with sweat. I had to say something to him. Anything. Even I knew that much.

But I couldn't.

I couldn't because if I did say something, said, "Hey," back, then what? Will would want to date me and Dad would get a real job and Grandma would fly home and never come back and Anna would be my best friend again?

None of those things were going to happen, not ever, and I didn't want that kiss to become something like that. I didn't want it to be one good memory that led to a lot of bad ones. I wanted it to stay what it was, one amazing moment, something that was strong and sweet enough to stand on its own. Something I could remember without any pain.

It was a good thing I didn't say anything too, because Will looked away. He didn't say anything else to me. He didn't mention the kiss.

I hadn't expected him to, but deep down, in a tiny, hopeful place I hated, it stung that he hadn't. But really, why would one kiss mean anything to Will?

Especially when it clearly didn't. After lunch, as I threw my empty soup cup away, I saw Will come into the cafeteria. He was laughing, and when one of his friends elbowed him he turned, puckering his face into an exaggerated fish-faced kiss. A joke.

I didn't have to guess what—and who—it was about.

I felt stupid for being so nervous before. For spending so much time thinking about that kiss. For thinking it was amazing.

I was angry, too. I knew he was just a guy and there were plenty more in the world, but I wasn't going to get a chance to do my first kiss over again and it wasn't fair that it had been ruined.

I faked a headache in my last class and got a pass to the nurse's office. I didn't go there, though. I went to the gym. I knew Will's schedule, and last period he worked in the coaches' office because the internship he was supposed to have ended when the sponsoring company went bankrupt.

I was walking past the trophy case when the gym office doors flew open and Anna came out, her arms so full of photocopies that all I could see was the top of her head. One of the copies slithered off the top of the pile and hit the floor.

"Crap," she said, and then kicked off one of her shoes, nudging the copy with her foot. I saw her toes try to grab it, and suddenly thought I might cry.

She was still Anna. My Anna, who could pick things up with her toes and who once, on a bet, had picked up two quarters in a row. Twice. Todd had to drive us to the movies, pay for our tickets, and buy us popcorn because of that.

"Here," I said, and picked up the copy, handing it to her.

She froze for a moment and then said, "Can you put it on top of the stack?"

I did.

"Thanks," she said, sliding her shoe back on and gingerly shifting the stack of copies to the side a bit, just enough so I could see her face. She was grinning, actually grinning. "I guess the wonder toes don't work like they used to. I guess my glory days ended with the quarters, huh?"

I couldn't move. I couldn't speak. She'd talked to me. After months of silence, she'd talked to me.

"I thought Todd's head was going to explode when we both ordered large popcorns," she continued, and made a face, a mirror of Todd's expression as it had been that night.

"Oh, I know," I said, laughing as I remembered how mad he'd been, and because I was so happy she was talking to me. Finally, she was talking to me. "The best thing, though, is that I actually caught him trying to do it later and he couldn't."

Anna grinned again. "Not everyone has my wonder toes. I loved how your dad used to say that. 'Anna and her wonder toes!' My dad hardly ever noticed me and . . . well." She gave me a look, and it was a real Anna look, sad and strong at the same time. "You know how he is."

I did. "Have you talked to him lately?"

"He called last week," she said, her voice suddenly wobbly. "He's getting married again. Her name is Becky and she's great, she's wonderful, he wouldn't shut up about her. And then he didn't even ask me to come to the wedding."

"You must be so pissed," I said. "I swear, if you looked in the dictionary, his picture would be right next to the word 'ass.'"

She laughed. "It should be, shouldn't it? And I am pissed. Everyone's told me how sorry they are, but no one's seen . . . no one else has seen how mad I am. God, I miss you so—"

She broke off and looked at the floor, then shook her head. "I gotta go," she said, talking so fast the words practically fell over each other, and before I could say anything, before I could even think anything, she walked off.

I stared after her, stunned. She missed me. She remembered the quarter thing. She remembered being friends with me.

Anna *missed* me.

I looked around, my mind spinning. Maybe I could find her and we could talk, really talk. She must have the period free, running errands for cheerleading or something, and if I caught up to her now—

"So, wonder toes. I guess now I know how to become a successful cheerleader."

Will. He was leaning against the wall by the gym door, hands in his pockets.

"Did you just stand there and listen to us talk?"

"What was I going to do, say, 'Hey, Anna, sorry to bother you while you're messing with Kate's mind, but can you not turn the photocopier off when you're done with it because some of us have stacks of health forms to copy'?"

Now I remembered why I'd come down here. "She wasn't messing with me. She was talking to me. But then I wouldn't expect you to know the difference, you pig dog weasel loser."

"Wow," he said, sounding surprised and a little angry. "You kiss me, ignore me, and now you're calling me names? That seems a little strange, but then you're—"

"I kissed you? Is that the story you're telling?"

"Now I'm telling stories about you?"

"I saw you at lunch."

"Lunch? I didn't say anything about you at lunch."

"Right. Funny thing, I don't trust liars."

"Fine," he said, and yanked his shirt collar to the left, baring a mouth-shaped bruise near his collarbone. "Someone saw this earlier, I've been getting shit for it all day, and so at lunch I threatened to give everyone one of their own." He made the face I'd seen him make before.

"So your friends run around looking down your shirt? And I didn't give you that . . . thing."

He laughed. "Sure. It was just some girl who shares your name and looks just like you. And I'd like to see you try to hide this all day. Are you part vampire?"

I started to laugh, then stopped myself. "Look, I didn't do—"

"What? Give me this?" He moved toward me, touching the bruise with one finger. "Should I refresh your memory?"

"You're not funny," I said, and poked his chest with one finger.

He grabbed it and leaned in, pressing his lips to my neck right below my ear. I felt the warmth of his mouth, a sharp quick nip from his teeth, and then he was grinning at me again.

"Now we match."

I stared at him, my mouth hanging open to somewhere around my knees. His grin faded and that look, the intense one from last night, came back again. The bell rang and he didn't move. The look didn't change. I heard people coming out into the hallways, a wave of sound building toward us.

He kept looking at me. I wasn't sure I was still breathing.

"Miller! Where the heck are those copies?" someone

yelled, and I looked over and saw one of the coaches frowning at us.

Will blinked, like he was waking up, and looked over at the coach. I walked away, promising myself I'd figure every-thing out later.

# thirteen

**Instead, I ended up kissing Will again.**

Work was boring, and by seven, the mall was pretty much deserted. Dad went off to buy himself a coffee, and Mom stopped by right after he left.

"You just missed Dad," I said. "Coffee run."

She didn't seem surprised. "So, how are things?"

"Slow. Also, Dad gave Todd fifty bucks for some audition he claims to have, but I bet Todd's just going to—"

"Kate," she said in her warning voice, "aren't you a little old for this?"

"Isn't Todd a little old to be living at home?"

She sighed. "When I asked how things were, I meant with

you. You've been so quiet about everything lately. I don't know how your classes are going, or if you're dating anyone—"

"Mom, please. Do I look like the kind of girl guys want to date?"

"Yes," she said, like I'd asked the silliest question in the world, and I looked down at the floor so I wouldn't do something embarrassing like hug her in public.

"School's fine," I muttered. "And no guys."

"What about Anna?"

"I saw her today."

Mom and Dad knew what had happened with Anna, sort of. I'd said we weren't talking as much now that she had a boyfriend. There are some things you just can't tell parents, and "Hey, my best friend thinks I'm a loser" is one of them. They think stuff like that isn't possible, which is sweet, but wrong.

"That's good. I thought I saw that boyfriend of hers the other day, but he was with a redhead so I guess it wasn't him." Her stomach rumbled, and she blushed.

"Hungry, Mom?"

She sighed again. "When I got home tonight, I made dinner, and the first thing Mother—Grandma—says to me is, 'Darling, you aren't twenty anymore, so don't eat like you are.' I'd been looking forward to boxed macaroni and cheese all day, and she ruined it for me."

"I'm sorry," I said, and rested my head on her shoulder for a second. Poor Mom. Grandma was annoying, but she wasn't my mother. "You should find Dad and have coffee with him."

"I can't. I've got an interview."

"Interview?"

"Selling cosmetics in the department store Dad's banned from," she said, and gave me a weak grin. "If I get the job, he'll have to sneak in to visit me. Can you see him doing that?"

Sadly, I could. "But why would you want to work there when you already have a . . . Oh. You're getting a second job. We need money that badly?"

"Well, I guess I don't have to wonder if you've noticed we're having money problems," she said.

"Mom, why don't you ask Dad to go back to work?" I said, but she didn't answer, just shook her head, silencing me as Dad called out, "Sharon?" from the end of the corridor that led out into the main part of the mall.

"I have to go," she said, and went to meet Dad. The two of them talked briefly, far enough away so I couldn't hear them, and when Dad got back he told me to take a break.

"Did Mom tell you why she's here? Because it doesn't seem fair that she has to get another job so you can sit here with these stupid . . ." I trailed off, shamed by the shock and hurt in his eyes. "Dad, I—"

"Kate, please go take a break," he said, and his smile was so horribly fake I practically ran away from the booth.

I felt bad for making him upset, but I was mad too. I didn't ask for him to fall in love with stupid vitamins. I didn't ask to work in the mall. I didn't ask to have things get so screwed up that Grandma had to come out.

For once, I wished he and Mom were the kind of parents who yelled at each other. But Dad was incapable of getting mad, and any time Mom did get upset with him, they always talked about it in private, and worse, acted like everything was fine in front of me and Todd.

I went down to the food court but didn't feel like sitting there surrounded by people with shopping bags and sodas who were having fun at the mall. It just made me think about how the mall was the last place I wanted to be anymore.

I went outside, the food court's neon glow casting bright shadows, and saw Will. He was in his Sports Shack uniform, wolfing down a burger like he hadn't eaten all day. There was a little bit of mustard right above his upper lip, and when he saw me, he licked it away, swallowing his last bite, and then looked at me, the food court lights shading his face strange colors.

The way he was looking at me made me think about earlier, and I put a hand to my neck. His mouth hadn't left a mark, but I swear I still felt it.

He grinned at me then, like he knew what I was thinking, and I don't know what it was about his smile, but when I saw it, school and my parents and Anna and vitamins and everything else didn't matter. I couldn't even think about any of it.

And I liked that feeling. I liked it a lot.

I wanted to feel it again, in fact, and when he said "Hey," just like he had that morning, I said, "I gotta go back to work, but I'll be at our storage locker behind Toy World in about ten minutes."

He looked at me, his eyes impossible to read, but from the way he'd stilled, I knew I'd surprised him.

That made two of us.

I couldn't believe what I'd just said. I never did stuff like this, not ever. Anna was the one who had ideas and who was never afraid to say what she thought. Anna was the one who dared to do stuff, who talked me into getting my ears pierced even though I was afraid, who'd turned herself into someone new. I just followed her lead, happy to go where she wanted. And then she was gone and I had turned quieter, pulled into myself. I guess that one kiss with Will had destroyed part of my brain.

Or, deep down, I really wanted another moment like the one I'd had last night. I wanted to kiss him again.

But when I got back into the mall, the momentary surge of whatever it was that had made me talk to him like that faded, and after several minutes of standing in the corridor that led toward our storage space, I leaned against the wall and sighed.

I couldn't do it. It was a mistake, and I knew it. I had to go back to work.

Besides, what were the odds he'd even show up?

Low. Nonexistent, even, because when Dad sent me to grab a few bottles of Garlic Gels for a display he wanted a couple of minutes after I got back to the booth, Will wasn't there.

Disappointment washed over me, and I told myself I was being stupid, that I knew he wouldn't have shown.

I still felt disappointed anyway.

I looked at the shelves Dad had stacked full of vitamins, and started digging around for the Garlic Gels. I found a box of them wedged in the back and pulled them out, blowing out a breath at the weight.

I heard a noise, looked over my shoulder, and then almost dropped the box. Will was standing a little ways behind me, leaning against the wall, like he was trying to look relaxed but couldn't quite get there. He watched me wrestle the box onto another already over-crowded shelf without offering to help, and the overwhelming urge I'd felt to kiss him started to seem a lot less overwhelming.

"Don't worry, I'm fine," I said.

"Like you'd have let me help you," he said, taking a step toward me. "Besides, right now I'm supposed to be counting shoelaces in our storage overspill. Guess now I'll have to stay late to do it."

"I didn't ask you to do that."

"I didn't say you did." He took another step toward me.

"Good," I said, but my voice came out all wobbly and cracked.

Then he kissed me. He touched the sides of my face, my neck, and then rested his hands on the small of my back, pulling me closer, and my whole body burned. He tasted like cinnamon, which surprised me because I'd just seen him eating a burger, and then I realized he must have eaten a mint or something and it just . . . melted me.

I could have kissed him forever, I think, but once again vita-mins messed up my life. The corridor door creaked open and Dad yelled, "Kate, did you find those Garlic Gels yet?"

I jumped like he was right next to us and Will touched my shoulder, whispering, "Your dad, right?"

"Yeah, I gotta go." I tried to pretend I didn't notice that him whispering in my ear had given me goose bumps, and walked off before he could notice. Or say anything.

I could say I don't know why I walked away like that again, but that would be a lie. I walked away so I would be the one who left, and I left so I wouldn't have to see him do it first.

"Hand 'em over," Dad said when I reached him, and I blinked at him before remembering I was supposed to be bringing back vitamins.

"How come you're not at the booth?" I said, hoping to change the subject. "I mean, didn't you tell me someone always has to be there during mall hours?"

Dad blushed. "Well, it gets sort of boring out there sometimes, and you were gone for a while." He looked at me. "You weren't able to find them, were you?"

I shook my head, and he went and got the vitamins. I sat in the booth and wondered what the hell had just happened. I'd basically asked Will to make out with me. Why had I done that? What had I been thinking?

I hadn't. That was the problem.

I couldn't face going to school, afraid that Will might say something and equally afraid that he wouldn't, and in the morning I tried to convince Mom I was sick. I got up when she said Grandma would stay at home with me, though, and before I knew it, I was walking into first period, dreading what was going to happen.

Only nothing did.

I walked into class and Will was talking to Jennifer M. smiling and nodding and not noticing me at all. I wanted to smack her. And him. And then go home and spend the day eating ice cream.

It was a really distressing feeling.

"Did you understand the reading?" Jennifer S. asked when I sat down.

I looked at her, totally not caring that Will was still talking to Jennifer M. In fact, I hoped they hooked up. Her insanely jealous boyfriend, who played football and had a neck the size of my leg, would break Will in half.

"Sort of," I said, and Will looked over his shoulder at me then, clicking the pen he was holding over and over really fast. For a second, I thought he looked nervous.

"So . . . about last night," he said, and as soon as he did, I knew what was coming. The "Look, last night I was drunk/in a really bad place/etc., and I just don't see you that way" speech. I'd heard Todd make it about a million times, and that was always how he started it.

I didn't want to hear it now, especially not in front of everyone.

"I don't care about it, just quit clicking your pen, okay?" I said, and looked back at Jennifer S. "Did you understand the reading?"

"All I remember is that when people get certain kinds of anemia they end up eating stuff like paint."

"And dirt," Will said, butting in just like always. He looked at me again. "You don't care?" He almost sounded hurt.

"Yes. I don't care, so please spare me the speech."

"Speech?"

"What are you, an echo?"

He stared at me for a moment, and then grinned just like he had last night. "What kind of speech am I supposed to make?"

Flustered, I looked at my desk, and kept looking at it until class started.

Of course, it ended up being group day. And guess who was in my group?

That's right. Jennifer M., who I was still having residual feelings of irrational hatred for; Kim, who actually thought being student council treasurer meant something and spent all his time discussing ancient movies from the 1980s; and Will.

"But there aren't killer robots around now, Kim," Jennifer said when he finally paused to take a breath mid-rant about some movie no one but him and a bunch of ancient people had ever seen. She turned to me. "Let's focus on the reading. Kate, what did you think about the section on blood typing?"

I'd read it last night, while worrying about what had happened with Will, and remembered nothing about it. "I thought it was . . . well, it was interesting. What do you think?"

Jennifer sighed. "You didn't do the reading, did you? Will, please tell me you did the reading. Never mind, I know you did. What did you think about the blood typing stuff?"

I could practically hear her eyelashes fluttering. I reminded myself that I'd hung out with her, and that aside from a tendency to pit Jennifer S. and T. against each other, she wasn't so bad. And who'd want Will, anyway?

I ignored the little voice inside me that said, "Me!"

"I think it's really complex," Will said. "There's a lot of stuff going on, you know?"

"Absolutely," Jennifer said. "You mean how blood types were discovered, right?"

"That's it. The evolution of it all," Will said.

Okay, how come she didn't get that he clearly hadn't done the reading either? I cleared my throat, and he looked at me, grinning again, and then glanced at Jennifer.

"Wow, are these your notes? You've even highlighted—yep, this is exactly what I was thinking. You've got to mention all of this when we get called on."

"Really? You think it's okay?" Jennifer said, and looked over at Jennifer T., who was talking to Jennifer S.

While she was distracted, Will leaned toward me. "You need to work on your bullshit skills," he whispered.

"Oh, please. If I had dimples and pretended everything she said was interesting, she'd be all over me too," I whispered back.

He laughed. "So you're saying you're immune to the Will Miller charm?"

"I'm definitely immune to anything you call the Will Miller charm, you loser."

Will stretched, still grinning. His shirt rode up, showing a little bit of his stomach, and I watched Jennifer turn back toward us and stare at that little patch of skin like she'd been hypnotized. Honestly, it was so sad the way some girls got totally stupid over—

Will tugged his shirt down, and I looked up to see him looking at me, grinning a slow smile that made me want to smack him. And then make out with him.

I glared at him. He winked at me and I slumped back into my chair. Stupid Will.

Stupid me.

# fourteen

**Work was fine. I stayed in our booth the whole** time, even eating dinner there. Dad said he admired my dedication and asked if I wanted to straighten up our storage space.

"After all, you've gotten a good look at it now, right?" he said, and I said, "Sure," trying not to blush.

Back in the corridor by the shelves that held box after box of Perfect You vitamins, I tried to put them into some kind of order and didn't think about Will. I didn't wonder if he was at work. I didn't wonder what he was thinking about, and if he was thinking about me.

Not much, anyway.

In the morning, I woke up before my alarm went off because Mom and Grandma were arguing. I got up and opened my door a little, peeking out at them. Mom was standing by the bathroom door, which was open just enough for me to see that Grandma was inside fixing her hair.

"So what you're saying is that I'm on my own like always," Mom said. Her voice was quiet, just above a whisper. At first I thought it was because she didn't want me or Todd to hear, but then she wiped a hand across her eyes and I realized she was try-ing not to cry.

"Darling, I'm not even going to respond to that. I'm here, aren't I? I want to help you." Grandma picked up my hairspray, made a face at it, and then picked up her own.

"And how are you going to do that? I told you what we needed last night, you said you'd have to think about it, and now you've told me 'no'?"

"That's not what I said. I said I'll help you."

"What does that mean?"

"It means it's not my job to save you from your husband's choices. You chose to stay with him, you live with what he does. Does that sound familiar, darling?"

"So, this is really about Daddy and something I said to you before I went to college? You can't seriously be comparing Steve to him, Mother, and I sure as hell hope you aren't saying I'm like you."

"No, you made that quite clear before you left. And then you didn't say a word to me or your father until you graduated with no job and a mountain of student loans."

Mom flinched. "That's not fair. I came home because I read that Daddy was ill, not because I wanted money. I've never asked you for anything, but the life Steve and I have built . . . we're in danger of losing it."

"Not if he gets a job."

"He has a job."

"Oh, Sharon, please. You married a child and frankly, it's time he grows up. I'll help you, but I'm certainly not going to support Steve's absurd fantasy."

"You have no idea what you're talking about. Steve's amazing. He's actually capable of emotion, and he would do anything for me or the kids."

"Would he?" Grandma said, and I saw Mom look at the floor, her face turning a dark, shamed red. "As I was saying, if I did what you asked, it would only delay the inevitable. Steve's little dream is just that, darling, a dream, and putting off his wake-up call for a few months or even a year won't change a thing. I will help you, though, and all I ask is that you think about what I said. A marriage isn't supposed to be—"

"That's enough," Mom said, looking back up at Grandma. Her face was still red but her voice was icy cold. "Keep your damn money. I don't mind work, unlike some people, and I know more about marriage than you ever will."

"Darling, that's a bit melodramatic, even for you, and I think we both realize I know plenty about marriage. I did survive mine, after all."

Mom took a deep breath, let it out slowly, and then said, "There's no point in you staying here any longer."

"You want me to leave?" Grandma seemed shocked and, weirdly, hurt. I didn't think that was possible.

"Yes, Mother, I do. I want you to leave as soon as possible, and if I'm ever stupid enough to ask you for anything again, just pretend I'm a child. You won't be able to ship me off to boarding school like you did then, but it should still be easy enough for you to ignore me."

"Darling—"

"I don't want to hear it, Mother."

"What do you think life at home would have been like if I hadn't sent you away?" Grandma said. "Do you think your father would have decided to give up his little blue pills? Do you think he would have been around more, or noticed either one of us if he was? Do you think I would have somehow become a better person? A better mother? Getting you out of that house was the most unselfish thing I've ever done."

"The only thing," Mom said, but her voice was shaking.

"You may be right," Grandma said. "But still, I won't support Steve and his ridiculous scheme. However, I do want to help you, darling. I won't mention what I said last night again, but I will give you enough money for this month. I don't want you working two jobs, especially when one of them is selling those hideous cosmetics."

"What's the catch?"

"No catch. I just want to see my family. Is that so hard to believe?"

"Frankly, yes, but I'll live with it. Once the month is over, though—"

"Yes, darling, I understand. 'Thank you for the cash, now get out.'"

Mom shook her head. "Mother, you trying to do guilt is like . . . well, it's like me trying to sell forty-dollar eyeliner."

"Oh, I'm not that bad at it, darling," Grandma said, and shut the bathroom door.

I crept back to bed and wondered what Grandma had said to Mom about Dad and their marriage. It must have been really . . . well, typical Grandma. As far as Dad and his vitamins went, I had to agree with her, though. Dad's dream was a stupid one and I didn't care if it got crushed.

In fact, I'd love it if he got a real job again. It would mean part of my life would go back to the way it used to be. It would mean no more working at the mall, no more piped-in music or tiny booth or people staring at Dad and his vitamins and then looking away like he embarrassed them.

No, there was nothing I'd miss about working at the mall.

Well, one thing. With one person. But it had happened, it was over, and that was that.

Still, I was relieved to get to first period and find out Will wasn't in school.

Or at least I wanted to feel relieved. I was actually sort of disappointed when I walked into class and didn't see him, but the disappointment could have come from having to face biology so early in the morning. Or because I had to hear Jennifer M. talk about her new purse, which was just as annoying as it sounds.

No, I was pretty sure the disappointment I felt had nothing to do with Will.

Then Jennifer started talking about him.

"I heard Will isn't here because Monica is a complete wreck and he can't deal with it," she said. "You know they were sort of together for a while, right? Well, supposedly she went to see him at work last night, and he had a hickey from some other girl. I mean, okay, they weren't actually together anymore, but still. He's always got a girl waiting, you know?"

I drew a little box on the edge of my open notebook page. I did know. Everyone knew about Will. Unlike Sam, who was so popular that hooking up with him required a level of social standing that almost no one had, Will was attainable. Hell, I'd attained him. I scribbled over the box I'd drawn.

Jennifer M. leaned in closer, lowering her voice. "I heard the other girl is some random mall skank."

How flattering. I drew another box and scribbled it in, pretending the paper was Jennifer's face.

"Well, it is Will," Jennifer T. said. "He's been with at least half the girls in school, so who's left for him, you know? I feel bad for Sam, actually, because people say stuff about him and random girls sometimes, but you know it's just because he hangs out with Will."

"But Will hasn't been with hardly anyone this year," Jennifer S. said, looking at Jennifer M. "I mean, besides Monica, I've only seen him with a few—"

"Please," Jennifer T. said to Jennifer S., rolling her eyes at me and Jennifer M. "Like you know anything about guys. You can't even get one to look at you."

Jennifer M. laughed, even though she looked a little uncomfortable, and Jennifer S. crumpled, slouching down in her desk. She looked like she was going to cry.

"Sorry," she said to Jennifer T., who acted like she hadn't said anything at all and started talking to Jennifer M.

And there was yet another reminder why I didn't hang out with the Jennifers anymore. Anna never made me feel like crap for saying stuff the way the Jennifers sometimes had. Of course, Anna had also just stopped talking to me.

But she'd also spoken to me again, out of the blue, and said she missed me.

Maybe we could be friends again. I wanted that more than anything, and thought about it all through my first few classes, wondering if there was something I could do to make Anna talk to me again.

I went to the bathroom after lunch, and passed Diane on my way in. She was leaving, and called out, "That stupid song actually sounds decent when you sing it, Anna," practically yelling in my ear and yet still managing to act like she didn't see me.

Anna was standing by the sinks. I watched her look at herself in the mirror and then make a face at her reflection as she fiddled with her hair, which was pulled back into a made-to-look-messy knot.

"It looks great," the girl standing next to Anna said, and I realized it was Tara. *The* Tara. "And you really did make that crap song sound way better. You want to come to lunch? I'm so not doing it here today." She looked around, and just like Diane, looked right through me.

"Oh, I guess Diane left. Too bad for her. Look, I'm feeling like Chinese, so be in the parking lot in five, okay?" She glided out before Anna could say anything in reply.

As if anyone ever said no to Tara.

"Damn," Anna whispered, and frowned at herself in the mirror. "I've got three dollars. How am I going to pay for lunch?"

Was she talking to me? There was another person in the bathroom, but it was just a freshman who skittered past both of us as soon as Anna finished talking, clearly stunned from being in a room with Tara. And Anna.

"Did we look like that last year?" Anna said, and now I knew she was talking to me.

"I'm not giving you any money." I was proud of how strong my voice sounded. I did want to talk to Anna again, but not like this.

"I didn't ask you for any," she said, sounding surprised and a little angry. "I was just saying I only have three dollars. Mom got laid off again. It's like every time she gets a job and starts talking about taking a vacation, I know what's coming."

I didn't say anything, but there must have been something in my face, an expression Anna knew, because she added, "She still wants to go to Chocolate Village. What is it with that place, and how long has she been promising to take me there?"

"Free chocolate, and since you actually wanted to go."

"I told her to try and take college classes again, but she . . ."

"Won't."

"Yeah. She says she's too old and that—well, you know." The

bell rang and she jumped. "Oh, shit, I gotta go. Tara hates wait-ing. See you later, Kate."

"Okay," I said, and waited until I knew she was gone before I let myself go and spun around in a circle, grinning and giddy. Anna had talked to me again, and even said she'd see me later.

Please, oh please, let her mean it.

# fifteen

**Dad and Todd decided to go to the movies about** ten seconds after Dad and I got to the mall.

"I'm not in a real hurry to go home, you know?" Todd said to Dad, who nodded in weary, Grandma-fearing agreement. "Plus, I know someone who works at the movie theater, and when I was getting us coffee this morning she said that if we showed up before three, she could get us in to see anything for free."

"Any movie?" Dad said, cheering up enough to do a weird half turn, half dance thing I hoped no one saw.

"Yep."

"I'll bring you back something to eat," Dad said as he and Todd practically ran out of the booth, like food made up for him sticking me with watching over his precious business.

Not that there was much to watch over. There weren't any customers, of course, so I did some homework and then tried to rearrange the bulging cabinet below the cash register. Why did Dad keep buying more vitamins?

Mom called the booth after I'd given up fiddling with the cabinet and had gone back to trying to decipher geometry problems. She wanted to talk to Dad, and she sounded tense.

"He's not here."

She sighed. "Where is he?"

"With Todd." It's not that I wanted to protect Dad, who was making me work by myself, but I knew that him skipping out on his "dream job" to go to the movies was the sort of thing Grandma was thinking about when she'd called Dad a child. And even though I'd thought that before myself, it had sounded so mean when Grandma said it.

"So he's left the mall?"

"No! He's just at the movies."

"The movies," Mom said, echoing the words like she didn't quite believe them. "All right, you tell him . . ." She sighed again. "Just tell him I called to say hello."

"Do you want him to call you?"

"No. I mean, it's not necessary. Oh, and Kate—when he does get back, tell him I said you deserve an extra-long break for working so hard."

It was nice that someone noticed. "Thanks, Mom. I will."

Dad came back well after any movie he could have seen

would have ended, eating ice cream and offering me a half-empty box of mushed gummy things, oblivious to my growling stomach and glares.

"Mom called," I said, throwing the candy in the trash.

"Okay," Dad said, and didn't move toward the phone or even ask me what she'd said. "You know, the neatest thing happened when I was watching the movie—which, by the way, wasn't very good. The special effects were terrible and—"

"Dad."

"Okay, sorry, got a little off track there. Anyway, I started thinking about how business is kind of slow and then it hit me. An ad!"

"An ad?" Dad on television? I'd never be able to leave the house again.

"A movie ad. Most of the mall restaurants have them. I could say something like, 'Mention this ad and get thirty percent off your next purchase.' What do you think?"

"Mom said you should let me take a long break."

"Sure, of course. But what about the ad? Should I make it twenty percent off instead of thirty? I'd better call the theater manager and ask about rates."

I didn't feel like sticking around while Dad ignored the fact that Mom had called and went ahead spending money on a business he'd cheerfully abandoned to go to the movies, so I left. He was so caught up in sketching out ad ideas I'm not even sure he noticed me walking away.

At the food court, my warm juice box and sandwich looked pathetic among the mall food. I wished I had something fun to do, or even a magazine to look at, but all I had was homework. I was now a girl who brought her own food to the mall. And worked on her homework. I might as well just have LOSER tattooed on my forehead.

An hour and several false starts on an English paper later, I gave up pretending my so-called break was better than work and decided to head back. I was throwing my trash away when I saw Will. My heart kicked into overdrive, clanging up into my throat, and my juice box missed the trash can and landed on the floor, the cartoon character side of the box facing up.

"My next door neighbor loves those," Will said. "He's six."

"Is that supposed to be an insult? Because you're the one discussing juice boxes with a six-year-old."

"We talk about cereal too." Will grinned at me, and I remembered kissing him in a way that was amazing and scary. Amazing because, well, kissing! Scary because I didn't like how happy I was to see him.

I bent down and picked up the juice box, not realizing I'd end up crouching right next to him, so close that if I reached out I could rest my hand on his leg and then—well.

I know I'm supposed to not be thinking about that kind of stuff, his body, I mean, but the fact is, I was. I did. I do.

I backed up a little, trying to clear my head and suddenly afraid everyone in the mall could read my thoughts, and smacked into a table as I stood up.

"Hey, watch it," the guy sitting there said. "You almost knocked over my food."

I stared at the man, who had a pathetic scrub of a mustache

sprinkled with crumbs from an open bag of potato chips.

"Don't worry, I'm fine," I said. "I'm sorry your chips wobbled. It must have been very traumatic for you."

"Don't give me any crap, kid," the guy said. "I've had a long day, and I have to go to my second job soon. Maybe when you grow up you'll realize life isn't all about you."

"Oh, but I already know that, because clearly it's all about you." It was a great exit line. Too bad I spoiled it by forgetting the juice box I was holding until the little bit that always lurks on the bottom spurted onto my hand. I tossed it into the next trash can I passed, hoping stupid mustache guy wasn't watching, then wiped my hand on my jeans and crossed out of the narrow food court hallway.

"Kate. Hey, Kate, hold up for a second."

Will. I stopped and turned around, giddy because he'd come after me. (Me!)

"Sorry about that guy," he said.

"Yeah, well, if I had that kind of mustache, I'd be in a bad mood too." Wait, had I just implied that I had a mustache of my own? Why did I do stuff like that? Why?

Will laughed, and I relaxed. A little.

"Good point. But then, he is what life is all about. Which is kind of frightening." He shoved his hands into his pockets and fell silent.

I didn't want to look like I was waiting for him to say something else, even though I was, so I forced myself to smile in what I hoped was a polite and not oh-please-kiss-me way, and turned to go.

"Can you meet me later?"

"What?" I was mid-turn, and stopped so fast that I barely managed not to trip over myself.

"I have to break down boxes over where we—over by the trash. I'll be there around nine, and well . . . you know."

"You want me to meet you? Around nine?" I knew I sounded stupid, but Will had just asked me to meet him. Guys did not ask me to meet them.

"Yeah," he said, and then blushed. Will BLUSHED. I didn't know he could do that. I know I should say he suddenly seemed vulnerable and I felt a connection to his soul or whatever, but the truth is I just wanted to tackle him and then make out for the next three thousand years. "It's just . . . today has really sucked, and when you're around stuff doesn't seem so crappy."

"Oh. Okay." I didn't say anything else. I couldn't say anything else.

"Okay," he said, "later," and that was that.

I watched him walk off, sure I was in a dream because there was Will, walking. There was Will, who wanted to meet me. There was Will, who said I made his day better. Well, made it less crappy. But still!

So I made up some excuse, which Dad totally bought because he's Dad and also because he was distracted by the sketches he was still making for his ad, and met Will at nine. I think we were making out before the mall door clicked all the way closed behind me.

At one point I bit his lower lip, and then he did this thing where he sucked on mine and when I touched his face, a quick, careful brushing of my hands along his jaw as I slid them down onto his shoulders, I could feel a little bit of stubble. Just that difference, the slight roughness of his skin, made me feel like I was boneless. Breathless.

Stupid.

I'd been so happy that Will asked me to meet him that I'd overlooked the fact that he asked me to meet him so we could make out. So he could hook up.

Yeah, he'd said being with me made his bad day better. Sort of. If I didn't think about it too much.

But I was thinking about it.

I pulled away. He had his eyes closed, and I watched as they opened. If he'd looked annoyed, I would have known for sure that he just wanted me to stand there and make out with him. I would have known I was as stupid as I was afraid I was.

But he didn't look annoyed. He just looked surprised.

"I don't get this," I said.

"Get what?"

"You know . . . this. I don't even like you."

"You don't like me?" He sounded amused, sort of. Really more like upset and trying to sound amused, like how Dad sounded when he talked to Grandma.

"It's not—I mean, you're just so . . ."

"What?"

"Well, you. Like the first time we met, you made fun of me."

"I don't remember . . ." He trailed off. "I hate it when you look at me like that, like I've proven you right on some theory you have about me."

"Is that your way of saying you do remember?"

He shrugged. "All I did was ask for a pen."

"Oh, yeah?"

"Fine. I'm sorry. But it was my first week at JHS too, and it wasn't like I was in a place where I could say, 'Hey, leave that cute girl alone.' I couldn't even find the cafeteria."

"But it's not like you were nice to me afterward, either." I wasn't going to say anything about him thinking I was cute. I wasn't. (But he thought I was cute! Me! Cute!)

"Hey, I tried. You're the one who called me an illiterate jackass and then practically spit on me if I so much as looked at you after that. And if you don't like me, how come we're here?"

"I—well, everything's just sort of . . . happened. And anyway, it's not like you like me, either." At least I hadn't made it a question. At least I wasn't asking him if he liked me. Not really, anyway.

He looked at me for a moment, a strange, almost hurt look flashing across his eyes, and then he kissed me again.

I hadn't asked the question, but I had my answer anyway, didn't I? It was there, in his silence.

And it hurt. Stupid, I know, but it did.

Stupider still? I kept making out with him.

# sixteen

**Not just that night, either. I started meeting Will** every night at work. Sometimes we met by the trash bins. Sometimes we met by Dad's storage space. One night, we made out inside a closed store. The back door had been propped open a little, probably so the empty racks and pulled-down lights could be taken away, and in that small, shadowed space, it was like the whole world faded away. All I could think about on the ride home that night was how soft the skin on Will's back was, and how it had felt to touch it. To be able to touch him.

We'd been meeting every night, and we never talked about it. But the morning after I'd spent the whole ride home thinking about the two of us in the dark of that closed store, in our own little world, he said, "Kate," in the hall after first period, and used the voice.

The voice was how he talked to girls. Other girls. He'd never used it on me.

I'd thought about hearing the voice before, back when I didn't know what it was like to kiss the skin behind his ear. I'd thought about him saying my name like that back when the pressure of his mouth against mine was a dream.

I didn't want him to say it now.

I didn't want to hear the voice because if I did, what happened between us would be out there, in the open. Real. And I didn't have a good track record with that. Real life had me friendless and selling vitamins at the mall. Real life had me sharing a bathroom with my brother and grandmother.

So I definitely wasn't all that interested in dealing with Will and reality, especially not at school, in front of everyone. "Forget it, I'm not going to tell you what we're supposed to study for the test. No one held a gun to your head and made you fall asleep in class."

"I—" he said, and touched my shoulder, stopping me. "Look, not that I don't appreciate your complete lack of interest in whether or not I pass biology, but—"

He was interrupted by Sarah, who cheered with Anna, and who was cute in the I-know-it way only girls as cute as she was could get away with. "Hey, Will, why didn't you get back to me about coming to last night's game?"

That, right there, was reality smacking me in the face. Hard.

"I had to work," Will said. "I should have called you back. Sorry."

"Oh, no, don't worry about it," Sarah said, and leaned in, pressing her breasts against his arm. "Just don't forget you owe me now." She shimmied off, hips swinging and twitching her little cheerleader flip skirt.

"Why doesn't she just do a super deluxe cartwheel backflip and flash you already?" I muttered, and then glanced at Will.

He was looking at me, and it was a strange, intense look, like he was trying to see inside me.

"Quit giving me the death stare," I said. "I'm not telling you what's going to be on the test. Besides, you've got bigger problems than that. I mean, you owe Sarah, and we all know cheerleaders are the mafia of high school. Who else can get people to pay ten bucks for a crappy car wash?"

His lips twitched. "She's not that bad. And look, I was just supposed to help out with this thing at the game last night. It wasn't a big deal or—"

"Spare me any stories about you and the creation of school spirit through dance routines and 'JHS Rules!' painted on your bony chest."

That night, at the mall, pressed up against the wall by Dad's storage space, Will laughed when my hands slid under his shirt, my thumbs rubbing over the skin below his ribs.

"Not too bony?" he said.

"What can I say, I'm a giver," I told him, and felt something inside me go weak when he laughed again, his eyes crinkling at the corners.

"I—" he said, but I kissed him before he could say anything else.

And before I could think of him shirtless. With Sarah.

On the way home, Dad said, "You've been really eager to take out the trash or put extra products back in storage recently. I'd love to give you a raise or, well, pay you, but—"

"Dad, I'm just trying to help." I didn't want him to keep talking. It felt strange to take praise for stuff I was doing to have frequent makeout sessions. Plus, I wanted to think about Will, not Perfect You's craptastic vitamins.

"It's just that you haven't shown much interest before, so I thought maybe—well, I know your friends must come to the mall, and I thought that maybe working with me was embarrassing and you were hiding."

I looked over at him. He was clutching the steering wheel and smiling his stupid, fake grin. I sighed. "It's not that bad. Working with you, I mean."

"Really?"

"Really, Dad," I said. "But I still won't wear a carrot hat tomorrow."

"But it's a great promotion. I know you weren't that impressed when I read you the leaflet about the new All-Vegetable Tablets, but people like vegetables."

"Dad."

"Well, they should."

"You don't even like vegetables."

"I like some vegetables," Dad said. "And you know, you really are a good daughter, Kate."

"I'm still not wearing the hat," I said, and then we pulled into our driveway and both let out a groan. Grandma had just gotten home.

She'd started going shopping during the day, driving all the way down to the big mall in Faron. It was a long drive, a couple of hours each way, and she always got back around the time Dad and I got home, and then asked us to help carry her bags in.

Dad didn't bring up the carrot hat plan again, not that he'd have been able to get a word in anyway. Grandma had started talking before I'd even gotten out of the car, apparently not noticing that I couldn't hear her.

"There's one truly wonderful thing about shopping here," she said as I was struggling under an armful of slippery dress bags. "No one has the foggiest clue about fashion, and so you get treated like royalty if you're willing to spend more than twenty dollars for an outfit."

Dad coughed behind the armful of bags he was carrying, the closest he'd ever get to telling Grandma to shut up.

"That's not true," I said to her. "It's at least thirty dollars. Maybe even thirty-two."

As usual, Grandma was completely oblivious to all sarcasm and said, "Well, darling, thirty-two dollars is hardly an improvement, is it? Careful with that top bag. It has presents inside." She said the last bit like it was something to look forward to.

It wasn't.

Grandma mostly bought stuff for herself, but sometimes she came back with presents for me or Todd or Mom. Tonight Todd got a suit, which he refused to try on and held like it might bite him before he put it on the floor.

Mom got a long red evening dress. The bottom fanned out

into a curve that trailed across our living room floor, the tiny beads that had been sewn onto it sparkling in the light.

"What am I supposed to do with this?" she said to Grandma.

Dad turned up the video game he and Todd were playing. He was fake smiling, but not very well. He knew a fight was coming, and Dad hated fighting. I figured he'd get up and "go for a walk" in about thirty seconds.

Grandma cleared her throat. "Darling, surely you must have an occasion to dress up for sometime, and red is a wonderful color on you."

Mom looked at the dress, and then held the price tag out toward Grandma. "So you'll spend this kind of money on a stupid dress but you won't—" She broke off, clenching the tag in one fist.

"I spend my money how I see fit."

Mom frowned, then looked at Dad. "Steve, turn that damn game down."

Dad looked at her, shocked like she'd slapped him. Mom's mouth quivered, and she turned back to Grandma and deliberately dropped the dress on the floor. "I don't want this. In fact, you can take it and—"

"Mom, can I have a sandwich?" Todd had abandoned the game and was leaning back on his elbows, looking at Mom upside down.

"Sure," Mom said, visibly relaxing a little, though her voice was still tight. "Steve, honey, did you get anything to eat tonight?"

Grandma glanced at Dad and Todd, and then back at Mom. The sadness on her face surprised me.

"No," Dad said. "I got so busy working on sketches for the ad that I forgot."

"An ad?" Grandma said, actually talking to Dad for once.

"Mother, come help me in the kitchen," Mom said.

Grandma ignored her. "Steve, tell me about this ad."

Dad looked anxiously around the room. Mom clenched her hands into fists by her sides. Todd shot me a look, a panicked, this-isn't-good look.

I glanced around the room, desperate, and then saw Todd's suit on the floor.

"I want a present," I said, inwardly bracing myself. "Grandma, did you get me something?"

Todd rolled his eyes at me but turned back around, satisfied that Grandma would forget about Dad and his ad in order to get the "Oh, Grandma, thank you" speech I was going to have to give.

"Of course, darling," Grandma said, and handed me a box. Mom looked at Grandma, then Dad, and then went into the kitchen. I opened the box.

I got a pair of suede boots. Bright purple suede boots.

"I thought you needed something fun," Grandma said.

"Thank you," I said, and wondered what kind of person would look at me and decide I needed neon purple boots.

"Of course. You're a pleasure to shop for, darling," Grandma said. "Imagine how nice it is to give someone something they don't leave on the floor." She glanced at Todd's suit, and then picked up the red dress, smoothing the fabric across her lap. Her hands were shaking.

"Mother," Mom said from the kitchen, her voice low and furious, and I bolted to my room, saying, "I should really go do my homework."

I worked on my English paper some more, finishing as Grandma completed her endless nighttime bathroom routine. With the coast clear, I snuck out to the kitchen to get something to eat.

Mom and Dad were still up, and they were talking in the dining room. They never did that unless they were discussing something really awful, like how they were going to pay for Todd's braces. They'd closed the door most, but not all, of the way, and I could hear and see them from where I stood.

"You said you liked the idea I came up with for the ad," Dad said.

"It's not that, Steve. How are we going to pay for it? And the house? And our cars? And everything else?"

"I know we don't have a lot of money right now, but things will pick up and get better, and the ad can only help. I know it."

"Well, things certainly can't get much worse," Mom said. Silence fell then—too much silence—and I could practically hear Dad's mouth curl up in a too-bright smile.

"Honey, don't—please don't look at me like that," Mom said. "It's not that I don't believe in you. You know I do. I just think that now isn't the right time to take money we don't have and use it for an ad."

"But I already paid for it," Dad said. "I had to split it between the last two credit cards because it wouldn't fit on one. I . . . I thought it would be okay."

"No, you knew it wouldn't. You just went ahead and did what you wanted, just like always, you selfish—" Mom broke off and pressed a shaking hand to her mouth, then touched Dad's arm. "I'm sorry. I was channeling my mother there, wasn't I? Oh, Steve, having her here is making me crazy. I'm acting like I'm Kate's age again and I—well, we don't need that, do we?"

I stood there for a second, stunned and so mad I wanted to scream. Acting my age? Mom had no idea! If she was my age, she'd be stuck going to school and doing homework and working a crappy job and dealing with a slug of a brother and knowing her family had no money and having no best friend and getting ugly purple boots from the world's worst grandmother.

There was no way Mom could handle my life. None. She couldn't even handle her own.

Her life, which was two jobs, a husband who'd decided selling vitamins was his life's dream and who didn't care that we were running out of money to pay for it, a son who got a college degree and then came home to pursue a career in couch surfing, and a mother who drove everyone crazy.

I went back to my room. I was still mad at Mom for what she'd said, but I also saw that someone actually had a life worse than mine.

Mom.

# seventeen

**The next day, Anna smiled at me before last period.**

I was going to class, and saw Sarah walk up to Will and do that thing only girls like her can do, the one where they grin and toss their hair and manage to somehow stand like there's a spotlight shining on them, showing off how perfect they are. I hate girls who can do that.

I also wish I could do it.

Anyway, the important thing is that I wasn't jealous. I thought I might be, because of the making out, but I felt fine. Not fine as in "Oh, I hope Will and Sarah get together and come make out by me at work" fine, because that would be insane. But fine as in "I knew he'd end up with someone like her."

"Ow," someone said, and I looked away from Will and Sarah and realized I'd walked right into Jennifer S.

"Sorry," I said.

"It's okay," Jennifer said. "It's my fault for stopping like that, but these shoes are killing me."

I looked at her a little more closely and realized she was limping when she walked, like she had blisters. "Are they new?"

"Yeah. I got them the other day with Jennifer T., and we thought it would be fun to wear them today, only she didn't wear hers. But she told me they looked cute. What do you think?"

"Very cute," I said, even though they looked like regular shoes to me. I felt bad for Jennifer S., who was clearly the non-best-friend in the Jennifer M., T., and S. friendship, the one who got left out, behind, and ignored. I knew what that felt like, and for a second I could picture me and Jennifer S. becoming friends. Real friends, even.

Granted, all we had in common was that our friends didn't like us anymore, and after spending the better part of the fall semester hanging out with her and the other Jennifers, I knew that was all we'd ever have in common, but still. It was something.

"I almost bought another pair of shoes, actually," she said. "There were these amazing purple knee-high boots I really wanted, but Jennifer said these were cuter."

Never mind.

I slowed down then, so I wouldn't have to try and make conversation with her anymore, and ended up walking right by Will and Sarah, who were still talking. I only looked at them for a second, I swear, but naturally that was the one second Will chose to not be looking at her and saw me.

"Hey Kate," he said. "Hold up for a second."

He smiled at Sarah and then walked toward me. Sarah dismissed me by not even looking at me and told him, "I'm going to come visit you at work soon," brushing one hand slowly down his back before she swayed away.

"Oh, the lingering back touch," I said. "Must be serious." I could have bitten off my tongue as soon as I said it. For someone who wasn't jealous, I sure sounded like it.

And since I wanted to rip off her hand and jump up and down on it, I was kind of feeling it too. Not a good sign.

"Not that serious," he said, grinning at me. "Like she said, she hasn't even come to see me at work. Now, if someone did that, and then let me buy them a slice of pizza or something, it might be serious."

I wasn't going to read into that. I wasn't. I was going to say something clever. Or at least sort of clever.

"Uh," I said, sounding like an idiot instead, and that's when Anna walked by, holding Sam's hand, and smiled.

Really smiled. At me.

It was like she knew what was going on with Will and saved me from myself. It was like she was my friend again. I mean, I knew that wasn't what her smile was about, I did. But if she hadn't smiled, I probably would have told Will something stupid like, "I like pizza," or worse, "I'll come see you at work."

Luckily, I didn't say anything like that. I was so startled by what had happened (Anna smiling! At me!) that all I could say to

Will was, "I . . . bye," which wasn't clever, but also wasn't begging for a date.

Why had she smiled at me? I couldn't figure it out. Not in last period, not on the way to work, and not when I was at work.

"Hello," Dad said, interrupting my thoughts and waving one hand in front of my face. "Earth to Kate." He made his terrible so-called spaceship noises. "Come in, Kate."

"Funny, Dad. I was just thinking."

"Is everything all right?"

"Yes," I said, dragging the word out. Talking to Dad had punctured my super secret fantasy thoughts, which were that this year was a dream and I'd wake up tomorrow and find out everything had gone back to normal. No more vitamins, no more working in the mall, no more Grandma hogging up the bathroom and making everyone crazy, and Anna would be my best friend again.

"Good. I'm going to get some coffee, okay?"

I nodded, staring down into our display case. If everything did go back to normal, the only thing I'd miss would be Will.

That was a scary thought for a lot of reasons, and it made me think about what he'd said earlier, which, naturally, gave me more to worry about. What had he meant with all that stuff about seeing him and pizza? Did it really mean something? Or was he just talking? Why couldn't guys come with a decoder?

"Kate?"

I looked up. It was Anna. Here. Now.

I made myself blink. She was still there.

"Hi," she said.

"Hey." I didn't know what else to say.

"How's work going?" She was biting her lip the way she did when she was nervous.

"Okay." Was I making her nervous? I couldn't be.

She nodded but didn't say anything, just looked around like she was searching for something. Probably an exit.

"You can go," I said, and was proud of how normal I sounded. My voice wasn't shaking much at all.

She looked at me. "I know."

I refused to look away first, even though I really wanted to. "Why are you here?"

"I just . . . I saw you over here."

"And?"

"God, Kate," she said. "What do you think? I wanted to talk to you."

"Me? Why would you want to do that when you could be hanging out with Diane or laughing at me because my dad sells infomercial vitamins?"

She sighed. "I suck for that. It's just that I . . . look, Diane was really upset. Her mom was pretty freaked out by your dad's party thing."

"Right," I said, my voice tight, and shoved my hands into my pockets because they'd started to shake. "God forbid Diane, who used to call you Fat Ass, should be upset."

"Nice," she said, looking off the to the side again and shaking her head. "Real nice, Kate. Bring up—"

"What, the truth?"

She looked at me. "You . . . you're so you, Kate," she said, and then she smiled. "I saw you talking to Will before last period today. Does he still drive you crazy?"

She had no idea. "Pretty much."

Her smile grew wider. "I really do miss you, you know."

She'd said it before, but it still felt so good to hear. The thing was, why did she miss me now? And what about before? "Is that why you stopped talking to me?"

"I . . . I had to."

"You had to?"

"Things changed for me, Kate, and I . . . I like who I am now. Life was never as easy for me as it is for you."

"Easy for me? Oh yeah, Anna. Having my best friend act like I don't exist? Piece of cake! Getting stuck working at the mall with my dad selling crap vitamins? Joy! Yeah, I can see why you would want my easy life."

"I don't mean—it's just that you've always known who you are," she said. "You never . . . well, you didn't spend years in love with a guy who never noticed you were alive. You didn't have birthday parties that didn't work out like you wanted them to. You didn't . . . things were different for me than they were for you."

"But you were the one who never cared what people said, who—"

"Always listened anyway," she said. "I can still hear what people used to say about me. To me. And I just . . . I got tired of it. I didn't want to be me anymore."

"Well, you aren't."

"But I am," she said. "That's just it. I'm still me. You see it, don't you? See me?"

And looking at her, made over into someone blond and thin and beautiful—I did see it.

I saw Anna, my friend.

# eighteen

**We made plans to meet later, down by the ATM.**

"I have to go home for a while first," Anna said. "I don't want to, but Mom's job hunting, and you know how she is."

When I nodded, she hugged me. "See, that's why I miss you. You do know exactly what my mom is like. I'll see you at nine, okay? And I won't be late, I promise."

"Oh, come on," I said, grinning at her. "There's no way you've changed that much."

She laughed and hugged me again before she walked away.

I went on my dinner break so happy that even hearing Dad obsess about yet another new promotion plan, this one involving me and shrimp, couldn't get me down.

Then I thought of something.

What if she didn't show up?

I put the bag containing my sandwich, a small box of raisins, and a container of warm orange juice on a table in the food court and sat down, slowly taking everything out. She'd show up. I was almost sure of it. After all, she'd said that she missed me. She'd even said it more than once.

But she'd said that back before school started too.

"Hey, where's your juice box?"

I looked up and saw Will standing next to the table, a slice of pizza on a paper plate resting in one hand, a soda in another. Today his name tag said SHOE GUY. I wanted to kiss him so bad I couldn't think straight for a moment.

"What? Oh, right. No juice box today," I said, and put the carton down, poking at the plastic wrap covering my sandwich with one finger. It oozed jelly at me.

"Can I sit down?"

I knocked my juice over. Thankfully, I hadn't opened it yet. "What? Why?"

"Because when I eat standing up, people look at me strangely."

I laughed. "That's not why they look."

"Nice," he said, grinning, and sat down.

I didn't know what to do, so I picked up my juice and opened it. Then I realized I didn't have a straw. I know you're supposed to be able to drink from the carton, but there was no way I was going to try that. I'd have been better off just pouring the juice directly onto my shirt.

I glanced at Will. He was looking at me, and I didn't know

why. I didn't know why he was sitting with me. After we'd started meeting at night, I'd sometimes seen him on a break when I was taking mine, but I'd always left before he could see me, even if it meant killing the rest of my break sitting by our storage area.

"How's work?" he said.

This was exactly why I'd always left. I didn't want him to talk to me like this, like he had to.

"Fine," I said. "You?" What was I doing? I sounded like a freak. A boring freak.

"Well, let's put it this way. I just spent an hour pulling tissue paper out of sneakers so some guy could try on fifteen pairs before deciding he didn't really want new shoes after all."

"I can top that. I just found out that tomorrow I'll be handing out shrimp."

He grinned at me, and I tried not to stare at his dimples. "I'll be up close and personal with other people's feet for hours. I win."

"Have you seen how people act around free food?"

"Strangely enough, I have," he said. "It really isn't pretty, so maybe I don't win after all. We can talk about it later, if you want. I'm supposed to hit the trash and break down boxes at nine."

"I'm meeting someone then," I said, and he didn't say a word. He didn't do anything. He just sat there, his smile fading and his slice of pizza suspended halfway between his plate and his mouth.

"Anna," I added stupidly, like he would somehow care.

"Oh," he said, and put the piece of pizza down only to pick it up again, like he'd forgotten what to do with it.

Then we just sat there for a while. I wanted to leave, but

everything was so weird I was afraid to, and so he ate his pizza and I stared at the table, ignoring my sandwich and picking at my raisins, hoping I wasn't chewing too loudly. Or getting bits of them stuck to my teeth. How could sitting with him be so much harder than making out with him?

"So, what about this weekend?" he said, and I looked at him, startled.

"Weekend?"

"You know, tomorrow—well, tomorrow night, Saturday, and then Sunday? Traditionally known as the weekend. Are you doing . . . are you working?"

"Probably." I felt . . . well, I felt like crap. For a second I'd actually thought he was going to say something else. Ask me out. I was so stupid.

I stood up, grabbing my stuff and squeezing my empty raisin box into a ball. "I've gotta go back to work."

He stood up too. His face was red. "Me too."

We both stopped at the same trash can, sort of walking together but not really, and after we'd tossed our trash we just sort of stood there. It was horrible, but I couldn't bring myself to leave.

"I don't have to go back right away," he finally said, glancing at me.

"Same here," I said. I felt like I should have been upset with him for what he hadn't said before, but the truth was I knew him asking me out wasn't going to happen, that it was just a stupid dream.

Plus I really wanted to kiss him.

For some reason, he decided he had to have another slice of

pizza and then didn't eat any of it. I ate it as we walked back to Dad's storage space instead, sucking cheese off my fingers and making a face at him when I caught him looking at me with a very intense expression, almost like how he looked right before we kissed.

"It's just cheese," I said.

He shook his head, shoving his hands into his pockets and glancing at Dad's ever-growing vitamin stash.

"Kate, look, about this weekend," he said, and I kissed him before he could say anything else. So I could pretend he'd done more than ask me if I was working.

So I could pretend he'd asked me out.

I spent the rest of the night in a weird mood. I was really happy and really not happy at the same time. I couldn't wait to see Anna, but I was still afraid she wouldn't show up, or that she'd show up with Diane and laugh at me.

And then there was the Will thing. Until tonight, I hadn't ever thought about going out with him. Making out with him, on the other hand . . . well, that had been the subject of a whole lot of fantasies, but that was it. I hadn't ever thought about more because I knew Will. He was always hooking up with someone. Plus I'd seen Sarah with him, and who'd pick kissing me over kissing her?

But he'd bought me pizza. Despite what he'd said, I knew he'd gotten that extra piece for me just so I'd have something to eat other than the raisins I'd picked through. And that was so unexpected, and so sweet, that I couldn't help but . . . well, like him. A lot.

Plus he was a really good kisser.

At a quarter till nine, I couldn't stand it anymore and told Dad I was going to meet Anna.

"Oh, sure," he said distractedly. "Hey, do you think a new display would help? Mall management said no to my shrimp idea, but I was thinking of setting up shells, and maybe some sand. A beach-type thing, you know?"

"Sounds great," I said, my voice flat, and grabbed my stuff. I didn't know why I told him anything. All he cared about was stupid Perfect You.

"Kate—"

"What?"

"Have a nice time," he said. "I'm glad you and Anna are talking again. I know you must have missed her."

I guess Dad wasn't always completely clueless.

Anna wasn't by the ATM, but then I was early and she was always late for everything. When I used to meet her at the mall to go shopping, back when being at the mall was something I liked instead of my job, I always told her to meet me twenty minutes before I actually got there so she'd show up when I did.

I sat down on a bench and waited. Then I waited some more. When it had been what felt like two hours, I asked someone walking by what time it was. It was only 9:01, and I told myself to relax, that Anna would show.

But I was so afraid she wouldn't.

I got up and walked down to the main mall corridor, hoping I looked casual and not worried. I stopped and stared in the window of a shoe store, pretending I was looking at a truly ugly pair of heels. Then I went into the only store in the mall that sold decent jeans and flipped through the first rack, the one by the door, as I glanced toward the ATM in what I hoped was a not totally pathetic way.

Anna still wasn't there. I flipped through the jeans again. I pretended I was reading a price tag.

I looked up, and saw Anna standing with Diane by a rack at the back of the store. She was looking at me.

Then she bit her lip and looked away.

I turned around, bumping into the rack, which gave a protesting wheeze. I walked away fast, heading toward the ATM. I stopped halfway there, my eyes stinging, hot with tears I wasn't going to shed. Not here. Not now.

I turned back toward the main part of the mall again, blindly trying to get away from everything, even myself, and saw Anna standing there, hands clenched tight around the shopping bags she was holding.

"Don't be mad," she said, her voice pleading. "I didn't know Diane was going to be here. I ran into her right after I talked to you, and she wanted me to go with her to get some shoes and then look at jeans and I—"

"Didn't want to meet me anymore."

"That's not—Kate, come on. Would I be here if that was true?" She sounded so much like herself, so Anna, that I felt my eyes sting again. "Besides, you've actually saved me. Shopping with Diane is—well, she's kind of . . . you know."

"Actually, I don't."

"Score one for you," Anna said, grinning. When I didn't grin back, she sighed. "The thing about Diane is that she's kind of insecure about everything. You wouldn't believe how much she obsesses over jeans. She's convinced the back pockets make her butt look huge." She rolled her eyes at me the way she used to whenever someone like Diane would push past us like we didn't exist.

She was making fun of Diane. She knew Diane wasn't some amazing person just because she was popular and had the ability to make others feel like dirt! She was still my Anna.

I grinned back at her. "So she's afraid of back pockets?"

Anna's grin grew wider and she moved in closer, nudging my leg with one of the shopping bags she held.

"She is! This one time, we tried on jeans for something like four hours, and she—" Anna looked over her shoulder real fast, and then turned back to me. "She didn't like any of them until I said, 'Oh, I love these!' about some random pair. It was weird, like she needed me to want something so she could get it and I wouldn't be able to."

"Really?" Actually, it didn't sound weird to me. It sounded just like Diane, and I couldn't believe Anna would put up with it. She used to talk so bad about Diane every time we saw her that I thought Anna really hated her.

"Yeah, it's crazy. You want to sit down?"

"Sure," I said, and we sat on the bench where I'd waited before.

"So, I'm thinking of getting my hair cut really short," Anna said, looking around and then smiling at me. "I sort of fried it the first time I dyed it because I did it myself. Does it look totally weird blond?"

"No, it looks good."

"Thanks. I'm always afraid Mom is going to drag out photos for Sam to see and it's like, 'Hi, Mom, let's not remind him I used to be a fat ass with bad hair.'"

"You weren't ever—"

"Oh, please. I was disgusting. Fat and boring."

"Hey, that's my friend you're talking about."

She smiled at me again, but this time it was different, almost sad. "You're so nice to me, Kate. I—hey, is the mall closing?"

"What? Oh, yeah," I said, as the mall closing chimes dinged. "It's sad, but now that I work here, that sound is the best noise—"

"Oh no," she said, jumping up and grabbing her bags. "I totally forgot I was supposed to go home and hear about Mom's job search, and you know how she is when she thinks I'm ignoring her." She started frantically digging around in her purse. "Where are my keys? Where the hell—?"

"Here," I said, and took her purse. "I'll get them." They were in the bottom, stuck under her wallet just like always, except now she had a car key next to her house key. I'd seen Anna's car around and always wondered what it would be like to ride in it. Maybe I'd find out now.

"This sucks," she said when I handed them to her. "I don't want to go, but Mom—"

"I know." I did. Anna's mom was intense, and not in a good way. She loved Anna and didn't care much about anything else, which meant Anna got whatever she wanted but was also basically her mom's only friend, as well as her shrink.

"I want to give you a ride home, but I need to go. I hope

you aren't mad, because I really don't want you to—"

"I'm not mad, and everything will be okay with your mom."

"Promise?" she said, like she always did whenever she was worried about talking to her mother.

"Promise," I said, just like always too, and she hugged me then, hard, saying, "I miss you so much, you have no idea. Thank you for putting up with me."

I felt pretty good after she left. Almost great, even. I would have to catch a ride home with Dad, but that wasn't a big deal. Anna talking to me—now that was a big deal. And it had been fun. It even felt like we'd never stopped talking at all, especially toward the end.

I walked back to the main part of the mall, which was now mostly empty, and then, for some reason, I stopped. I don't know why I did this, but I went back the way I came. I passed the store I'd seen Anna and Diane in, and Diane came out as I walked by.

She didn't seem to notice me, and I followed her past the bench I'd sat on with Anna, and then down to the door I'd seen Anna leave through. I pretended I was using the ATM as she went outside, and heard her say, "Okay, why were you acting so weird before? And where did you run off to?" as the mall door swung closed.

She had to be talking to Anna. The bottled-up tears from before stung my eyes again, and I leaned against the door until the feeling passed, telling myself not to look.

I did anyway.

There was nothing to see except a car out by the edge of the parking lot, pulling onto the road. I didn't try to see if I recognized it. I didn't want to. Anna had talked to me. She missed me. That meant something. I knew it did.

It had to.

But part of me knew it didn't mean enough. A part of me hated how pathetic I was around Anna, how desperate I was to have her talk to me. I couldn't help myself, though. I missed her enough to take crap from her that I wouldn't take from anyone else because I wanted her to come back to me for real. Be my friend again for real, be the Anna who had always been part of my life.

# nineteen

**The next day, I ran into Will right after last** period ended.

"Locker run," he said, like those two words explained something. Which they didn't, because I knew exactly where Will's locker was, and it wasn't here.

Obviously, however, I couldn't say that.

"I'm going to meet my ride," I said, and was sorry as soon as the words were out. What if Will thought I was asking him to walk with me? I didn't want to be pathetic.

More than usual, I mean.

He nodded. And walked with me! "Are you going to Jennifer T.'s party?"

I didn't know Jennifer was having a party. I looked at him, to see if he was kidding, and he looked back at me, smiling, but there was something tentative, almost fragile, in his eyes. I looked away, afraid that if I didn't I might do something stupid like tell him how much I liked him.

"I wasn't invited."

"I heard her ask you in first period."

Had she said something about a party? Now that he mentioned it, I did remember her babbling at me during biology, but I'd been so busy wondering if Anna would say anything to me (she hadn't, she didn't even look at me once all day) that I didn't really listen. "Oh, I thought you were talking about something else. But yeah, I think I might go."

"Me too."

"Really?" We were walking almost close enough for our shoulders to touch, and I had a sudden (and insane) desire to tell him about last night, about talking to Anna. To ask him what he thought. I wondered what he was thinking now, and wished I could ask him why he was asking me about Jennifer's party.

"Yeah. See you around?" he said, and gave me that look again, the intense one that made me want to shove him up against a wall and kiss him until I couldn't breathe.

"Sure." I was proud of how calm I sounded. Almost sophisticated, even.

Then I walked outside, saw my father sitting in his car wearing the stupid carrot hat he'd been talking about, and realized I was never going to be sophisticated.

Not that it stopped me from asking Dad if I could take the night off. Or telling him to never ever wear the carrot hat when he was anywhere near school.

"In fact, just don't wear it when you're not at the mall," I said.

"I forgot I had it on," he said, grinning at me. "It's just so comfortable that I—"

"I'm still not wearing one, Dad. And what about tonight? I don't have to work, do I?"

"I'd like to give you the night off, honey. But what if it gets busy?"

I looked out the window and forced myself to take a deep breath. "It's not usually busy. And I worked by myself when you and Todd went to the movies. And that time you did that thing at the library."

"Your mother has to work tonight, so she won't be able to take you anywhere."

"I'll get a ride." I didn't know how I'd do that, but I'd think of something. If necessary, I'd even ask (shudder) Grandma.

"Big plans?" Dad actually sounded curious, and when I glanced at him he was looking at me strangely, almost like I'd grown horns. Or was wearing a carrot hat.

"Not really. I just want to go out, that's all."

"You're growing up so fast," he said, and I realized he was looking at me so strangely because he was doing that choked-up thing parents do when they realize that you're sixteen and not, say, three. "You know, if there's ever anything you want to talk about, or any questions you might have—"

"Dad, if I don't know about sex by now, I'm pretty much doomed, don't you think?"

"Maybe I wasn't talking about . . . that."

"I heard you say the exact same thing to Todd after you caught him and his girlfriend doing it in his room."

"All right, all right," Dad said hastily, his face bright red. "So you've heard my little speech about being responsible before. I still mean it, though. You can talk to me about anything."

I knew he meant it. He'd die of embarrassment if I ever did ask about sex, but he'd at least die trying, and that was nice to know, especially since a lot of the time it seemed like he saw me as a vitamin pack mule. "Thanks, Dad."

"Hey, Kate," he said when I was getting out of the car at home, "have a good time tonight, okay?"

I nodded.

"You're a special girl, and I hope you know that you should wait until you meet a guy who appreciates you for who you are before—"

"Tonight isn't about a guy, Dad." And it wasn't. Not exactly. I mean, I was just going to a party, and if a certain someone happened to be there, then he was there. It wasn't like it was a big deal or anything.

I reminded myself of that a lot, especially after I'd changed clothes for the fourth time. And after I caught myself having imaginary conversations with Will. (Good—Him: "Kate, you're so beautiful, I can't stop thinking about you." Me: "You're so sweet. Tell me more." Bad—Him: "Oh, hey, Kate. I didn't see you. I was too busy making out with Sarah." Me: "I didn't see you either, because I was looking for my . . . my date." Him: "Date? You? Oh, that's funny. Sarah, isn't Kate funny?")

Once I'd finally found something to wear that wasn't totally hideous, I went to the bathroom to brush my teeth. Grandma was already in there, examining two identical-looking eye shadows.

"Bought these today, darling," she said. "Which one looks best?"

"Whichever one will let you let me use the bathroom."

She laughed but didn't move. Typical. "You look nice. Are you going somewhere?"

"To see some friends."

"What time are you leaving?"

What time? Great. I'd spent so much time thinking about Will asking me if I was going to be at the party that I hadn't thought about the actual party. "I'm not sure. I mean, soon."

Grandma frowned at the eye shadows. "Maybe I should have bought a third color too."

I gave up and grabbed my toothbrush, then headed to Mom and Dad's bathroom.

By the time I'd gotten my breath as minty fresh as I could and left a message for Mom saying I'd call by midnight for a ride home, I realized I still needed a ride. I hyperventilated in the front hall for a while, trying to figure out how I could get Grandma to take me there without having to talk to her on the way, and just when I'd realized it wasn't possible and I'd have to spend the night at home, Todd came in and said, "Hey, loser, Dad said you were going out. Guess he was wrong."

"Not that it's any of your business, but I am going out. What are you doing here?"

He grinned at me. "Dad said I could take off early. He felt bad because I had to stay and help out this afternoon so someone could go home and get ready for her big night. So, how is standing in the hall working out for you?"

I saluted him with my middle finger. "You're such a disease."

"Todd, darling, is that you?" Grandma called from the living room. "Come here and say hello."

Todd's eyes got wide. I grinned at him and, in my loudest voice, called out, "Grandma, he's—"

"Stop," he whispered, cutting me off. "What do you want?"

"A ride," I whispered back.

"Fine," he said, and jerked his head in the direction of Grandma's voice. "Tell her I'm not here."

I rolled my eyes at him, but said, "He's not here, Grandma."

"I thought I heard him."

"No, it's just me." I looked at Todd, who was edging toward the door, and clamped one hand onto his arm. "And I'm going now, Grandma. Bye!"

"That was so wrong," Todd said when we got outside. "I can't believe you were going to rat me out to Grandma. I'd never—"

"Spare me," I said, and got in the car.

Jennifer's party had definitely started by the time I got there, because Jennifer S. came up to me as soon as I walked in. She was upset because Jennifer M. and T. weren't talking to her.

"I even heard them say they don't like my shoes!" she said, and then burst into tears.

"They're nice shoes," I said, looking around for Will.

"You think?" She sniffed, and wiped her eyes. "I like yours."

And that's how I ended up discussing shoes with Jennifer S. for two hours while she pretended she wasn't watching everything Jennifer M. and T. did, and I pretended I didn't care that Will wasn't there.

That's right. Wasn't there. Will hadn't come.

I'd really thought he would, that he'd asked about tonight and the party because—well, because he'd wanted me to be here. I was so stupid.

I wanted to go home, but as soon as I told her I was leaving, Jennifer S. started to cry again and begged me not to go because she didn't want to be alone. I could relate to that.

Naturally, I ended up standing by myself, holding a drink that was so strong my nose stung every time I lifted the cup toward my mouth. I finally ducked outside and dumped it, tossing the cup away as I came back inside.

Will wasn't coming, Jennifer S. had forgotten me now that Jennifer M. and T. were talking to her again, and there was no reason for me to stay. I started looking for a phone, wishing for once that I still had a cell. They'd been one of the first things to go when money got tight, though, and I hadn't cared since I wasn't getting any calls.

I finally found a phone in the living room. Actually, it was Jennifer S.'s cell phone, and I borrowed it out of her purse right after she'd run up to me and said, "Get this. Jennifer T. is mad at

Jennifer M. because she totally disappeared with her boyfriend even though she swore she was going to help with the party. Can you hold my purse? Jennifer says I need to look more stream-lined."

She didn't even wait for me to say anything before she thrust the purse at me and ran off, so I felt justified in using her phone. Virtuous, even, because I didn't even look at her text messages, just called home.

Grandma answered and said Mom and Dad were talking, but that she'd tell Mom to come get me.

"If Mom sends Dad, tell her to remind him that I left the address on my note."

"What? I'm sorry, darling, this phone is beeping at me. Your brother is certainly a popular young man."

I snorted. He was, but that was because none of the girls who called seemed to understand that when Todd said, "I'm an actor/potter/poet," he meant, "I live at home, and am one with the sofa."

"Of course," Grandma said, "I doubt these young women realize his primary career is watching television."

Huh. Maybe Todd wasn't totally off when he said I sounded like Grandma.

Oh crap, I sounded like Grandma.

"I gotta go," I said, and hung up. And then, just when I'd realized I'd wasted my whole night AND was capable of thinking exactly like a woman who lent new meaning to the term pain-in-the-ass, I saw Will.

# twenty

**He'd clearly just come from work, because he was** in his Sports Shack uniform, and he'd brought Sam with him. You could actually hear everyone fall silent for a moment because Sam didn't come to parties like this. He went to parties thrown by people like Tara. Or Anna.

Anna wasn't with Sam, though. I wondered about that, but only for a second, because Jennifer M. appeared, trying too hard to act casual around Sam and practically flinging herself at Will, who didn't seem to notice me even though I was basically right in front of him.

I dropped Jennifer S.'s phone back in her purse and set the whole thing down on a chair, then went into the kitchen. My plan was to head out into the backyard through the door I'd used to ditch my drink before, and then circle around to the front of the house and wait for Mom or Dad to show up.

Sam and Will came into the kitchen too, Sam nodding at something Jennifer M. said and smiling the slightly bored smile he wore whenever he talked to anyone who wasn't someone. Will was sauntering over to a pizza Jennifer T. had miraculously produced despite the fact she'd told everyone there wasn't any food left ages ago.

I headed toward the door, reaching it just as I heard Will say, "No, man, I haven't been with anyone tonight. But maybe I can talk someone into leaving with me," grinning as the guys around him laughed and a couple of girls, including Jennifer M., giggled and shot him hopeful looks.

I laughed. I couldn't help myself. Will was so full of shit and tonight . . . tonight couldn't end fast enough. I'd dressed up and hoped and I was so tired of doing that, so tired of dreaming and being unable to stop it despite the fact that I'd seen, maybe better than anyone here, what dreams could do to you. Anna had a dream, it had come true, and she wasn't my friend anymore. My father had a dream, and I had to sell vitamins and share a bathroom with my brother and grandmother because of it.

A couple of people heard me laugh and looked over. I shrugged, like I didn't care that people were staring even though I did, but as I started to turn away I saw Will looking right at me, like he knew where I'd been all along.

"In fact," he said, still staring at me, "I know for sure that this uniform," he gestured at himself, "drives some women crazy. Make-out-with-me-behind-the-mall crazy."

Sam laughed, and most everyone else did too. But Will didn't, and a couple of the more observant girls didn't either. I saw Jennifer M.'s mouth open and her eyes light up as what he was saying sank in, and felt myself blush as she looked at me, connecting the dots of a story about Will and a mystery mall skank.

I don't think I'd ever wanted anyone to drop dead as much as I wanted Will to in that moment. Not only had he basically let everyone know that we'd hooked up, he'd made it sound like I was so crazy for him that I'd make out with him anywhere. He'd made me sound like I was just another girl in his never-ending parade of them.

He'd made me into what I'd always known I was to him: nothing. He'd made me into what I'd been stupid enough to pretend wasn't true.

I guess he saw me realize that because he grinned, that adorable, dimpled grin I'd prided myself on being immune to when I hadn't been immune to it at all, and said, "Hey, Kate, do you want a slice?" holding up a piece of pizza.

Maybe it was a peace offering, or even his stupid way of apologizing, but all it reminded me of was before. Of him buying me a slice of pizza. Of me thinking that him asking about the weekend meant something.

Of me pretending he'd asked me out.

I threw my shoe at him. I would have picked something better, but it was all I had to work with. At least I hit him in the head, my shoe connecting with a loud smack before bouncing off him and landing in the middle of the pizza.

Will stared down at the ruined pizza and then looked at me,

a mixture of shock, hurt, and fury in his eyes. Then he picked up
my shoe, went over to a window, and tossed it outside. I realized
what he was doing as soon as he picked it up, but by the time I
got to him he'd already thrown it and people were laughing.

"That was my shoe," I said.

"No, really?"

"You know what?" I said, so furious the words just poured
out of me. "I wouldn't run around saying that someone wants to
make out with you behind the mall. Because, really, how crazy
about you can she be? Just think about it. You, and the back of
the mall, where they keep the trash. Sounds like she's figured out
where you belong." Then I turned around and glided outside.

At least as much as anyone can glide with only one shoe on.

"You think I'm trash?"

I looked behind me. He'd followed me outside. His forehead
was still a little red from my shoe, and he looked pissed off.

Good.

"Let's see, you come in and announce you're making out
with me behind the mall because I'm so hot for you I can't help
myself? I guess I could have called you the most amazing guy
ever, but somehow that just doesn't seem to fit," I said, and started
digging around in the seemingly millions of bushes in Jennifer T.'s
backyard.

"I don't get you," he said. "One minute you're sticking
your tongue down my throat, and the next you're throwing
shoes at me."

"Look who's talking. You ask me about my weekend, but
don't ask me out. You ask me if I'm coming here and then don't

show for ages and then, when you do, you talk about taking someone else home and then make me sound like I—" I broke off and wished I'd get sucked into another world through one of the stupid bushes. A world where I hadn't just said all the things I had. A world where it wasn't so painfully obvious that I liked him more than he liked me.

He walked toward me. "I couldn't get here earlier. I had to work. And when I asked about the weekend, I wanted to—"

"I don't care."

"Then why did you bring it up? And why won't you ever let me finish saying anyth—"

"I brought it up to prove you're a jackass. A 'Hey, I'll make out with you because you work at the mall and no one else is around' jackass. A 'Hey, come to a party so you can hear me talk about how I can pick up someone else' jackass. A 'Hey, watch me throw shoes around' jackass." My voice was wobbly and my eyes burned, like I was going to cry. I told myself it was because I'd gotten a finger snagged on a branch.

"Wait, you threw your shoe at me because you think I kiss you just because you work at the mall?" he said, and then laughed.

I stared at him, incredulous. Laughing? Now? Great. I was SO glad I'd blabbed my brains out.

"You are the strangest girl I know," he said. "You won't even talk to me for more than ten seconds unless we're at the mall, so how could I ever kiss you anywhere else? And who do you think I was talking about when I said I wanted to talk someone into leaving with me?"

"I'm not strange," I said, straightening up and brushing dirt off my hands. "Just because I don't find your brand of bullshit . . . oh. You were talking about me?"

"Did you see me looking at someone else?" he said, and then he kissed me.

I forgot about finding my shoe.

In fact, I forgot everything and we ended up on the ground, tangled in Jennifer T.'s endless shrubbery and each other. I only opened my eyes once, registering branches and the shadow of Will's face, head thrown back as I yanked at the buttons on his shirt, and that sight was enough to dazzle me.

Well, that and the enormously bright light that suddenly blasted my eyes, causing Will and me to freeze, blinking like mole people.

"Kate, are you out here?" Jennifer M. said, sounding alarmingly close. "Jennifer T. said I should come look for you. And, hey, if you can hear me, have you seen Will? Because he— oh. OH."

"Hi," I said, registering her as a gossipy blur as I pulled my shirt down and tried to yank all the bits of whatever plant I was lying in out of my hair. "I was just looking for my shoe."

Jennifer, now swimming alarmingly into focus, held up something that looked an awful lot like my lost shoe. "It was right by the door."

"Thanks," I said, trying not to hate her for staring at Will like she wanted to undo all the shirt buttons he was refastening. (Not that I wanted to do anything like that. At least, not with her around.)

PERFECT YOU

"Oh, and your brother's here," she said, glancing distractedly at me before looking at Will again. "He's inside."

Todd? If Todd was here that meant something had happened because he was not the kind of guy to give up his weekend to drive me home. Especially not after I'd pretty much blackmailed him into driving me here. What could have happened? Something with Mom? Or Dad? Or both of them?

I ran inside, only to find Todd talking to Jennifer T. and looking down her shirt as she leaned forward to show off her cleavage. Somehow, when I'd seen her do what she called "the move" back when we were hanging out, I never pictured her using it on my brother.

"What's wrong?" I said, and Todd looked at me and started laughing.

"You look—" he sputtered.

"Shut up," I muttered, and dragged him to the door.

"What's wrong?" I asked again when we were outside, elbowing him after he kept laughing.

"Nothing," he said, grinning as we got in the car and he pulled out onto the street. "I went by the house just now to borrow some money from Mom—and say hi—but Grandma pounced as soon as I walked in and told me to come get you. Great hair, by the way. And the one shoe look? Very nice."

I made a face at him and slumped into my seat. Super. I'd left my shoe behind. Just like Cinderella, only I wasn't a princess. And I hadn't been at a ball. Or with a prince. I'd been rolling around in the bushes with Will.

When we got home, Grandma was awake, drinking diet

soda and reading a fashion magazine, folding down the pages that had something she liked. Most of the pages were folded.

"Todd, you got two phone calls from a young woman named Amy," she said, still flipping through her magazine. "Must all of your friends phone so late? Also, your mother is not an ATM." Then she looked at me and put her magazine down.

"I know, I'm a mess," I said, fidgeting under her stare and the fact that she'd put aside fashion in favor of me. Clearly, she knew something had happened.

"Mess? You've only got one shoe on," Todd said, knocking his shoulder against mine and taking great pains to pick a piece of shrubbery out of my hair, grinning at me as he did. "Maybe you should explain what that's about."

"Shut up," I hissed.

"Good night, Todd," Grandma said, rising from the sofa and gesturing for me to follow her, tucking her magazine under one arm. "Remember what I said about your mother."

Grandma didn't say a word to me when I followed her back to what was once Todd's room, but was now thoroughly hers. She'd even put pink sheets on his bed. Oh, I hope she left them there when she left. It would serve Todd right.

I waited for her to say something about my hair or my missing shoe, but she just sat on the bed and looked at me.

"Well?" I finally said, brushing my hands against my legs and hoping Grandma wouldn't notice the puffs of dirt that rose off me and drifted toward the floor.

"Well, what?" she said. "Move back a little, darling, so you don't get dirt on those bags next to you."

"Aren't you going to say something?"

"What do you want me to say?"

"I don't know," I said. "I mean, you must know that I . . . I mean, I guess you're probably going to say something to . . ." I trailed off. No need to go into details, and definitely no need to suggest that Grandma mention this to anyone. Like, say, Mom.

"I suspect what happened is tied up with the fact that your shirt is on backward and that a few minutes before you got home I had a nice chat with a young man named Will, who asked me to tell you that he has your shoe."

"Oh." I hadn't even noticed my shirt.

"He sounds like a very nice boy, although you might want to rethink rolling around on the ground with him, darling. Or at the very least, carry a brush when you go out."

"It's not like that."

"It's not?"

"Okay, it's sort of like that. But it's . . . complicated." Will had called? He'd actually called?

"The best things usually are," Grandma said, looking back at her magazine.

I went to bed before I cracked and asked her to tell me exactly what he'd said and how he'd said it.

I went to bed and pretended he'd told her to be sure to tell me that he'd call again.

# twenty-one

**When I woke up, my clock said it was after ten.**

That couldn't be right. The mall opened at ten, and Dad liked to get me and Todd up at eight because he was always so excited about his plans for the day that he couldn't wait to tell us about them.

I rubbed my eyes and got out of bed, deciding that Todd had messed with my clock as payback for having to drive me around last night, and went to the bathroom. Weirdly, Grandma wasn't in there fussing with her hair or putting on makeup, but I enjoyed not having to wait to use the bathroom for once.

After I got dressed, I checked to see if Grandma was in Todd's room, but she wasn't. I headed out into the living room, but that was empty too. Todd wasn't even there, and the blankets he slept with were neatly folded and resting on the far end of the sofa.

"Hello?" I said, starting to feel a little freaked out. Where was everyone? And since when was Todd neat? Or not on the sofa?

"Hey," Todd said, leaning out of the dining room door. "Can you please come in here?"

Now I knew I had to be asleep. Todd and I never went in the dining room, and he'd said "please." The last time Todd said that was during dinner right after he'd graduated from college. He said, "Please pass me the potatoes, Kate," and then asked Mom and Dad if he could move back in.

"Why did you say please? And why do I have to come into the dining room? Did you drive the car into the garage door again?"

"Hilarious. Just get in the dining room, will you?" he said, and then mouthed the word "Mom" at me.

"M—" I started to say, but he shook his head and gave me another look, the same one he'd given me the night I'd jumped into whatever was brewing between Mom, Dad, and Grandma and ended up with those awful purple boots. A things-are-bad-so-help-me-do-something look.

I went into the dining room and then stopped, frozen. Mom was sitting at the table. Her eyes were all red, like she'd been crying.

"Mom?" I said.

"Your grandmother's out shopping, so I thought we could—

should—talk now," she said, motioning at the chair across from her. The words sounded like Mom words, but her voice . . . her voice was so broken-sounding.

"What's going on?" I said as I sat down, and glanced at Todd. He was staring at the floor and, I swear, looked as upset as Mom did.

I sat down.

"This is hard for me to say," Mom said, and then talked about how things had changed since Dad had left his job (like I hadn't noticed), and how money was tight (like I hadn't noticed that either), and that sometimes, in spite of trying your hardest, bad things happened. I didn't say I already knew that, because I had a feeling she wasn't talking about Grandma visiting.

In fact, I had a feeling that, once again, my life was going to get worse.

"We're going to have to move," Mom said, and started to cry.

Move? Leave the house? My bedroom, the hallway I'd practiced cartwheels down, the bathroom where Anna and I had tried to highlight our hair with hydrogen peroxide, the kitchen where Todd and I argued over who got the last piece of cake—leave all of it? Lose all of it?

No. I couldn't have heard right. But looking at Mom, and seeing her cry, I knew I had.

"But Grandma . . . I heard her say she'd help you," I said.

"What?" Mom said, wiping her eyes, her voice suddenly sharp.

"I heard you talking to her one morning," I muttered. "She

said she'd help you but not Dad. So why won't she help with the house?"

"I can't ask her," Mom said, her voice tight.

"Can't?"

"Your father and I—we needed money to send Todd to college," Mom said. "We couldn't get a loan, because we had so many credit cards, but we were able to use them. The thing is, my mother had given us money for Todd's education when he was born, but things got tight and we . . . we did what we had to." She cleared her throat. "So that's why I can't ask her now. I don't want her to know."

"But—"

"Stop," Mom said, her voice rising. "Look, I've—I've tried, using our savings and then getting another job, but between paying the minimum on the credit cards, the mortgage, and everything else, we've fallen behind. Very behind. If we sell the house now, we should be able to pay off most of what we owe."

"But Grandma could help! She has money, and—"

"And you think my mother is going to just hand over what we need?" Mom said. "Do you really think she'd do that with no strings attached? That she wouldn't constantly remind us of how we spent money she'd set aside for Todd on other things?"

"She might." If I poured a lot of liquor into her diet soda first.

"I'm not going to discuss this with you any further," Mom said. "Your father and I have to sell the house, and as hard as it's going to be for all of us, it's something we have to do." She stood up. "A real estate agent is coming by in a few hours, and I need your help cleaning. Will you please—?"

"No," I said, and got up too, slamming my chair into the table. "I can't believe how stupid you and Dad are. That's right, I said stupid. And if you want the house cleaned, you do it, because you're the one who screwed up and lost it."

"Hey," Todd said, staring at me angrily, "don't—"

"Shut up," I said. "I'm going to have to move because you spent four years learning to burp the alphabet only to move back in and lie around doing nothing."

"I'm getting a job," Todd said, his voice stiff and his face red with fury. He went over to Mom, hugged her, and said, "I'll come back as soon as I'm done and start cleaning up the backyard."

"Way to go, suck up," I said, glaring at him. "Now you're getting a job? I guess I'd better get one too. Oh, wait, I already have one. In fact, I'm late for it."

"Your father's given you the day off," Mom said. "He—we—thought it might be easier for you."

"Right, Mom. You mean it's easier for him. He doesn't have to deliver the bad news. He gets to come home tonight and pretend everything's fine. In fact, I bet he's actually glad Grandma's here because you won't tell her what's going on, and he thinks no one else will mention it to her. Well, guess what? I'm telling her everything."

Todd grabbed my arm and dragged me out of the dining room. "Stop it," he said, practically shaking me.

"Quit it," I said, and pushed him away. "All of this is your fault, you know."

"You think I don't know that?" he said. "Hearing that I'm the reason we're losing the house feels—"

"I don't care how you feel. No, wait, I do care. I hope you feel terrible. I hope you feel so terrible that—"

"That I wish I'd gotten a job instead of coming back home? That maybe I'd wondered why Mom and Dad always looked so freaked whenever I told them tuition was due? Guess what, Kate? I feel all that stuff."

He stalked into the kitchen and got out the mop, coming back and thrusting it at me. "But you know what? This isn't about me and, believe it or not, it isn't even about you. Mom is really upset, and she can't get the house ready for the real estate agent by herself. So shut up, grow up, and help out."

I stared at him, speechless, and then I started to cry. Not because of what he'd said, but because he was upset too and that, more than anything else, made me realize this was going to happen. It didn't matter that I didn't want it to. It didn't matter that it wasn't fair. What I thought and wanted didn't matter, not in this.

Not in anything.

# twenty-two

**Mom and I cleaned, the real estate agent came,**
and when she left our house was officially for sale. At least, I
assume it was. The two of them went out "to discuss things" after
Mom was done showing her around. I wasn't invited, even though
I'd just spent the last few hours wiping dust out of corners that
hadn't seen the light of day since before Todd was born.

Even though it was my house too.

I didn't say anything, though. I figured I'd said enough
earlier.

I lay down on the sofa, staring at the ceiling because I was
too depressed to even turn on the television. Today sucked. I
wished I could go out and do something, but where could I go?

What could I do? Nothing. There was no one who wanted to see me, except maybe Will.

Will. I sat up.

Will, who had my shoe. Will, who had called me. I could count the number of guys who'd called me on one hand, and until now, it had always been about homework.

I could call him back.

I could, but the thought of doing that made my stomach hurt. What if he wasn't home? Worse, what if he was? I figured I could get out "Hi, Will" on my own, but everything else—I'd have to write it down first, and then practice. A lot.

And what if I did all that and he just wanted to say, "You left your shoe behind" or, worse, "What? Oh yeah, I called. I gave your shoe to Sarah and she'll give it to you on Monday because I'm going to be really busy making out with her in between classes. And hey, by the way, what's going to be on our biology test?"

I lay back down on the sofa. No way could I call him. With my luck, why risk it? So far my sophomore year had rendered me friendless, and now I was heading toward homeless. And that didn't even include the fact that I wasn't allowed to drive, and had to work at the mall. Or deal with Dad and his Perfect You obsession.

No, life was bad enough already, and I didn't need it to get worse. Right? I looked over at the phone, then away. Then back at the phone again.

Then Grandma came home, and I knew not calling was

the right choice because she was more than enough proof that I didn't need to go around making life worse. It would just happen for me.

"Darling, what on earth are you doing?"

"Lying on the sofa."

"Well, get up, darling, and don't look so miserable. Let me tell you about my day. I had the most wonderful time shopping. Look at all the lovely things I got."

I sat up again, and was treated to a show of shirts and pants and then, frighteningly, underwear. I lay back down during that part of the show-and-tell, not that it stopped Grandma from talking.

She finally finished and headed back to Todd's room to stow her bags. "So, how was your day?" she called out. I thought about pretending I couldn't hear her, but she'd just come out and ask again, and at least there was a buffer zone when she was in Todd's room.

"Fine. I cleaned the bathroom." It hadn't been easy, mostly because Todd was a pig but also because I had to pick up each of Grandma's makeup/hair/skin products in order to clean under them. Or at least I did after Mom caught me cleaning around them.

"Did you talk to that nice young man who called last night?"

I was not going to answer that question. There was no way I wanted to discuss Will with Grandma.

Naturally, this meant Grandma came back to the living room and made me sit up, then settled down next to me on the sofa. "So, did you speak to—?"

"Yes, I talked to him. We're getting married tomorrow. Don't tell Mom."

Grandma patted my knee. "I'm sure things will work out."

"There's nothing to work out. I don't care if I talk to him or not."

She gave me a look I couldn't read, and then said, "Well, if he doesn't appreciate you, then it's his loss."

"Right, Grandma. Thanks."

"Kate, I mean it. Don't define yourself through some boy— or through anyone. It's not worth it. Not ever."

"You mean like you and—"

"Yes, like me and your grandfather. And your mother and father. Not that I don't think your father is a wonderful father. And he does love your mother. But I look at all your mother is doing, and I can't help but wonder—"

"Wonder what?" Mom was standing in the doorway, and she looked mad.

Grandma looked right at her, not backing down. "Wonder why you've given up so much for a man who is so selfish."

I didn't know it was possible for Mom to look madder than she already did until then. If looks could kill, Grandma would be dying in a really unpleasant way.

"I don't think I want to discuss selfishness with you, Mother. And I'd appreciate it if you'd keep your thoughts on my marriage to yourself, rather than try to sweep Kate into your ridiculous attempts at drama."

"Let's not do this, darling," Grandma said quietly. "I'm

leaving in a few days, and I don't want to fight. I want to spend time with you in your lovely home—"

Mom laughed, but it was a brittle sound. "It's not my lovely home. Not for much longer, anyway."

"What do you mean?"

Mom frowned, looking away from Grandma for the first time. "Darling, if this is about money, I told you—"

"No, Mother, it isn't about money. It's about the house." She paused, and I watched her take a deep breath. "We're selling it."

"Selling? But darling, isn't that extreme? Surely even Steve couldn't have run up enough debt—"

"You just can't help yourself, can you? You always have to get in a dig at my husband. God forbid you say you're sorry to hear we're going to have to move."

Okay, I'd heard enough. More than enough. I got up and edged my way to the hall, hoping to slip around Mom and make it back to my room before this fight got any worse.

"You wouldn't have to move if you'd leave Steve and let him sink on his own," Grandma said. "You know I'd take care of you, darling. You and the children mean the world to me."

"Really? Because I had no idea that meaning the world to someone actually meant 'I'll fix things for you, but only if you do exactly what I say and destroy your family.' Let him sink on his own? Listen to you!"

The phone rang then. I'd never been so happy to hear it, and that included the time Grandma called after I failed my first driving test and got Mom so upset that she forgot she'd told me I couldn't take the test again for another year and let me take it the next month.

"I'll get it," I said, eager to get away from both of them, and didn't even think about who could be calling until I'd already picked up. And then I thought, Will. WillWillWillWill.

"Hello?" Please let me sound normal. Please let it be for me. Please let it be him.

"Is Todd there?"

Of course. Everyone wanted to talk to Todd.

It wasn't until I'd taken a message and hung up that I realized I hadn't even thought it could have been Anna calling. I hadn't even hoped it was her. I hadn't thought about her once today. Not until now.

I didn't know if that was good or bad. It was like . . . it was like it was both somehow, actually.

During dinner, Todd came home and said, "I got a job," as he sat down at the kitchen table. He was going to work full-time at another branch of the mall coffee place, and I didn't even care that he acted like he was the first person in the world to ever get a job. It was just nice to see Mom smile.

Dad came home late, probably trying to avoid Grandma, who'd actually gone to bed early, claiming she was tired. I'd seen her face when she'd tried to help Mom clear the table after dinner, though, saw the sadness in her eyes when Mom stiffened and said, "I've got it, thanks," like Grandma was a stranger she was forcing herself to be polite to.

When Dad sat down in the living room, smiling at me and Mom and Todd, I figured we'd finally talk about the house, or at least discuss where we might move to. After all, we had to live somewhere, and Mom had already said it wasn't going to be in our house anymore.

"Is there anything to eat?" Dad said.

"Of course," Mom said, and we ended up back in the kitchen, the four of us sitting around the kitchen table just like we used to every night for dinner.

"So," Dad said, looking at Todd and me as Mom handed him a plate with a sandwich on it, "I guess you two know about the house?"

Todd and I nodded.

"Good," Dad said. "That's really good." He clapped Todd on the shoulder. "Dave at the coffee place told me about your job at their new branch. Congratulations." He leaned over and kissed Mom. "I'm beat, honey. Can you wrap this up for me? I think I'd better go get some sleep."

He yawned and started to get up, pushing his chair back from the table. I stared at him. That was it? I knew Dad didn't handle bad news well, but this was our house, not me failing my driver's test, or Todd doing it with some girl in his room, or even Grandma coming to visit. I must have looked upset, because when Dad glanced at me, he quickly looked away.

Like he did anytime he saw something he didn't want to see.

"I can't work tomorrow," I said, the words coming out strangled, like they'd gotten caught in my throat. I looked at Mom, waiting for a reaction. She wouldn't let this be it, would she? She'd say something, tell me I had to work, tell Dad we needed to talk about everything that had happened.

Mom didn't look at me. She just stared at Dad's sandwich, her mouth a thin, tight line.

"No problem," Dad said. "With Todd getting a job, I'll need to get used to working by myself a bit more anyway."

And that was it. That was all anyone said about the house, about how it would soon belong to someone else.

# twenty-three

**When I woke up the next morning, I looked around** my room.

I saw the smudges on the wall from where Anna and I had practiced handstands and rested our feet against it, scrabbling to stay upright before we fell. I saw the weird crack in the corner of my ceiling that I'd always thought looked like a spiderweb. I saw the shells I'd collected the summer me and Mom and Todd stayed with Grandma at her beach house. I'd forgotten how much I loved walking along the beach with her. She never got mad when I wanted to stop and pick something up. She said walking too fast was silly, and it was important to see everything you could.

I tried to picture my desk and my bed in a new room. I tried to picture myself in a new room. I couldn't do it, even though I knew it would happen.

Since I didn't have to go to the mall, I went for a walk, not even bothering to try and talk to Mom about driving. I just wanted to get away from the house, from everything that was already gone.

I ended up at Anna's.

Walking by her house made me feel better and worse. Better, because it brought back so many memories. Worse, because that's all I had. Memories.

I stood at the edge of her driveway, staring down at it and wishing I could walk up to her front door without even thinking about it the way I used to, when I heard Anna say, "Kate?"

I looked up, embarrassed, and saw Anna standing just inside her house, peering at me from the open door. I waved weakly, feeling like an idiot.

"What are you doing here?" She didn't sound mad, just surprised.

"I was out walking. I would have gone for a drive but Mom has this whole thing about me and driving and . . ." I forced myself to stop talking, aware I was babbling and that Anna had no reason to care about me walking or anything else.

"Oh," she said, and then, a second later, "Do you want to come in?"

And just like that, my friendship with Anna began again. It was like a dream but better, because it was real, because we went to her room and sat like we always did, me curled up in the over-stuffed chair that Anna's mom had picked up at a yard sale years ago, and that Anna had decorated with the butterfly stickers I'd given her when she turned eleven. It felt like coming home in the best way.

The stickers were gone, but the chair was still there, familiar and solid, and Anna lay on the floor like she always had, resting her feet on the bed, and told me all about Sam. She told me everything I'd always wondered about the two of them, answered all the questions I'd wanted to ask but hadn't been able to.

"So, that's how it happened," she said much later, her voice slightly hoarse from talking for so long. "Me and Sam. Our story. Wow. Our story. It sounds unbelievable, doesn't it? I mean, if you'd told me this time last year that I'd be his girlfriend . . ." She lifted her arms up and spread them out to the side, then giggled and crossed them over her chest like she was hugging herself. "I'm so lucky."

"You are." And she was. Being with a guy like Sam was the Jackson High equivalent of dating a movie star.

The thing was, I was the tiniest bit tired of hearing about Sam. Anna had talked about him before, of course, but he'd never been all she talked about.

"Do you miss choir?" I said. "I had to quit when everything with Dad happened, but in the fall we sang at least two songs at the winter concert that you totally would have gotten a solo for."

"Choir?" Anna said. "I swear, Kate, I totally forgot I was ever in it. I was the world's biggest loser back then, wasn't I?"

She laughed. I didn't. Anna seemed different, not just in how she looked, but in how she talked too. It was like Anna was there, but there was someone else layered on top of her as well. Someone new.

Someone who didn't care about any of the things she'd once cared about except Sam.

"I guess I do miss singing a little, but I can always do it for real later, you know?" she said. "I was talking to Diane about New York City, and—well, I can totally see myself singing there, you know?"

"New York?"

"Yeah, Diane wants to go to NYU, and she'll totally get in because her aunt or somebody works there, and since there's no money for me to go to school, I'm going to go out there with her and we'll get an apartment and I'll get a job singing." She pointed her toes up into the air, bouncing her heels on the bed. "Maybe I'll end up in a really famous musical or something. Wouldn't that be amazing?"

"Amazing," I said, but it came out flat, strangled-sounding. Anna was going to move to New York and live with Diane. We used to talk about moving to New York. How had she forgotten that? We'd talked about it for years and now . . . now it was like none of it had ever happened.

"Okay, something's going on," she said. "I can tell because you've got that 'I'm-thinking-too-much' look on your face. What's up?"

Where was I going to start? Her? Dad? Grandma? Todd and his new job? Mom? Finding out about the house? Will?

Will, who hung out with Sam.

"I was thinking about Sam," I said, rolling my eyes when she nudged me with one foot. "Not like that. I saw him on Friday night. At a party, I mean. Were you there with him? I didn't see you but it was pretty crowded, and I sort of ended up leaving in a hurry."

"Party?" Anna said, sounding startled. "What party?"

"Jennifer T.'s."

"Oh," she said, visibly relaxing. "That thing. I thought you were talking about . . . never mind."

"Talking about what?"

"Nothing." She waved a hand at me, grinning brightly.

I stared at her. She was trying really hard to act casual. Too hard. Plus her smile looked like Dad's did whenever Grandma was around, too wide and fake.

"Really?"

"Yeah. I'm just brain-dead because of everything with my mom, you know?" she said. "But anyway, I definitely wasn't at Jennifer's. Me and Diane went out, and I was supposed to go to this thing at Tara's, but she called at the last minute and said it was just going to be a few people."

"Oh," I said, confused as to what this had to do with Sam.

She laughed, but it was hollow sounding. "I forgot, you don't know that Sam and Tara hang out sometimes. See, he swore he wasn't going over there, but I thought he might drop by real fast or something. But instead he went to Jennifer's. I bet she loved that."

I looked at her, hearing something strange in the brittle tone of her voice. "Are you and Sam okay?"

"Of course." She looked away from me, staring up at her ceiling. "It's just that people like Tara can do anything, you know? And Sam says he loves me, but I—I guess I keep thinking it's all a dream, and I'm going to wake up and find out I'm still a nobody."

"Wait a minute—Sam's said he loves you?" WOW. I couldn't imagine anyone saying that to me, not ever, and Anna had just said it like it was no big deal. But I knew it must be.

"Yeah," she said, her voice shy and giddy, and in that was a glimpse of the Anna I knew, the one who dreamed about Sam and a perfect life. "Pretty amazing, isn't it? I still can't totally believe it, which I guess is why I worry sometimes. But anyway, you have to tell me how stupid the Jennifers were." She cleared her throat. "Did Jennifer T. throw herself at him?"

"No, but he got pizza when she'd told us there wasn't any food left."

She laughed again, sounding oddly relieved. "God, she's so pathetic. I bet Will talked him into going for some reason. Some girl, probably."

Me? Could Will have talked him into going for me?

"I totally get why you never liked him now, by the way," Anna continued. "You know how sometimes there are stupid rumors about Sam hooking up with random girls? It's all because Will hooks up with anything that breathes, and it's so annoying because it's obvious Sam has actual standards, you know?"

I nodded, stung, the brief flash of whatever I'd had before gone. I had heard rumors about Sam, but there was no way he'd kiss a girl like me, and I knew that. But Will would. He had.

And now I didn't want to know what Anna would think about that.

So I didn't say anything else about that night or Will, and

when I left her house, I felt—I felt like things weren't totally back to normal between me and her. I thought they could get there, though. Hoped they could. That they would.

At home, there was a huge FOR SALE sign up in the yard, and no one had called me.

No one called me all night.

I know I could have called Will, but I was afraid. Really afraid, and not like before, when I was afraid that I wouldn't know what to say, or what he'd say. Now I was afraid of everything.

Jennifer T.'s party changed things. I knew she'd tell everyone what she saw, and there was no way to escape the fact that people would know Will and I were . . . whatever.

But I hadn't truly realized what it would mean. Everyone would know. Anna would know. What would she think?

After today, I was afraid to think about it.

And he hadn't called. When I went to bed, trying to fall asleep but staring at my silent phone, all I could think was that everyone knowing meant disaster on an epic scale. I'd wanted to keep whatever I had with Will quiet. Mine. I'd wanted the ending I knew was coming to be private.

I knew what Will's silence meant, and I hated that tomorrow everyone else would know what it meant too. Just once, I wanted to lose something without the whole world watching.

# twenty-four

**In the morning, I saw Anna. And she saw me.**
I know she did, because she looked right at me. Then she looked
away, like she'd forgotten me all over again.

For a second, I hated her. I mean, really hated her. Anna and
I had talked, and I thought things had been fixed—or at least sort
of fixed—between us. So why was she doing this?

I went to my locker, tossing my books inside and ignoring
everyone around me. I didn't want to know if people were looking at me or talking about me, and when the warning bell rang
and emptied the halls, I ignored that too. Anna could have her
new perfect life for all I cared. It was her loss. Really.

Now if I could just get myself to believe that.

"Kate?"

It was Anna. Anna right beside me, like she walked up to me all the time, and I felt my anger evaporate as I watched her bite her lip, clearly upset.

"Don't be pissed at me," she said. "I saw your face when you walked in. I wanted to say something to you, I swear. I just—"

She broke off and looked down at the floor, and when she spoke again, she whispered. "I'm scared, okay? I know it's stupid, but I keep thinking 'what if Sam sees who I really am?' I mean, I've lost weight and everything, but I really don't care about pep rallies and I miss choir and I get so sick of hearing about Diane's new clothes or who she hates today that sometimes I just want to scream."

"I bet if Sam heard you sing he wouldn't care if you were in choir."

She gave me a look.

"Okay, he might care a little," I said. "But you can do whatever you want, you can be whatever you want. Remember how you always used to say that?"

"Yeah, and look how well that turned out." Her voice was flat. Angry.

"I just meant—"

She shook her head. "Don't worry about it. This morning is just stressing me out. You forgive me for earlier, right? Please? I don't want you to hate me. I'd go insane if I didn't know I could count on you being there for me."

"Since when were you ever sane?" I said, grinning at her, and she smiled back, eyes bright.

"Speaking of sane, is there something you want to tell me

about a certain party and a certain guy I thought you hated? Did you and Will really get caught—?"

"Don't say it!"

"It *is* true! Why didn't you tell me yesterday?"

"I was going to, but—" The final bell rang, cutting me off.

"Damn. Well, details later because the two of you—well, talk about insane, right?" Anna said as she headed down the hall.

I nodded even though I knew she couldn't see me and sagged against my locker, trying to ignore the weird mix of hurt and anger her last words had created. Anna had spoken to me at school. She'd told me she needed to know I'd be there for her.

Maybe things weren't exactly how they used to be, but now I knew for sure that Anna and I were friends again, and that was what I'd wanted. The final bell rang, but I didn't move. I was still processing everything that had happened.

And paralyzed by what I was afraid was going to happen when I finally made it to first period, where I'd have to face Will.

# twenty-five

**As I plodded to first period, my vision got all spotty** and my heart was beating so hard I could practically hear it thumping in my chest. It got worse and worse the closer I got to class, and by the time I got there, I was convinced Will could be lying on the floor naked and I wouldn't notice him because I'd be too busy dying.

I was wrong.

That's because Will wasn't in class. Or naked. He was standing in the hall, listening to Jennifer T., who'd clearly cornered him. Jennifer M. was playing lookout, and I saw her see me and then elbow Jennifer T., all the while moving so I'd have to walk right by them to get into class.

Will, who was clearly trying to figure out why they were

attempting to herd him into position by the door, looked around. When he saw me, he looked almost as freaked out as I felt, which made it very clear he was having "oh-shit-what-was-I-thinking-on-Friday-night" thoughts.

Great. I already knew he was having them, because he'd never called me back, but still.

"Hi," both of the Jennifers said to me, and then retreated into the classroom, leaving me and Will out in the hall. We looked at each other for a second.

He was the first person to speak. "Hey."

"Hey." My voice came out relatively normal, and I felt my heart pound even harder. Maybe he wasn't going to blow me off. Maybe he was going to say something amazing.

"Ready for the test?"

Or not. "I guess. You?"

I could go on, but I won't. The whole conversation, which probably was about ten seconds long but felt like it lasted for an eternity, was just like that, so politely bland it hurt. And when Mr. Clark showed up, reeking of cigarettes and crabbily asking, "You do realize your seats are inside the classroom, right?" I was actually glad to see him.

I fumbled my way through the test, trying to remember what I'd supposedly learned but mostly thinking about what the non-conversation I'd had with Will meant. I mean, I knew it wasn't a good conversation, but he had talked to me.

Of course, it wasn't like he'd had much of a choice, since Jennifer T. and M. had trapped him into being around when I showed up.

"Miss Brown, your test?"

"What?" I looked up and saw Mr. Clark waiting impatiently by my desk.

"The bell has rung. Your test?"

I handed it over.

"Thank you. I suggest you study a bit more in the future, as the tests are only going to get harder. That goes for you too, Mr. Miller." The scolding would have been more effective if Mr. Clark hadn't bolted for the door while he was talking, desperate to get his nicotine fix in the three minutes before next period started.

I grabbed my bag, careful not to look at Will, or at least, not look at him in an obvious way.

"Kate," he said, grabbing his stuff and walking toward me. "Sorry about before. The Jennifers sort of ganged up on me, and you know how that is."

I headed for the door. "Yeah, I saw your face. You should be thankful you've never had to go shopping with them."

You don't know how much it cost me to say that, to act like him not bringing up Friday night didn't hurt, but a year of disappointment had trained me well, and I was not getting cut off at the knees again. Will wasn't going to blow me off because I wasn't going to care. It was just that simple.

"Are you mad?" he said as I was getting ready to walk into the hall.

"What?" Where had that come from? I would never understand guys. "Do I sound mad?"

"Sort of."

"I'm not," I said tightly. Why wasn't he going away? I'd given him his out. What more did he want from me?

"Oh. Okay. It's just . . . you never called me back and your grandmother—who seems really nice—said you would." He reached into his bag and pulled out a plastic shopping bag. "Here's your shoe."

"Thanks." I stuffed it into my bag, my mind racing. Grandma had told him I'd call? I thought her "Darling, call him," stuff was her trying to give advice. Why couldn't she just say, "He asked you to call him," like a normal person? "She didn't exactly give me all of your message."

"Well, I said I had your shoe and that you should call me."

"To what, discuss ransom?"

He laughed. "No. I thought—" We'd walked out into the hall now, and I could see people watching us. Hookup aftermath viewing was truly Jackson High's most popular sport.

I saw Will look around, watched him realize our conversation had gone public. Very public.

"I thought that test would be easier," he said, two spots of dull red appearing on his face, and tossed off a "Later," before walking off.

And so I ended up standing alone in the hallway, undoubtedly looking like I'd just been blown off by a guy I was sure rumor had me conceiving triplets with. The worst part was, there was nothing I could do about it—and I still had the rest of the day to get through. Hell, I had the rest of the year to get through, not to mention the rest of high school.

Still, Will had blown me off, so at least that was over. We

were over. I told myself the burning feeling in my throat and behind my eyes was worry over the test I'd just taken, and not anything else.

I managed to make it through second period by pretending I couldn't see everyone looking at me, but then I ran into Will again. He was in the hall outside class when it ended. He looked liked he'd combed his hair with a fork, and said he'd meant to say something else before.

"Oh?" I said, my stupid brain churning up fantasies of him sweeping me into his arms and kissing me while people threw flowers and someone handed me keys to a new car.

"Yeah," he said, and glanced around. Once again, plenty of people were watching. "So . . . how do you think you did on the test?"

If only the world could have ended then. But it didn't, and so Will and I discussed the test again.

And then, after third period, I saw him once more. This time he looked like he'd combed his hair with a fork and had the wild-eyed look of someone who hadn't slept for three days. Topic of conversation? THE WEATHER. It was horrible.

The only good thing to come out of whatever was going on was that people weren't staring at us anymore. Instead everyone— even the girls—was looking at Will like he'd gone a bit crazy. It would have made me feel better except that every time he said, "Kate?" my heart started pounding and I started hoping for things I knew would never happen.

Hope was supposed to be a good thing, but it was starting to feel like every other four-letter word you're not supposed to say.

I didn't see him before lunch, though, and afterward I was sure I wouldn't see him again. I figured he was finally done doing whatever it was he was doing to me. Plus we'd exhausted every stupid conversation topic out there. I mean, what was left to talk about once you'd discussed the weather?

The fact that I had rice in my hair.

Yes, that's right. Apparently there wasn't enough humiliation in my life, because I did see Will as I left the cafeteria. In fact, I pretty much walked right into him.

"Hey," he said. "I—I was wondering if . . . do you know you have rice in your hair?"

"No," I said, hearing my voice crack and hating myself for it, for letting him get to me again. I headed for the girls' room, practically shoving him out of the way. He looked sad, but I knew I was seeing things. Will looked amused or adorable or sometimes bored, and I was the girl with rice in her hair.

I picked it out, a small sticky lump snagged in the ends of my hair, and tossed it in the trash, telling myself that when I had a real job and a real car and a real life, this would be funny. Or at least forgettable.

"Here," I heard, and saw Sarah standing behind me, holding up a small brush. "You want to borrow this?"

I'd actually rather have my eyes sewn shut, but you didn't turn down kindness from girls like Sarah. Well, some people would. People with actual self-esteem, for example. But I'd just lost all of mine and I'd have taken a nice gesture from anyone then.

"Thanks," I said, and took the brush.

"Sure," Sarah said. "I heard what Will said back there. And I saw him talking to you after third period too. It's one thing to be all . . . whatever after you hook up, but he's acting really weird."

"Yeah," I said, and dragged the brush through my hair as fast as I could, not wanting to discuss what had happened Friday night with her or anyone else. "Thanks."

"No problem," she said. "I've been there, you know? This one time last year, I hooked up with a senior, and when I saw him on Monday he called me Sandy and asked if his brother could call me. And his brother? Kim."

"Kim? 'I worship ancient movies' Kim?"

"That Kim," she said, and made a face. "It was the worst moment of my entire life, and I swore I'd always get a last name before I hooked up after that."

I nodded, not trusting myself to comment on anything she'd just said without mocking or laughing. Or both.

"Anyway," she said, tossing her brush in her bag and checking her makeup, "I just wanted to say that guys suck sometimes, you know?"

"They do," I said, and when I left the bathroom I felt—well, not great, but better, and it was thanks to Sarah, of all people. I almost felt bad for the stuff I'd thought about her before. I knew a better person would actually feel sorry, but then a better person probably wouldn't have had to watch Sarah rub herself up against the guy I liked.

Wait, make that used to like. And definitely wasn't talking to again.

Except that when I left my last class, Will was there.

I walked out into the hall and saw him. He looked like he was going to throw up and was clearly waiting for me because he said, "Kate," when I came out and then started walking toward me.

I can't tell you how terrible it felt to know I made him look like he was going to vomit. Next thing you know, he'd see me and go into convulsions. I couldn't wait to get out of school and away from him, and turned around, walking away.

"Hey," he said, following me, "I need to talk to you."

I ignored him. Or at least pretended to.

"Seriously, Kate."

I started to walk faster, but he'd caught up with me and fell into step beside me.

"Look, I've been trying to say something all day, and if you'd just let me—"

"Fine." I stopped in the middle of the hall, not caring if people saw. I'd had it. Screw trying to pretend my life wasn't a big ball of suck. Screw trying to act like I could somehow stop it from getting worse. "Say whatever it is you want to say already, because I can't take another fucking conversation about the weather with you."

His face got red again. "I wanted to see if you wanted to go out sometime. With me, I mean. And without—" He gestured around us, face still red but a smile springing to his face, dimples showing. "An audience."

Yes, my brain screamed. YES! But only part of my brain. The rest of it—the thinking part of it—remembered how people had looked at us after first period, and how their expressions had changed with every "conversation" we'd had. How they'd started to look at him, and how Sarah, of all people, had said something nice to me after lunch. How she clearly didn't think as much of him as she'd used to.

Will had made himself look like an ass, and I knew he was smart enough to know it. And what better way to redeem himself than asking me out, especially since Will never asked anyone out. He didn't date. Everyone knew it. I knew it.

This was a big gesture. A big moment, and I could guess why he'd done it. And when, out of the corner of my eye, I saw Sarah, I knew it had worked because she wasn't shooting me glances of solidarity. She was watching Will like he'd done something incredible.

He'd fixed things for himself. All I had to do was play along, and I'd get the date I'd dreamed of.

"No," I said.

"No?" He looked startled, which confirmed what I already knew, that him asking me out wasn't about me at all, but it still hurt. It hurt a lot.

"That's right," I said. "I don't want to go out with you. I don't want anything to do with you. You hook up with me, then humiliate me. I've had more than enough of you."

And so I did get to have a say, I got to end something before it could end on me.

It wasn't what I wanted. But then, what was in my life that I did want?

# twenty-six

**Work was weird. I didn't get to go home, not even** to make something to eat for dinner, because Dad had to close the booth down to come get me and was anxious to get back. Mall management didn't like it if stores were shut down during mall hours, and apparently Dad had already gotten in trouble for it.

When I asked him when he'd shut the store down, he muttered something about "taking a break" to look at video games with Todd "a couple of times." Figured.

"How come you never take me to the movies or ask me to go somewhere with you at work?" I said, and looked out the window. The mall loomed in front of us, just waiting to suck me in. I couldn't believe I'd ever wanted to spend time here.

"Well, I—you're always doing homework or fixing things in

our storage area," Dad said, and I cleared my throat, embarrassed that he thought I was working so hard when I'd mostly been making out with Will.

"Plus, whenever I ask you about coffee or getting something to eat, you always tell me to bring you something or say you aren't hungry or—" Now Dad cleared his throat. "Look, the truth is, I know you don't like working with me, and I wouldn't—I don't want to embarrass you. But if you want to do something together, I'd really like that. Like tomorrow, I'm planning on visiting Todd at work in the morning, before the mall opens, to hand out some free samples. You should come. You'd miss a little bit of school, but I bet you wouldn't mind that, right?"

"You're going to try and sell Perfect You stuff at Todd's job while he's working? Won't that get him in trouble?"

Dad shook his head. "No, it's not like that. I'm just going to put some samples by the door and say hello to anyone who picks them up. I think it'll be a great way to start building a client base."

How was that different from what I'd said? And how could my father be so clueless? "Todd wants you to do this?"

"I thought I'd surprise him," Dad said. "Thank him for pitching in. I know it's been hard on him, giving up his dream to take the first job that came along."

I laughed. I couldn't help it. I knew it was mean, but come on! Todd's "dream" had consisted of watching television, hogging the computer, bathroom, and phone, and going out.

"You think what your brother's done is funny?" Dad said. He didn't sound mad, just disappointed, the most negative emotion he seemed to let himself feel, and I sighed. I knew why Dad was upset, that he saw all of Todd's so-called dreams as reflections of the one he had, and that was both sad and really worrying. I thought losing the house might make Dad less enamored with his "dream job."

I guess I was wrong.

"I don't think it's funny," I said carefully. "I think it's great Todd's working. But maybe—maybe you should ask him if it's okay to bring all the Perfect You stuff with you before you visit."

"Oh." Now he sounded hurt and sad, but when I looked over at him he was smiling like always. Great. I wished he could get upset like a normal person. The way he always turned away from anger made me feel guilty for having any of my own.

"I mean, I'm sure he wouldn't care," I said, "but he's probably in some sort of training/new employee thing, and I bet that's keeping him really busy. He'd probably be too busy to even talk, you know?"

"I hadn't thought about that, but I guess you're right. Thanks, honey." He sounded cheerful, but as soon as we got to the booth he took off on an "errand" and I was left alone. I got out my homework and wondered why it sometimes felt like I was the parent and Dad was the kid.

I went to the food court on my dinner break, but even though I sat in the middle, visible to everyone, and lingered for an extra ten minutes, I didn't see Will.

I went out to the trash bins right before the mall closed, to throw out some expired vitamins that hadn't sold, but didn't see him there either. I told myself I wasn't going to check our storage space but I did, and stood there for a moment, alone.

I guess Will really had heard what I'd told him earlier. That was good. It really was. If nothing else, it was about time someone listened to what I had to say. That I'd ended things before they ended on me.

But the thing was, even though I'd meant what I'd said to him before, I still wanted to kiss him. I wished I'd never gone to that stupid party. I wished I knew why he'd asked me if I was going. I wished he'd been in the food court or behind the mall or waiting for me by our storage space.

I wished that he really wanted me.

Todd was asleep when we got home, curled up on the sofa with a blanket pulled over his head. It pretty much discouraged conversation, and for once Grandma wasn't lying in wait. Even Mom hadn't waited up, though I could hear the television on in her and Dad's room.

I went to my room and thought about doing homework. I didn't feel like doing it, though. I wanted to talk to someone about what had happened. I wanted to talk about life with Grandma and Todd, about losing the house, about how I'd made a pyramid out of fourteen bottles of Garlic Gels at work and it was the only time Dad had truly smiled at me all night.

Weirdly, the first person that came to mind when I saw myself talking about all of it was Will. I guess what happened at school had gotten to me more than I realized. Maybe . . . maybe he'd meant it when he asked me out. Maybe . . .

No, I wasn't going there. I'd seen everyone looking at us. I'd seen him see it too. I'd done the right thing. Plus Anna had said that me and Will together was insane. I was angry and hurt when she'd said it, but she was right, wasn't she? She'd known what I hadn't wanted to see. I should tell her that.

So I did.

I kicked off my shoes as I called her, curling up on my bed. "Hello?"

"Hey," I said. "It's me. Kate, I mean."

"I know, silly. What's up?"

This was familiar. This was how we always talked. "I hate vitamins. Also, my feet hurt."

"You know what I mean," she said. "What's up with you and Will?"

"Nothing."

"Come on, Kate. He asked you out in front of half the school, and you destroyed him. Sarah told me all about it."

Great. Remembering the way she'd been looking at Will the last time he spoke to me, I could just imagine what she'd said. "Did she tell you it was obvious he asked me out because half the school saw him talk to me about total crap and then run off all day?"

"She didn't say that, but I figured that's what happened. Because, okay, Will dating someone? Please. He's the king of hookups."

"So you knew it was a pity thing."

"I . . . Look, even if it was, so what? Will is okay but he's nothing special, you know? I mean, he totally blew Sarah off when she went out to the mall to talk to him this afternoon, and it's like, who does he think he is?"

"I—I don't know," I stammered, because I was too busy

thinking about the fact that he'd blown Sarah off to be coherent. "Maybe he was too busy to talk."

"Please," Anna said. "You know what I mean by talk, and since when is Will too busy to hook up with someone?"

Wait a minute. Not only had Will not talked to Sarah, he hadn't hooked up with her?

My mind was reeling. "Has Sam said anything to you about it?"

"No. Will and Sam only hang out because . . . well, they used to be friends, but then Will's mom talked Sam's mom into starting this stupid business, and now Sam says Will's accused him and Sam's dad of trying to stop it, which is so stupid that— hold on a second." I waited for Anna to click over to another call, but instead I heard her put the phone down and the faint sound of her mother's voice.

"Sorry," she said, picking up the phone again. "Mom's having a bad day."

"You okay?"

She sort of laughed/sighed. "Sure. I have to be, don't I?"

"Anna—"

"No, it's okay. I don't want to turn into mopey girl. I've got Sam. I mean me, fat Anna Dray, is with Sam. I have the perfect life, you know? And I have the perfect boyfriend."

She didn't sound like she believed any of it, though. She just sounded like she wanted to, like she felt like she had to.

"That's . . . good."

"Good?" she said tightly, and then sighed. "You know me too well, Kate. Things aren't totally perfect. Sam . . . well, okay, first, his feet stink, which just . . . it seems wrong to me. Plus he messed around with Tara over winter break."

"What?"

"Yeah." Anna's voice cracked a little. "I haven't—you're the only person who knows, okay? Tara told me a couple of weeks ago, all 'Yeah, Sam's great, and after we hooked up at Heather's over winter break he said he really loved you and I thought that was so sweet.' She was so upset when she realized I hadn't known about it that I felt bad for being mad."

"Anna!"

"You think she did it to be a bitch, right?"

"Yeah, I'd say casually mentioning she messed around with your boyfriend but hey, by the way, he totally loves you, qualifies as bitchy. What did Mr. Perfect have to say when you asked him about it?"

She mumbled something that sounded a lot like, "I don't know."

"You haven't said anything, have you?" I said. "Anna—"

"I can't say anything," she said. "He hates it when I get jealous. And it's Sam. Sam, Kate."

"I know it's Sam, but . . . okay, remember what you said last year when everyone knew that the senior Diane was messing around with was just using her to get back at his ex-girlfriend? You said it was stupid for Diane to pretend everything was okay just so she could be with some guy who didn't care about her or her feelings."

"Sam loves me, Kate," Anna's voice was clipped and cold. "And what happened to Diane was actually pretty terrible. She really loved the guy, and she just wanted him to love her back."

"Oh, come on. She just wanted to go to the prom because she'd have been the only ninth grader who went. We even heard her say that in the bathroom before lunch, remember?"

"No. But it's nice to know you think I'm like that, which I guess means you think I'm using Sam. What exactly am I using him for?"

"That's not what I meant and you know it." Had talking to her always been this . . . frustrating?

"Whatever. You don't know what it's like for me, okay?" Anna said. "When everyone knows who you are, there's all this pressure and you have to—"

"Anna, are you really going to lecture me about how hard it is to be beautiful and popular?"

She was silent for a moment, and then she laughed. "All right, I get it. I just—it's hard with Sam, but I don't want to give him up. I feel special when I'm with him. I am special when I'm with him."

"You'd be special without him."

"I wouldn't."

"Would."

"Wouldn't," she said, her voice soft. "People still remember who I was, Kate."

"You make it sound like you were a diseased yak or something."

I'd hoped she'd laugh, but she just sighed again. "Look, I gotta go watch a movie with Mom. She had a really bad day. Call me tomorrow?"

She wanted me to call her? I guess we really were friends again. "Sure. See you tomorrow?"

"Yeah," she said, and I heard the "but" in her voice before she said it, and felt something shrivel inside me. "But I have to spend time with Sam and Diane and everyone else, okay? And it's—it takes up a lot of time. You understand, right? Please say you do, because I meant what I said this morning. If I didn't know you'd always be there for me, I'd be lost. I really need to know I can always count on you."

"You can," I said, and we said good-bye.

The thing was, I did understand what she meant. Anna was being nice when she talked to me at school, acting like Sam, who would sometimes talk to people he didn't have to notice, only she didn't have Sam's lifetime of popularity to fall back on. Sam had always been liked, and until this year Anna was a nobody, and people knew that. Remembered it.

I hadn't thought about what her life was truly like now because I'd been so busy wondering why it was so easy for her to forget me, but it seemed like her perfect life wasn't perfect at all. I'd thought it was. She'd seemed so happy. Finding out that she wasn't, that she'd gotten the great life and the great guy only to have it be not-so-great was sort of depressing.

It was also sort of not-depressing. I felt bad for thinking that, but the truth was, I was glad Anna wasn't totally happy.

I was glad she felt like she needed me.

# twenty-seven

**Will didn't talk to me the next day. I hadn't realized** it, but I'd gotten used to talking to him, even if it was only to pretend he was annoying me while I thought stuff like, "I've kissed you! You've kissed me!" But he didn't ask me about homework or butt into any of my conversations, even when the Jennifers were complaining about the PSATs. In fact, when Jennifer M. asked me if I knew how she could do better for the four millionth time and I said, "Bribery," Will still didn't say anything. He didn't even smile.

I didn't see him at work either. I thought about going to Sports Shack to see if he was working, but what if he was? What was I going to say? "Hi, I know I said I didn't want to go out with you, and I know you only asked because you'd made yourself look like an ass, but the thing is, I kind of miss you?"

Besides, I didn't miss him. Not exactly, anyway. I missed making out with him. And hearing him talk about work. And how he never made fun of my crappy job, or even my dad. And the way he'd smile at me.

And the way I always felt like smiling when I was with him.

It wasn't even a relief to get home because things were so different there now. Mom was always picking up after Dad, trying to keep the house clean for potential buyers, and Todd had turned into someone who smelled like coffee, complained about how much his feet hurt, and wouldn't take phone calls after ten at night.

"Dad, I really need to get some sleep," he said when we were all sitting in the living room and Dad was trying to talk him into playing a quick round of a video game he'd picked up on his evening coffee run.

"Come on, one race," Dad said. "You should see all the stuff you can do. I played this level in the store for a while, and it was—"

"You left Kate alone so you could play video games?" Mom said.

"Not for long," Dad said. "I don't usually take a dinner break, but I like to get out and see what's going on and—"

"Buy video games even though we wrote up a budget and you promised to stick to it."

"This was a one-time thing, Sharon, plus it was on sale."

"I just think—" Mom clamped her lips together as Grandma appeared.

"I thought I heard voices," Grandma said. "Kate, darling, it's good to see you, but you look a little pale. Have you thought about wearing bronzer?" She glanced at Dad, but didn't say anything to him.

"Mother, Kate looks fine," Mom said. "I thought you were going to sleep."

"Oh, darling, I was, but then I decided I'd come say hello to my granddaughter. Also, Todd, what on earth was that strange note in the bathroom about?"

Todd, who'd managed to slump under his blankets while she was talking, lifted his head up. "I wanted you to know that I have to open the store every morning and that it would be great if I could use the shower before you get in there and do whatever it is you do."

"Darling, you could have just asked me. Besides, it's not like I take a long time in the bathroom."

"An hour and a half is a long time to some people," Todd muttered.

"What, darling?"

"Mother, just let Todd use the bathroom first in the morning," Mom said. "You can share with Kate while she's getting ready for school."

Great. I could hear Grandma now. "Oh, darling, are you wearing that?" "Oh, darling, is that how you want your hair to look?" "Oh, darling, I used all the hot water, but cold water is so much better for your skin." Shudder.

I glared at Mom, who pretended she couldn't see me. Great. Now she was treating me like she did Grandma.

"Oh, I'll just use your bathroom, darling," Grandma said to Mom, and I swear she winked at me.

"What?" Mom said, as Dad coughed dramatically, the closest to a "no" he could get.

"You have much better light in there," Grandma said. "Besides, Steve certainly doesn't rush in the morning, and you don't even wear makeup, never mind that there are some marvelous products out there. Tomorrow night, when you get off work, you'll have to let me show you what a little color can do for your face."

"Sharon has to work tomorrow night," Dad said, and when I looked over at him, surprised that he'd spoken, he was fake grinning at Grandma so hard his face looked like it might crack. "Remember how you refused to help out and she had to get a second job?"

Todd stuck his head out from under the blankets again long enough to give me a quick, eyebrows-raised glance. Had Dad finally cracked? Would he actually tell Grandma off?

"Sharon doesn't have to work tomorrow night," Grandma said, and shot my mother a look I couldn't read.

I guess Dad was able to read it, though, because he said, "Sharon?" and then he and Mom disappeared into their bedroom, their faces tense as they left. Grandma went into the kitchen to get a soda, and I poked Todd in the shoulder. "I want to watch television."

"Tough. Some of us have to get up and go to real jobs in the morning."

"Whatever, Todd. You've had a job for something like two days." I sat down next to him, nudging him so he'd move. "What's going on with Mom and Dad?"

Todd looked toward the kitchen and then back at me. "Grandma gave Mom some money tonight," he whispered. "Money so she wouldn't have to work. She made Mom swear she wouldn't give it to Dad, and I thought Mom would get mad and tear the check up. But she didn't. She just said 'Fine,' and took it."

"She must really hate selling makeup."

"I guess," Todd said. "I think she's mad that Dad isn't more upset about selling the house. Has he said anything to you about it?"

I shook my head.

"Me either," Todd said. "It's like none of this is real to him, and I think it's scaring Mom."

"Who's scaring your mother, darling?" Grandma said, coming back into the living room.

"No one. I'm just trying to sleep but Kate's bothering me. More than usual, I mean," Todd said, burrowing back under his blankets before I could hit him. Or before Grandma could start talking to him.

"Well, good night," I said, hoping to get away before she realized I was the only person left to talk to.

"Darling, let me come take a look at your room," she said, looping her arm through mine and walking us both down the hall. "How is school?"

"Okay. Lots of homework, which I should probably work on—"

"How do you like working at the mall?"

Wait a minute. Was this going where I thought it might? Was Grandma going to offer to buy me out of my job?

Oh please, let Grandma offer to buy me out of my job. Please, please, please let her offer. "Working there is hard. I mean, with school and homework and stuff—"

"Stuff? What kind of stuff?"

"You know. Regular stuff." I'd assumed mentioning that it was hard to work and go to school would lead to some cash.

"Regular stuff?"

Guess I was wrong.

"Well, I see people from school at work, and it's embarrassing and—" I could see her losing interest because she took Dad being embarrassing for granted. I took a deep breath. "There's a guy. Or was. And I don't want to see him anymore."

"A boy? Why don't you want to see him?"

"We were sort of . . . going out," I said. I knew "making out behind the mall" wouldn't work on Grandma. "And now we aren't."

"Why?"

"Because . . . just because."

"That's not much of a reason, darling."

"I guess I'm not the kind of girl guys want to be with, okay?"

I waited for Grandma to say something, but she just looked at me for a long moment.

"I want to tell you something," she finally said, her voice quiet. "You tell yourself that you aren't something or that you can't be something, and you know what? It will become true. You have to decide who you are and what you can do and then go after what you want. Because believe me, no one is going to give it to you."

"Grandma—"

She patted my arm. "Think about it, darling, all right? The world will knock you down plenty. You don't need to be doing it to yourself."

After she left, I called Anna because I didn't want to think about what Grandma had said. I just needed to talk to a friend. I needed to talk to my best friend.

"Hey," she said when she picked up. "Can I call you back in a minute?"

"Sure," I said, but an hour later, she hadn't called back.

The phone finally rang when I'd given up waiting and was brushing my teeth before bed, telling myself I was angry and only angry even as my eyes burned with tears. I ran back to my room, hearing Todd yell, "Some of us are trying to sleep!" as I grabbed the phone.

"Hello?"

"Hey, sorry it took me so long to call you back," Anna said. "Something . . . well, Dad happened. I didn't wake you up, did I?"

"No," I said, and felt bad for being angry when she'd been stuck dealing with her father. "What's going on?"

"Nothing. He called and left a message about the wedding, and Mom—well, she just can't seem to get over him. I think I hate that more than I hate him. And what if—what if I end up like her one day?"

"That won't happen. You aren't like your mom or dad. You're you, you know?"

"Yeah. I wish I was somebody else, though."

"Come on, you're great. You look amazing, you're popular—"

"You think I look okay?"

"No, I'm just saying that so you'll let me eat lunch with you."

There was silence after I said that. Really awkward, weird silence.

"I'm kidding," I said. "We don't even have the same lunch block, remember?"

"I know," she said, but I could tell she didn't. She didn't know my schedule like I knew hers. That hurt a lot, but her clearly not wanting to eat lunch with me hurt more, and I had to force myself to relax and release my death grip on the phone.

"How's Sam?" I said, hoping that changing the subject would make things better.

It turned out Sam had spent the afternoon hanging out with Tara after he'd given her a ride home from school.

"What do you think that means?" Anna asked.

I had a feeling now wasn't the time to say exactly what I thought about Sam. "What do *you* think it means?"

"He hooked up with her."

"Maybe you should say something to him, then."

"Like some sort of jealous girlfriend? I already told you how he is about that." She sounded pissed.

"I know. But—well, don't you think you deserve better?"

"Who's better than Sam? He's the guy everyone wants to be with."

"I don't want him."

"You know what I mean. People who stand a chance with him."

I pulled the phone away from my ear and stared at it. Had she just said what I thought she did?

"Kate?" Her voice was faint. "Kate, are you there? I didn't mean it like it sounded, I swear. Kate?"

"I'm here," I said, my voice tight.

"Don't be mad at me, okay? Tonight with Mom was . . . it was bad, Kate, plus there's all the Sam stuff. Everything's really hard for me right now."

"I know, but why did you say what you did?"

"Because I'm an idiot."

"Anna—"

"I am. Thoughtless, too. Forgive me?" She sounded so sad. Worried, even. And over me.

"Yeah, of course," I said, mostly meaning it, and totally meaning it when she said, "Thank you, Kate. You always make me feel better. You're a real friend, you know. The best."

"Really?" I said, overwhelmed. She'd just said I was her best friend again!

"Yep."

I took a deep breath. She'd just said what I'd been dying to hear, and I . . . well, now I could ask her this. "Look, about Sam— has he . . . did he say anything about what happened at the party? With Will and me, I mean?"

"No. Well, he knew what happened, of course, because Jennifer actually came running up to him and said he had to be the first to know." She laughed. "If she tried any harder, I swear she'd explode. It's pathetic what girls will do to try and get Sam to notice them."

"But Will didn't say anything?" I didn't know if that was good or bad.

"No, but you know how Will is, Kate. His whole life is basically random hookups. So why would he mention it, you know?"

I felt my heart sink. Bad. Definitely bad.

"And besides," Anna said, "Sam says all Will ever talks about is that business thing their mothers are doing. It drives him crazy. Oh, that's him on the other line. I gotta go, okay?"

"Sure," I said, but she was already gone.

# twenty-eight

**I thought about what Anna had said all through** school, and was pretty depressed by the time it was over, especially since Will hadn't spoken to me again. I'd told myself over and over that I'd known exactly what Will and I were, not a couple, not anything, but realizing I truly was just another hookup hurt more than I thought it would. Or wanted it to.

At work, I ended up alone for most of the afternoon because Dad had decided to target the department store again.

"Weren't you banned from there?"

"Not exactly," Dad said, pulling on his carrot hat. "And I know most of the security guards, and we get along fine."

I looked at the counter so he couldn't see my face. Of course he got along with the security guards. He was always buying them coffee. And while it was nice he did that, it hadn't helped our money situation. Or resulted in any sales.

"I'll be back in half an hour, tops," he said, and I settled back into the chair by the cash register with a sigh.

Half an hour turned into two. I got a lot of homework done, as I'd stopped pretending we were going to have customers and focused on getting through my biology homework. I didn't think I'd failed the last test, but I knew I had to do better on the next one.

Thinking about biology class made me think about Will. I wondered how he'd done on the test, and if he was at work. Then I told myself to stop thinking about him.

It didn't work.

I put my homework away and watched people walk by. It was amazing how many of them were able to pretend our booth didn't exist, like they could sense all the unsold vitamins and somehow knew to stay away. An older woman who actually looked like a grandmother, white-haired and sweet-faced, walked by and politely asked if I knew where the discount shoe store was, then thanked me when I told her. I couldn't imagine my grandmother saying the words discount and shoe in the same sentence, much less looking like an actual grandmother.

I straightened a display that didn't need to be fixed while I thought about what Grandma had said last night, about how I had to decide who I was and what I could do. It sounded like pretty good advice, I guess, but being me sure hadn't paid off so far.

I flicked a finger at the pyramid of vitamins and sighed. "This sucks. I suck."

"No, you're just annoying."

I looked up and saw Todd smirking at me. "What are you doing here? Wait, let me guess . . . you need money. Well, you can forget it, because Dad isn't here and I'm not giving you anything out of the register."

"Nice. I come by to say hi to my little sister and my father after selling gallons of coffee to people who apparently have no idea what a tip jar is, and this is what I get?"

"Yep."

"You really do sound like Grandma sometimes."

"Shut up!"

He grinned. "Where's Dad?"

"Down by the department store."

"Free samples?"

"Yeah. You gonna go see him?"

"Is he wearing the hat?"

"What do you think?"

Todd made a face. "Hey, did I get any calls?"

"What, here?"

"Yeah, here."

"No."

"You sure?"

"Yes, Todd, I'm sure no one called to request the honor of your craptastic, I mean fantabulous, presence."

"Hey, I like that," he said. "I am fantabulous. And you know why? I know how to have fun. Now, I know this will be hard for you to understand, but I'll try to explain it to you. Fun is—"

"Hilarious. I know what fun is, moron. It's just hard to have when I'm either stuck at school or here."

"Oh, stop feeling sorry for yourself. So you have a job, big deal. I have a job."

"Todd, you're twenty-three. You're supposed to."

He shrugged. "You could do stuff, you know. Talk to people. Go out."

"I go out."

"One party doesn't really count, Kate. You should stop moping because you and Anna aren't friends—"

"We're still friends."

He gave me a look. "Fine. I just imagined that Anna never calls or comes over anymore."

"She calls!" Actually, she only called me if I called her and she was on the other line, but still. I glared at Todd.

"Okay, so you and Anna are talking. But still, you should put yourself out there more. Do stuff, let people know who you are, you know? Because you aren't that bad, really."

"Wow, thanks."

He ignored my sarcasm. "So, are you sure you don't want to give me any money?"

Wordlessly, I opened the cash register and pulled out two rolls of pennies. "Go nuts."

"Later, Grandma," he said, and walked off. I ignored that, but I couldn't ignore what he'd said. Or that it was basically the same thing Grandma had. And that maybe what they'd said made sense.

It was a lot to think about, and when Dad finally got back, I said, "I'm going on break," and left.

I headed for the food court, but the smell of pizza made me think of Will and I ended up stopping outside it and staring blindly at a store window.

I had to stop thinking about Will. I'd got what I'd wanted when I'd told him off, when I'd ended things before they could end on me, and had the memory of making out with him on top of that.

It should have been enough. I should have been happy with that. But I wasn't.

I was angry.

As soon as I let myself think that, I realized how true it was. I was angry. Why did Will blow me off the way he had? Why couldn't he have just ignored me? Why did he have to make me think that he was going to ask me out for real?

Why did he have to make me think he cared?

He didn't have to do that. In fact, no one held a gun to his head and made him kiss me in the first place. No one forced him to come outside that night at Jennifer's. He was the one who'd asked me if I was going, after all, and now he couldn't be bothered to talk to me? I was the one who had every reason to ignore him! I mean, I'd ended up talking about the WEATHER because of him.

The more I thought about it, the more I wanted to know why he'd done what he had. And it wouldn't hurt him to apologize either.

Plus, in spite of everything I'd just thought and knew, I— well, I wanted to see him.

So I went to Sports Shack. Will was there, standing by the

shoe department talking to two sales guys around my dad's age. He saw me walk into the store.

I know that because he looked right at me. And then he turned around and walked off.

The old guys glanced over at me, and then back at him, grinning. "Will, where you going?" they said, laughter in their voices, but Will just kept walking, heading out of sight.

The old guys looked at me again.

"Hey, what did you do to him?" one of them asked.

I walked over to them. Their name tags proclaimed them HAROLD and TIM. "I didn't do anything. Yet."

They both laughed, and I decided I liked them. "Can you get him for me?"

"This ought to be good," Tim said, grinning, and Harold nodded before yelling, "Hey, Will, the girl you ran away from is out here waiting for you!"

We stood there for a moment, and then Tim shrugged and said, "Guess he's not coming."

That was going to get him? Please. "Why don't you really go find him? And when you do, tell him he can pretend my sister isn't pregnant all he wants, but when the baby comes and has his webbed toes we won't even need a paternity test."

Tim and Harold stared at me, and I mean really stared. Mouths open, eyes bulging, the works.

"Uh," Harold said, and then I heard laughter coming from the back of the shoe department, near a door that clearly led into a stockroom. Will's laughter. I hadn't heard it in a while, and it was nice to hear him laugh. To know I could still make him laugh.

No! I was here to be tough! To get answers and an apology!

"Excuse me," I said to Harold and Tim, and headed for the stockroom. I thought they might say something else, but when I looked back they were both off talking to other salespeople, their expressions eerily close to the ones the Jennifers wore when they were sharing particularly good gossip.

Will stopped laughing when I came into the stockroom, though a smile still quirked the edges of his mouth. "Didn't know you had a sister."

"Yeah, well, it's hard for her to get out, what with the baby coming and everything."

"Right. So did Harold and Tim run off to tell everyone?"

"I think so. They looked like the Jennifers do whenever they've heard something good."

He laughed. "I hadn't thought about that but they do, don't they?" He started to take a step toward me, then stopped. "What are you doing here, Kate? Telling me off at school wasn't enough? You want to do it again over the store intercom or something?"

"I probably should," I said, and he sighed, looking hurt.

"Don't do that," I said, because I'd expected him to look angry, not upset. "Don't act like any of this bothers you. You're the one who came after me at Jennifer's party and then acted so strange at school that you had to 'ask me out' so people wouldn't think you're a total jackass."

"Wait, did you just air quote me?"

"I guess I should have spoken slower," I muttered. "Figures that gestures would distract you."

"No, hold on," he said. "What exactly does 'ask me out' mean?"

"You know what it means," I said. "And I want to know why you couldn't just leave me alone."

"Look, I'm sorry that my humiliation was hard on you, but message received! You don't want to go out. I get it."

"Your humiliation? You're the one who pretended to ask me out!"

"Who said I was pretending?"

"Oh, please. It was obvious."

"I'm sorry I didn't ask you out in a more Kate-approved manner, but I did mean it."

"Sure you did."

"I meant it, Kate," he said and looked at me like he did right before he kissed me, a look I'd thought meant something. A look I'd thought meant that maybe he really liked me.

"Fine," I said, furious all over again. Why did he have to do this to me? Why did he have to make me think he cared? "How's this? 'I, like, totally want to go out with you!' Is that a proper response, or should I start screaming like I've won the lottery too?"

"Don't bother," he said through clenched teeth, the look he'd been wearing before replaced by one of extreme frustration. "I don't want to go out with you when it's obvious you don't want to go out with me."

"I knew it," I said, and to my horror, felt a sharp stinging in my throat and behind my eyes. "I just . . . never mind. This was stupid."

He stared at me, and now he looked surprised and sort of worried, like he'd just realized something. "I'm going to come by your house around seven on Saturday," he said. "If you want to go out with me, you just have to be there. Okay?"

"You don't know where I live."

"How do you know?" he said, and then leaned over and kissed me.

I went back to work with my ears ringing from Harold and Tim's shock—and then snickers—when they found me and Will in the stockroom. And the rest of me was tingling from all the kissing.

And from the fact that I had a date. Not that it was a big deal or anything. It was just a date. With Will.

I had a date with Will!

# twenty-nine

**I was really excited about my date for about half**
an hour, and then I started freaking out. But between school and
work and weirdness at home, I had almost no time to worry.

Almost meant I still had some time, though, and it turned
out there was a lot to worry about. What was I supposed to wear?
Was anything I owned okay for a date? And what about my hair?
Should I try and do something with it, like wear it up? But what
if doing that made my ears look big or my face look lopsided?

What if my face was lopsided?

And, most importantly, what did "date" actually mean? Was
it a real date? Or was it a pity thing, to make up for how he'd
treated me at school?

I didn't want a pity date, but I was pretty sure this wasn't one even though I was also sure he hadn't really meant it when he'd first asked me out at school. But when he'd asked me out again, no one had seen us or made him feel like he had to do it, so that made it real. Although it had only happened after I'd basically cornered him at work.

The truth was, I didn't know what to think. So I avoided him.

I knew it was the worst kind of stupid, but I couldn't help myself. Things at home were really weird, with Mom and Dad having lots of closed-door conversations in the dining room, and Todd had started to say things like, "We had to let the new guy go today because he wasn't a team player." I wanted something in my life to not be ending or weird or both. I wanted to pretend my life was normal, that I was normal.

Plus I really wanted to go out with Will.

So when I was at work, I avoided leaving our booth, and at school I became a great student, the kind who was studying when she walked into class, ignored conversations around her to focus on the teacher, and even stayed after to ask questions.

Or at least I pretended to become a great student, and faked all those things.

Naturally, since this was me, it didn't work, and on Friday night, Will came by the booth.

Dad was, as usual lately, gone, off trying to convince people shopping in the rest of the mall that they really wanted to buy vitamins. We now had so many unsold boxes that there was nowhere to sit behind the display case, and we sat in chairs by the register all the time.

"Hey," Will said. "Haven't seen you around much."

"It's been busy," I said, and then added, "at home and stuff, you know?" since it was obvious there wasn't a swarm of customers flocking around the booth.

"Sure," he said, and tapped his fingers against the display case. Today his name tag said NO I IN TEM.

"Nice name tag," I said, desperate to change the subject to something—anything—that wasn't remotely date-related.

"We got the 'no I in team' speech yesterday," he said, grinning at me. "It was very motivating. There was even a video. So today Hank is 'NO I IN SALE' and Tim is 'NO I IN SHOE.'"

"Hey Kate," Dad bellowed, appearing at the end of the corridor that led out into the main part of the mall, like he somehow knew that the universe wanted me to be even more uncomfortable and embarrassed. "Did we get more of the Garlic Gels in yet? I know we're down to our last bottle!"

I shook my head at him, and felt my face turn red as Will glanced at all the bottles of Garlic Gels stacked on top of the display case.

"Sales tactic," I said. To my surprise, he didn't laugh, just said, "We do something like that when we have shoes we can't sell. Signs that say 'Only a few pairs left!' and stuff."

"Oh," I said, surprised he was being so cool about my father, which meant that Dad decided to come back right then and embarrass me more.

"I think they were really interested," Dad said as he walked into the booth, completely wrapped up in his Perfect You world like always. "Maybe I should take some bottles with me, not samples, and try to sell them that way. I know mall management doesn't like that but—oh." He paused, finally noticing Will. "Hi there, fellow mall employee! Work at Sports Shack, right?"

Will nodded.

"Thought so," Dad said, like noticing Will's uniform was a major accomplishment. "You look familiar."

"I've been here before," Will said, and held out his hand. "Will Miller."

Dad shook it, his face lighting up. "Miller? Is your father Dan Miller? Because if he is, I'd love to talk to him about doing a promotion with his Ford dealership because—"

"My father's a fisherman."

"Really?" Dad said. "I didn't know there were fisherman in Jackson. I mean, there's the lake, but it's so small and I hear that pollution—"

"He lives in Alaska."

"Oh, that makes more sense," Dad said. "Lots of fish there. In fact, I once met a guy who worked in a cannery in Alaska and he told me that—"

"Dad," I said, cutting him off, "Will has to get back to work."

"I do?" Will said, and then looked at me. "Oh, right. I do. Mr. Brown, would it be okay if Kate walked back to Sports Shack with me?"

"Sure," Dad said. "In fact, I've been trying to get her out of here lately, but she keeps insisting that she can't take a break, which I think isn't healthy, but—"

"Dad," I said again. Was it possible to die of embarrassment? Because if it was, I was going to.

"All right, I'll be quiet," Dad said to me, and then told Will, "Nice name tag, by the way. Very creative."

"Thanks," Will said.

"Okay, we're going now," I said, glaring at Dad. Days of pretending I cared about school and sitting in the stupid booth for nothing, and now I had a new worry. What if, after everything that had just happened, Will decided to call the date off?

I looked over at him. He was staring straight ahead, not looking at me. Great. He was definitely going to tell me Saturday night was off.

I figured it would be best to treat the situation like a bandage and just rip it off. Get it over with. End it before I spent more time thinking about how much I wanted to go out with him.

"Look, about Saturday—" I said.

"That's why you're avoiding me, right?"

"What do you mean?" I hadn't expected him to notice that.

"Well, I haven't seen you since I asked you out, so . . ."

"I've been at school," I said, and when Will gave me a strange look, added, "Well, I have been. And then there's work. Plus, everything at home has been crazy. Like, seriously crazy. I mean, you met my father. Now imagine a whole house filled with people like that."

"Your dad seems okay to me. And I bet he would never make you watch a video on teamwork."

"No, just vitamin infomercials."

Will grinned at me. "I had to sit through a thirty minute presentation on how to measure feet."

"I have a carrot hat."

"Really?"

I nodded. He cleared his throat. "I . . . look, are you avoiding me? I mean, if you don't want to go out with me—"

"I want to go out with you," I said and it was true, but wow, did the truth sound like I really liked him. And I did like him. I liked him a lot. But I didn't want to like him that much. I was afraid to.

Plus maybe I should have let him finish his sentence. What if he was going to say, "If you don't want to go out with me, that's fine with me because I don't want to go out with you"?

"Hey," Will said, touching my arm. "I . . . me too." He looked toward the mall exit, and then back at me. "Do you want to—?"

I knew what he was asking. He wanted to go make out with me. My heart started hammering in my chest. He wanted to kiss me AND go out with me! Why had I been avoiding him again?

"Kate!" Dad yelled. I looked back and saw him frantically waving his arms at me. Great. He talked about me not taking breaks and now . . . I sighed and looked back at Will. His face was red. I had no idea why, but it was cute.

"I guess I'd better go," I said, and started to walk away before Dad decided to yell more—or worse, come after me.

Will grabbed my hand.

"See you tomorrow?" he said, and the grin he gave me when I said, "Okay," sent me floating back to the booth.

"What's wrong?" I asked Dad when I got there. He'd stopped waving his arms around, but was watching me pretty intently.

"Was Will the person from school you ran into the day you sold those Chocolate Chews?"

"What?" Since when had Dad developed a memory?

"You know, the day you sold Perfect You's specially formulated kids' vitamins, the ones with the song. 'Choose Perfect You Chocolate Chews—'"

"Dad, don't sing. And yeah, I saw Will that day."

"You started organizing the storage space around then, right?"

"I think so."

He gave me a look. "Are you two an item?"

Parents! "An item? Dad, ew."

"Are you?"

"We're going out tomorrow night. It's not a big deal." I mean, it was, but I clearly couldn't tell Dad that.

"You're my daughter. Everything you do is a big deal. And no more going off and making out with boys when you're supposed to be working, okay?"

"Dad!"

He grinned at me. "Not as dumb as I look, am I? Now, have you seen my pen?"

I grinned back at him. "It's behind your ear, Einstein."

# thirty

**When Dad and I got home, Mom told him it looked** like someone was going to make an offer for the house.

"Now we really have to think about where we're going to live," she said, and at first I thought she was angry because her voice was so sharp it almost hurt to hear it. But then, when Dad said, "Sharon, honey, don't worry so much. Anyone can get an apartment," and she nodded, hands shaking, I saw that she wasn't mad. She was scared.

I couldn't understand why Dad didn't see it, but as he and I sat eating chicken salad sandwiches, and he tried—and failed—to get her to smile, I realized he did see it. He knew she was frightened, but he couldn't stop pretending everything was fine.

And Mom—she didn't say anything to him. She just sat

there, arms crossed, fingertips trembling, silent. Waiting for Dad to say something that he never would—and that I didn't think he could.

I left the kitchen then, not wanting to see any more. Grandma was in the living room, draping bracelets against a rainbow of shirts piled on her lap.

"Are you working tomorrow, darling?" she asked. I wasn't sure if she was talking to me or Todd, but Todd emerged from his blankets and said, "Of course I am. All I do is work. My life is coffee and this sofa."

From the kitchen I heard Dad laugh, fake and nervous, and then say, "Sharon?"

Grandma stood up, carefully folding the blouses she was holding across her arms, and glanced toward the kitchen. "I think I'll go to bed. Kate, darling, come with me."

"In a second," I said, looking at Todd, and as soon as Grandma left, I asked him, "What's going on with them?"

"What do you think? They're—" Todd said, and then broke off, a sad look on his face. "This has been a pretty crappy year for you, huh?"

"You think?"

He sighed. "Fine. Don't forget to take out the trash in the morning and yes, it is your turn."

"You're so annoying," I said, but he'd already pulled the blankets back over his head.

I woke up late, and both the trash bags I lugged outside broke right before I could toss them in our bin, leaving me a pile of garbage to clean up. Not the best way to start the day of my

ELIZABETH SCOTT

date, and things only got worse from there. Mom wasn't up when Dad and I left for the mall, so I had to leave her a note asking her to pick me up at five, and hope that Grandma didn't lose it.

At work, Dad acted weird, and given how he usually acted, that was saying a lot. He'd seemed okay when we first got to the mall, but then Mom called the booth and whatever she said made him really upset because he said, "I'm going to get coffee," and practically ran away. It took him a long time to come back too, and when he did he just sat and stared at our display case, like he was looking for something inside it.

"Dad, if you need to go out for a while I can handle everything here," I said, and when he looked at me his smile was so painfully false I had to look at the floor.

"Are you kidding me? Miss out on a Saturday, the busiest day of the week?" he said. "This is what I live for."

"Mom's still coming to get me at five, right? I know you guys must have talked about . . . tonight, and I left a note, but I just wanted to make sure."

Dad was silent for a moment. "I don't know if she's coming," he finally said.

"You don't know?"

He shook his head. What was going on?

"Well, can you call her?"

"I really need to reorganize the display case, honey. But you can call and ask."

Great. Not only was Dad avoiding Mom, he was clearly not talking to her. Or worse, was afraid to talk to her. Weren't parents supposed to be, you know, adults?

216

I called home. Grandma answered the phone.

"Hi, it's me," I told her. "Kate, I mean. Can you make sure Mom comes and gets me at five today? Because I need to come home. I—I'm sort of going out tonight."

"Darling, what did you say?" Grandma said. "Your mother's outside honking at me. Why on earth are car horns so loud? And how can she expect me to change my shoes so quickly? I mean, my outfit needs a certain kind of heel and—"

I ground my teeth together. "Remind Mom to pick me up at five, okay?"

"Darling, we'll see," she said, and hung up.

I slammed the phone down, which made me feel a little better, especially since I pretended it was Grandma's head.

"Did you talk to your mother?" Dad said.

I looked over at him, but he was kneeling, rearranging bottles inside our display case, and I couldn't see his face.

"No. Look, Dad, is something going on?"

"Everything's fine," he said, looking up at me, and he smiled so brightly I knew he was lying. I also knew that no matter how much I asked, he'd keep smiling and telling me that everything was fine.

Things went rapidly downhill after that, and by the time five o'clock rolled around, I'd decided I'd walk home if I had to because I desperately wanted to get out of the mall and away from Dad, who'd gotten quieter and quieter as people walked by, seemingly unaware of him standing eagerly by the box of free samples he'd put out. I'd wanted Dad to wake up and see that his dream wasn't coming true, but seeing him so drained, so unable to try to talk to people or even fake smile, was frightening.

"I'm going," I told him. "You want me to ask Mom to call you?"

"I'm sure we'll talk later," he said, skimming his fingers over all the bottles on display like he needed to remind himself they were there.

"Are you okay?"

"I think I can handle working by myself tonight," he said, and his smile was so sad I had to look away. He knew what I was asking, but he wasn't going to answer. I don't think that he could.

I headed out of the mall, determined to ask Mom what was going on, only to find Grandma waiting for me.

"Hello, darling," she said, motioning for me to walk beside her out to the car. "How was work?"

"Long."

"Where are you going tonight?"

"Out."

She laughed. "Darling, I was able to gather that from your extremely garbled speech on the phone earlier."

"I have a date. With the guy who called before, the one who had my shoe."

"That sounds lovely," she said, and I looked over at her. She was smiling at me, and seemed genuinely happy.

"I guess. Mom's going to be mad, though. I haven't said any-thing to her about Will or tonight."

"Darling, don't worry about a thing," Grandma said as we got in the car. "I'll talk to her."

Nightmare visions of Mom freaking out as Grandma mentioned the night I'd arrived home in a rather disheveled manner, not to mention the phone call that made it real clear who I'd been getting disheveled with, danced through my head. "I'll do it."

"The thing is, darling," Grandma said, her hands tightening on the steering wheel, "your mother isn't feeling so well, and I think it's best if you let her rest. I'll talk to her for you later, all right?"

"Mom's sick?"

"She just needs some rest," Grandma said. "Besides, I'm sure she'd want you to go out and have a good time. What are you going to wear? How about those lovely purple boots I bought you?"

"I'm, uh, saving those," I said. "I think they might be better for later in the year." Or never.

At home, Mom was in her bedroom, but her door was shut. I could hear her moving around, though, opening dresser drawers and then closing them, but when I knocked and said, "Hey, Mom, I'm home," she just said, "Hi, honey. Can we talk later? I'm sort of busy right now."

"Oh," I said. "Sure."

By the time I was ready, I'd changed clothes four times. Well, four times plus two more. Also, it was seven o'clock.

7:02, actually.

I went out into the living room and sat on the sofa, reminding myself that no one showed up for a date on time. Or at least, that's what I'd heard.

"What are you all dressed up for?" Todd said, coming out of

the kitchen with a sandwich and sitting next to me. "Wait a minute . . . are you going out? Like, with another person?"

"Why are you here? Shouldn't you be working or out mooching off some girl?"

"You are going out! Awww, Kate has a date, how cute. What's his name?"

"Todd, darling, leave your sister alone and finish telling me about this customer who hurt your feelings," Grandma said, also coming out of the kitchen, a glass of soda filled with ice, just like always, in one hand.

"I didn't say my feelings were hurt," Todd said, flushing as I laughed. "I said . . . hey, stop laughing, Kate."

"Why? Am I hurting your feelings?"

Todd threw a blanket at me, and I retaliated by kicking him and stealing the remote. Soon we were yanking it back and forth, flipping through the channels at maximum speed and volume.

"Children," Grandma said, and then, when we ignored her, sighed dramatically and left the room. Todd and I grinned at each other for a second before we started fighting over the remote again.

"Is someone at the door?" Grandma called a moment later. It sounded like she was back in Mom's room. "I think I hear something."

"Just total silence from Kate's so-called date," Todd said as he yanked the remote away from me. "Admit you made the whole thing up and I'll let you have half the sofa till I go out."

I took it back. "So, are you going to tell your date how a mean customer hurt your little feelings?"

"Don't worry, children," Grandma said, coming back into the living room. "I'll get the door."

Todd and I looked at each other and rolled our eyes. I turned the television down, figuring that would make her happy, and made a face at Todd when he took the remote away again.

"Sucker," he said, and as I stuck my tongue out at him and jammed my elbow into his side, Will walked into the room, followed by Grandma.

Perfect. Just perfect.

"Oh, hey, your date did show up," Todd said, grinning at me. "I guess you didn't make the whole thing up after all."

If looks could kill, Todd would have died a slow, gruesome death. But they couldn't, so I settled for mashing my foot into his.

"Well, I can see we shouldn't wait for Kate to introduce us," Grandma said. "I'm Rose."

Thank you, Grandma. I glared at her, but of course she didn't see it.

"Hi, I'm Will," Will said. "I think we've spoken before. I called—"

"Oh yes," Grandma said, beaming. "The young man with the shoe. You know, you have really lovely teeth. Not that I'm saying you're unattractive or anything, mind you, although I do find young men's hairstyles rather odd these days."

"Um, thank you," Will said.

"Me and Will should probably get going," I said, but Grandma shook her head.

"Darling, we're chatting," she said, and smiled at Will. "Tell me, have you had braces?"

I stared at her. Why, oh why, had the universe gifted Grandma with the power of speech? WHY?

Will shook his head, looking a little confused. Todd shot me a sympathetic look, which just showed how bad things were.

"Okay, we're going now," I said. "Grandma, will you tell Mom I left?"

And then, before she could say anything else, I grabbed Will's arm and headed for the door. I didn't run, because that would have looked desperate.

I just walked really, really fast instead.

# thirty-one

**Outside, I dropped his arm, mostly because I** wanted to keep holding it and knew that would look strange or desperate or both. And right now I needed to appear normal. Or as normal as I could after what had just happened.

"Sorry about all that. My grandmother . . . well, it's like there's her world and then the real world."

"Hey, at least your grandmother talks to you," he said, heading toward a car parked at the end of our driveway. I followed, and then I was getting into a guy's car. I was getting into Will's car!

Normal, I reminded myself. Speaking is normal. Passing out because you have gotten into someone's car isn't. "Your grandmother doesn't talk to you?"

He shook his head. "Nope. My mom's mom died when I was little, and my dad's mom hasn't talked to us in years."

"My mom and grandmother didn't talk for a long time when my mom was younger," I said. "Sometimes I think they should have kept the silence thing going. Family stuff is weird, isn't it? Everyone knows about my dad and his vitamin thing, but no one knows how freakish my grandmother is, and I've never heard anyone at school talk about your . . ." I trailed off.

He grinned at me before he pulled out onto the street. "So, you listen when people talk about me, huh?"

"No! I mean, I hear stuff sometimes, but it's hard not to since you've hooked up with half the girls in school."

"I haven't hooked up with half the girls in school."

"Okay, a third."

He looked at me for a second, then back at the road. "Did your father get fired for trying to sell Perfect You stuff during a meeting, or because he sold his boss a bottle of vitamins that made him sick?"

"What? That's not what happened. He quit his job and then he started selling all the Perfect You stuff."

"But I heard—"

"You heard wrong."

"Exactly," he said. "Do you see what I mean?"

Now I looked at him, thinking about what he'd said.

"Just so you know, the ten-second rule is in effect," Will said. "One more and you officially agree with me."

"You wish," I said. "And okay, you're saying people make up

stuff about how many girls you've hooked up with? You forget, I've seen you in the halls at school."

"How many girls have you seen me with this year?" He looked over at me, grinning. "I know you know."

"I don't!" I did. Four. "But why would people make up stuff about you?"

"Why do people make up stuff about your dad? I figure they need something to talk about."

"How profound."

"Is that your way of saying I'm right?"

"It's my way of saying you're full of crap."

He laughed. And then didn't say anything.

"Ten-second rule," I told him.

He looked over at me. "Okay," he said, his voice quiet. "I did hook up with a bunch of girls freshman year. Some stuff happened right before school started and I . . . I don't know. I was hanging out with Sam a lot back then, and we'd go to parties where all these girls would be throwing themselves at him, and even Sam can only handle so many at one time, so—"

"Let me guess. You helped him out."

"I hate it when you look at me like I'm something you've found on the bottom of your shoe, Kate. I wasn't lying to you before."

"You just said you hooked up with tons of girls after telling me you hadn't."

"It was last year, and it wasn't tons, or a third of the school, or half, or anything like that. But people talked, and you know how that is."

"I suppose next you'll be telling me you only did it until you realized that, deep down, you hated yourself and that being with all those girls made you feel less empty inside. "

"Wow, that's insightful," he said, his voice low and furious. "You know what I don't get about you? Why you always think the worst about me, and why, in spite of that, you still seem to like me. At least sometimes." He turned the radio on, turning it up so loud there was no way he could hear anything I had to say.

But I didn't have anything to say. I just sat there, wondering if he was right about me. Did I always think the worst about him?

I used to. But Will was the only person to ever ask me about Anna. He also hadn't ever said anything bad about Dad, or even laughed at him, and that horrible day when everyone at school found out about Dad's new career, he'd been the one person who hadn't cared about what had happened. He'd just wanted to know if I'd run off crying. If I was okay.

And when things with Anna started to change, when we became friends again, he'd been the one person—the only person—I'd thought of telling. That I'd even wanted to tell. Recently, whenever something happened, he was the first person I thought of. The first one I wanted to talk to.

"I don't always think the worst about you," I said. Actually, I had to shout it, only I shouted when the song that was playing got quiet and so I ended up sounding like . . . well, me.

His mouth quirked up at the corners briefly, and then he leaned over and turned the radio off. "Okay, I heard that."

And then he didn't say anything else.

"All right, what is this?" I said when I couldn't stand the silence any longer. I think I lasted about thirty seconds.

"What's what?"

"The whole silence thing."

He shrugged.

"Okay, so I'm, what, supposed to forget everything you said about last year? I mean, you admitted that—"

"Everything I said? Why would you even listen to a guy who'd use girls to forget how empty he felt?"

"Look, I was mad."

"Never would have guessed."

"And now you're mad."

"Let's just say your little speech didn't make my day."

"I don't think you're that kind of guy, okay? I just—" I took a deep breath. It was weird, but I really wasn't used to talking to anybody. Really talking, that is. "What happened last year? Besides the stuff we both already know about, I mean. You said something happened before school started . . ."

He was silent for a moment.

"My father," he finally said. "I found out that the guy who'd left me and mom when I was six and hadn't ever bothered to send money or even call, was living in Alaska with a girl who's maybe five years older than me, and that they had a kid. He was so proud of that, of his new son, that he'd made a fucking website devoted to him and then had the nerve to track down Mom's e-mail address and send her a link to let her know he'd put his life back together, and hey, wasn't she happy for him and his new family?"

"Oh."

"Yeah. And I . . . look, it messed me up. I'm not saying that as an excuse for last year because—well, because it sounds like something he'd say. Or that I imagine he'd say, anyway. But it really sucked to have my father finally show up in a fucking e-mail about his new family and to have him not say he was sorry or even ask about—" He broke off, shaking his head. "Never mind."

I could guess what he hadn't said. "He didn't even ask about you."

"Not a single question. Not even a 'Tell Will hello.' It's like he forgot I exist. And all last year I went to that website and saw pictures of him and his new family and I just—I didn't even hate him, you know? I mean, I did, but more than that, I wanted to know why he left in the first place."

I nodded, thinking of how I'd felt when I'd first seen Anna hanging out with Diane, of how much I'd longed to hate her and even did, a little, but mostly wanted to know what I'd done to make her forget me, and why it was so easy for her to do it. "I know what you mean."

"Yeah?"

"Yeah." And now I knew there was someone else who understood what it was like to wake up one morning and find out you didn't matter anymore. Strange that of all people, it would be Will.

We slowed down and turned into the parking lot of the pizza place everyone went to.

"Do you want to go in?" he said.

228

"I don't know. I sort of feel like casual conversation about pizza crust preferences and toppings isn't going to work now."

"Yeah," he said. "We could get a burger or something and then go to the park."

"Sure, because I wasn't listening when you admitted that you spent plenty of time last year doing stuff just like this."

His mouth quirked up again. "I never did this."

"What, talked first?"

"Funny," he said. "I meant, I didn't do the whole dating thing."

"That makes sense."

He looked startled. "Why?"

"Because you knew things were going to end anyway, and so why pretend they might work out when they never do?"

"That's . . . not the reaction I was expecting."

"What, you wanted applause?"

He laughed. "No, I thought you'd, I don't know, yell some more or something."

"But you're right," I said. "Things do end. I mean, this year I lost my best friend, even though it turned out to be for just a little while, and then my father quit his job, and now—"

"Wait, you're talking to Anna again? Why?"

"What do you mean, why? She's my best friend. Wouldn't you hate it if Sam stopped talking to you?"

"Sam not talking to me? I think that'd be a dream come true for both of us," he muttered.

"But you two hang out all the time and—"

"I know, I used him as girl bait."

"That's not what I was going to say."

"Really?"

"Yes, Mr. I-Think-I-Can-Read-Minds-But-Can't. I was going to say, aren't your mom and his mom friends too?"

"They were, back when my mom was catering on the weekends to earn extra money and did all of Sam's mom's dinner parties. Now they're business partners, which means Sam's mom spends all her time drawing up menus for people to look at and my mom spends all her time worrying about how she's going to make a puff pastry thing for sixty people all by herself. I even had to miss school a while ago to help out with some brunch thing because Sam's mom can't be bothered to do any actual work."

I had a feeling that day was back when I'd listened to the Jennifers speculate that he'd skipped because of trouble with a girl. "So, you're mad at Sam because of his mom?"

"No, I'm mad at Sam because he's a jerk. I just . . . I guess I realized I was turning into my dad with the whole girl thing and—well, I didn't want to, you know? But he didn't get it. Still doesn't. Plus he and his dad keep telling his mom to quit working with mine, and if that happens my mom will be stuck trying to keep their business going. And she doesn't have the kind of money that Sam's parents do."

"That sucks."

"Yeah. Now Sam mostly uses me as a cover story for when he wants to ditch Anna and—" He broke off.

"It's okay. Anna knows he cheats on her."

"I guess it would be hard not to know," he said. "She doesn't care?"

"She's afraid he'll dump her if she says anything. Hey, how come you asked me why I was talking to Anna again?"

"Because of what she did when school started, and because you don't usually put up with crap from anyone."

"Anna isn't—it's not like that."

He looked at me. I looked away, staring out the windshield and feeling what I'd just said ring weirdly hollow inside me, like it wasn't true. I shook my head and looked back at him. "Speaking of crap, I put up with you, don't I?"

"That's because you want to make out with me."

"I don't—"

"Liar," he said, and then he kissed me and I forgot about everything for a while.

We ended up leaving the pizza place parking lot to get tacos and eat them at the park. I learned Will didn't like guacamole ("It's green and slimy—how is that food?") and that his mother had been Sam's father's secretary before she started catering full-time. ("Probably another reason why Sam's dad is such an ass about everything. My mother isn't around to do all his work for him anymore.")

I also learned why he was working at Sports Shack.

"You know what really sucks," he told me after he'd dumped all the guacamole out of his third chicken taco, "is that I was supposed to get a raise after I finished my training period at the Shack, only to find out the policy's changed and now I have to wait another three months. It sucks because it's not like rent's going to get any cheaper."

"Rent? On what?"

"Our house. You know, a place where people live. You must have heard of them."

I swatted his arm. "You're working to help pay the rent?"

"Thanks for sounding so shocked. You work to help your dad, right? Is it so hard to believe I'd work to help my mom?"

"No. I just—I don't know. I always thought you were—"

"Yeah, I know what you thought about me."

"Am I allowed to finish a sentence?"

He grinned, leaning into me. "I don't know. Are you?"

"I always thought you were a jerk, but you aren't. Not all the time, anyway," I said, elbowing him. "You . . . you surprise me."

"I surprise you?" He caught my arm in his, sliding his hand down so it tangled with mine.

"Yeah. You're not so bad, you know?"

"You like me," he said, grinning again.

"I didn't say that."

"Close enough," he said, and kissed me again.

By the time we left the park, it was after eleven. We got back to my house by 11:20, and were kissing by . . . well, about two seconds after 11:20.

"I have to go," he said after a few minutes, and then kissed me again.

"Okay," he said, a couple of minutes after that, "I really have to go. I'm supposed to be home by 11:30. Plus I have to get up and go to work tomorrow. Are you working?"

I nodded, dazed from all the kissing.

"Can I come see you when I get my break?"

"I don't know, can you?" I said, teasing him, and okay, trying to sound like it wasn't a big deal that he'd asked that, but inside I was cheering.

He leaned in and brushed his lips against my cheek, moving slowly toward my mouth. "You're so cute when you're trying to be mean. I used to say stuff just to get you to look at me like you are now."

I pulled away, frowning at him. "'Cute' is one of those words people use when they know you're smart enough to realize 'you've got so much personality' means 'you're ugly.'"

"Your ability to take compliments is definitely one of the things I like best about you," he said, grinning.

I forced myself to ignore his smile, but it was hard. "And what do you mean, you used to say stuff to get me to look at you? You were a pain in the ass on purpose?"

"Oh, please. For you and me, it was flirting. Besides, it was the only way I could get you to talk to me."

"You're making me sound like a freak."

He leaned over and put one hand on either side of my face and then moved his mouth so it hovered over mine, so close we were almost kissing.

"I don't think you're a freak," he said, and then he kissed me again.

"So what do you think I am?" I said when we separated.

He laughed. "I just think you're you."

"That doesn't really answer the question."

"I think you're stubborn and smart and sort of bossy and beautiful," he said.

"I'm not stubborn or bossy." He thought I was beautiful! ME!

"You're right. You're obstinate and occasionally domineering."

"You're not funny," I said, trying not to laugh. I did anyway.

"You have a nice laugh too," he said, and kissed me again. This time we didn't separate until his phone beeped.

"Sorry," he said, pulling away and flipping it open. He grinned when he saw the screen, and then held it out toward me.

*I will keep doing this until you call and say*
*you're on your way home.*
*Mom*

"I love how she signed it, like I wouldn't know who it's from," he said.

"I can't believe she spelled everything out."

"She's psychotic about that stuff," he said. "Back before my dad left, she was working on a degree in literature. I have to hide all my English papers from her. Hey, is that your grandmother?"

I looked out the window and groaned. Grandma was looking at us from the kitchen window, her orange silk bathrobe shining brighter than the kitchen light. "I should go before she comes out and starts talking about your teeth again."

"So, next time should I show up with my dental x-rays?"

"Who says there's going to be a next time?"

"Who says there won't?"

I was silent for a moment. I liked the thought of him coming over again. I liked the thought of having another night like tonight again.

"The ten-second rule is still in place, you know, so now we have another date," he said.

"Really?"

"If you want," he said, looking at me so intensely I really had no choice but to kiss him.

So I did.

# thirty-two

**I expected Grandma to pounce on me as soon as** I came inside, especially since I'd seen her in the kitchen, but the house was quiet and dark when I walked in, and Grandma's door was closed, no light shining out from underneath it. There was a light on in Mom and Dad's room though, but they didn't say anything when I knocked, and if they were awake, they weren't talking to each other.

So, free from discussing where I'd been with anyone, I went to bed. I was more than happy to, because I wanted to think about Will and everything that had happened tonight forever. Especially those last few minutes in the car. They had been amazing. The whole evening had been . . .

It had felt like the kind of night that could change your life.

I fell asleep happy, with the promise of seeing Will again tomorrow burning warm inside me.

I woke up with a start right before my alarm was supposed to go off and heard a muted thump out in the hall.

"Dad?" Todd said, and there was something in his voice, a mix of bewilderment and panic, that made me tense. Todd didn't panic. Not ever.

"Sorry," Dad said, and his voice was flat, empty of his usual enthusiasm. "I didn't mean to bump into you like that. I'm a little distracted."

"Dad—"

"We'll talk later, okay? I'll come see you at work."

Their voices faded as the two of them headed toward the living room. I got up, threw on some clothes, and cautiously opened my door. Peering out into the hall, I saw that Grandma's room was empty, and wondered where she was.

That's when the shouting started.

"This is not a punishment!" Mom yelled, and I wondered what Grandma had done to make her so mad. No wonder Dad sounded so strange. He didn't like Grandma, but he really hated it when Mom got angry enough to yell.

"You guys, what's going on?" Todd said, and he sounded more panicked than he had before.

"Ask your mother," Dad said, and although he wasn't yelling, he was talking louder than he usually did. "She's the one who's decided I'm not fit to live with anymore!"

Those last few words did come out as a yell. I froze for a moment, stunned by what he'd just said—and by how he'd said it—and then I ran to the living room.

"That's not what I said," Mom said as I came in. She and Dad were standing on opposite sides of the room, Dad by the hallway that led to the front door and Mom by the sofa, one hand braced on the handle of the sliding glass door that looked out onto our backyard. Grandma was sitting in the recliner, and Todd was in the middle of the room, looking back and forth at everyone.

"I asked you to make a choice," Mom continued, her voice shaking now. "You did, and it's a choice I'm not comfortable with, so I think it's best if we . . . if we live apart for a while."

"Since when?" Dad said. "You've never doubted me before. But now," he glared at Grandma, "you've suddenly decided things aren't working? I know your mother gave you money, Sharon, but you don't owe her—"

"Suddenly?" Mom said. "This hasn't been sudden. I begged you not to cash in all your retirement money. I begged you not to buy so many Perfect You products, or to at least wait until you sold some of what you had. I begged you not to make the children work for you. I begged you not to throw that party. I begged you not to buy that ad. And you know what, Steve? You did what you wanted anyway. What I said—what I thought—it wasn't important to you at all."

"How can you say that? You and Kate and Todd are my life!"

"Are we? Then why didn't you listen when I told you we had no money? Why did you ignore the budget I begged you to stick to? Why did you choose to throw away our home—our home, Steve—for goddamned vitamins?"

"I can't believe you're saying this," Dad said. "It isn't . . . none of this is fair. If you'd only—why can't you—?"

"Don't you dare try to blame my child for this," Grandma snapped. "You chose to throw away your retirement money, you chose to ignore everything Sharon said. She showed me the credit card bills, you know, and how you could buy expensive coffee and worthless video games during this time . . . I admit I never thought you were right for my daughter, Steve, but I certainly never thought you'd be cruel enough to wreck her life like this."

"Damn you, I haven't wrecked anything!" Dad said, and we all froze. Seeing him mad was a million times worse than all his fake smiles because it was so clear he was falling apart.

"Look," he said, staring at Mom, his voice softer now, pleading, "I've got it all figured out. We'll rent the house I told you about, the one that needs a little work, and we'll save as much as we can. After a few months of that, plus Todd's paychecks from the coffee place and the money your mother's given you, we'll be able to move somewhere nicer. And then, once business picks up, we'll have just enough to live on and we can use Todd's paychecks to help pay down our debt."

"No," Mom said, at the same time Todd said, "What?"

"I've sacrificed enough for you, Steve," Mom said. "I got a second job. I stretched money as far as I could while you kept spending it, and I am not going to live in a falling-down house and let my son pay off our debt. It's not right. We deserve better."

"I just think that if we all help each other out for a little while longer—"

"Hold on," Todd said, and turned to Dad. "Did I hear you right? You want me to give you my paychecks?"

"Not forever. Just until we get things together. It's for the family, Todd. Your mom and I did what we had to in order to send you to college and now—"

"Hey, you had money to send me to college," Todd said.

"We didn't—"

"You did. Mom told me about it."

Dad shot Mom a hurt look, and Grandma sat up straighter, her eyes darting from Todd to Mom.

"Look, I feel bad that you guys had problems," Todd said, "but Dad, I took the job at the coffee place to save up enough to move out on my own. Not to—not to support you." He swallowed. "I mean . . . I want to help, okay? But I don't want to take care of you."

"But that's not what I'm saying," Dad said.

"But it's what you're asking," Todd said, and looked at Mom, turning away from Dad.

"I'm going to work now," he told her. "Call me if you need anything."

"Todd," Dad said, but Todd just shook his head and walked out.

It was so quiet after he left. Horrible, deadly quiet. I looked at Grandma and was startled to see there were tears in her eyes.

"Is this it?" Dad said, breaking the silence. He was staring at Mom, looking broken. "You really want me to go?"

"No, but I . . . I need you to grow up," Mom said. "And I hope that time apart will help you—"

"Grow up?" Dad said. "This isn't you, Sharon. I know it isn't. You sound like your mother."

Mom flinched. "I'm not saying you have to give up your Perfect You business, Steve. You can still do it part-time. I just . . . I need you to get a job. A real one."

"But I have a real job," Dad said. "And it's—I'm living my dream, Sharon. My whole life, I've wanted to do something that makes me happy, and I have that now. Please don't ask me to give it up."

"I don't make you happy? Our life isn't enough for you?"

"Of course you make me happy. It's always been you and me, hasn't it? And I know the two of us, together, can do anything. Things will turn around, Sharon. Just trust in that. Trust in me."

"I can't," Mom whispered, and Dad staggered back like she'd hit him.

"Why did you do this?" he said, turning to Grandma. "Why did you have to ruin things?"

"I didn't," Grandma said. "You did. Didn't you listen to a word Sharon said? Or are you completely incapable of hearing anything other than yourself?"

"Mother, please," Mom said, her voice cracking.

"Me? You're accusing me of not hearing Sharon?" Dad said. "You sent her away when she was a child, like she was a gift you could return, and now you sit there and try to tell me that I—"

"Stop it," I said, and then said it again, louder, shouting, and Mom and Dad and Grandma stared at me like they'd never seen me before. I don't think they'd even noticed I was there.

"See," Dad said to Grandma. "Look at what you've done

to Kate. Honey, go get in the car and we'll go to the mall in a minute."

"Me?" Grandma said. "Kate, darling, come over here and sit on the sofa and rest for a bit. You don't have to go anywhere."

"Both of you stop it," Mom said, glaring at Dad and Grandma. "Kate, please go to your room and I'll come talk to you in a bit, okay?"

"No," I said. "I'm sick of listening to all of you." And then I walked past them, grabbing a pair of shoes as I went outside. I heard their voices, raised again, as I slammed the front door closed behind me, but I didn't stop to listen.

I didn't want to hear anything they had to say.

# thirty-three

**I sort of wanted someone to come after me, if only** to tell me that everything would be okay, or at least as okay as things could be when you woke up and found out your parents were splitting up, but no one did. I stopped at the end of our street for a second, waiting, but no one else was around, and the front door to our house was still closed.

I kept walking, trying to think of something I could do. Some way I could fix things. But there was nothing. I wished I could talk to someone, that I could tell Will what had happened.

I could call him. Go home, lock myself in my room, and call him. Except I'd have to deal with my parents and Grandma, plus Will was probably on his way to work already.

Also, I was pretty sure that everything I wanted to say

wasn't the kind of thing you went around telling someone after only one date.

I still wanted to call him, though. But how would I even start the conversation? "Hey, I had a great time last night, and by the way, I got up this morning and my mom asked my dad to move out. How are you?"

No, I couldn't call him. At least not with that as my opening line. But I . . . I could ask Anna what to do. I could tell her every terrible thing that had just happened. After all, we were talking again.

When I got to her house she was outside, setting up a couple of lawn chairs in her front yard.

"Hey," I said. "What are you doing?"

She looked up and blinked, clearly surprised to see me, and then she moved away from the chairs and came toward me. "What's wrong?"

"Dad's moving out," I said, and my voice came out faint and wobbly.

"Oh, Kate," Anna said, and wrapped one arm around my shoulders the way she used to whenever I got upset about something, and led me inside.

"How did you know something happened?" I asked as we walked in and she was shutting the door, careful to close it quietly.

"Well, your hair is, um, a little messier than usual," she said, grinning. "Plus you looked about the same when you found out Todd was moving back in, remember?"

"Except then I was mad and now—" I said, my voice cracking as I wandered around her living room, touching the top of the chairs I'd sat in so often, the side of the sofa I'd lain on to watch television.

"Here," Anna said, nudging me with one hip and handing me the cordless phone she and her mom had always kept on their coffee table. "Call your mom."

"I don't want to."

"You said that last time too, but remember how she showed up here, totally furious because you hadn't called?"

I nodded and took the phone.

Grandma answered before the first ring had even finished. "Hello?"

"Hi, Grandma, it's Kate."

"Darling, where are you?"

"I'm at Anna's. What's—is everything okay with Mom and Dad?"

"I'm glad you called to let us know where you are," she said, and her voice was softer now, soothing. "Your father has already left for work but he's going to pick you up after school tomorrow so the two of you can talk about what's going on. That's all right with you, isn't it?"

"Dad's left?"

"I have to go now, darling. Your mother is very upset. Please come home before dark, and call if you need a ride."

"Upset? What do you mean, upset? Is she—wait a minute, is that Mom crying?" I froze, sure that was the sound I heard in the background.

"I—well, yes, darling, she is crying." Her voice got fainter for a moment, like she'd turned away from the phone. "Sharon, sweetheart, she could hear you, and I'm not going to lie to her. What? Darling, you don't have to do this now—" Her voice came back over the line strong and clear. "Kate, I have to go. Don't forget to call if you need a ride."

"Bye," I said, but Grandma had already hung up. I stood there for a second, then clicked the phone off and stared at it.

Anna took it out of my hand and passed me a pint of ice cream, open with a spoon already planted inside. I took it and automatically sat down on the sofa, the place where we'd always discussed our biggest problems, the ones we didn't want her mother to hear.

"Tell me everything," Anna said, and so I did.

Her eyes got wide when I told her about Dad yelling. "I can't picture it," she said.

"I know. I heard it, and I'm not sure I believe it happened. But it did."

"Do you think that maybe your mom is just really mad and that later she'll—hold on," she said, and got up, silently mouthing "Mom" at me.

"Do you need something?" she called back toward her mother's bedroom, and there was a faint noise, a whimper that was familiar and sad. Anna left the room, and after a moment I heard the peculiar scrape of her mom's bedroom door opening. It hadn't worked right since Anna's dad kicked it open during one of the big fights he and her mom had right before he left, but her mom would never get it fixed.

Anna came back a few minutes later, smiling brightly but biting her lip.

"What's wrong?" I said.

"Nothing."

"You're biting your lip."

She sighed and flopped down onto the sofa next to me. "You know me too well. Can you put the ice cream away?"

"I just got to a big bunch of chocolate chips," I said, and grinned at her, offering up a spoonful.

"I can't," she said, glaring at me. "Sitting around eating ice cream was my problem before, remember?"

"Sorry," I said, hurt and hating the way she was looking at me, how she talked about the past like it was all horrible. "I'll put it away."

When I got back from the kitchen she motioned for me to sit next to her on the sofa and then rested her head on my shoulder. "Ignore me, okay? I got home late last night and Mom had waited up because she wanted to talk about some guy she'd met, and then she got upset about being single and unemployed and now she's . . . she's a mess. What if I end up like her, Kate?"

"It won't happen," I said.

"Why not?"

"Because you'd never make your whole life about somebody else," I said. "You're really strong, you know what you want, and you go out and get it."

"I did lose all that weight," she said slowly. "And I got Sam. And I'm going to move to New York with Diane. I've always wanted to move to New York."

"See?" I said, ignoring the pinprick of hurt at how I still wasn't the person she wanted to move to New York with anymore.

"So, what do you think about everything with my parents?"

"It's not really a surprise, I guess. I knew something would happen when I heard about the whole vitamin thing. I just figured it would be something like you guys losing your house, you know?" She laughed.

I didn't.

"Oh, I'm just kidding," she said, nudging me, and I knew I should tell her she was right, that we'd lost the house too, but I couldn't. It felt . . . it felt like she wouldn't see it for the loss it was.

"Everything will be okay, Kate," she said. "Seriously."

"It doesn't feel like it will be. It feels like everything's falling apart." I let out a breath I hadn't known I was holding. There. I'd told her that, how lost I felt. I could tell her the rest now and she'd understand. I knew she would.

"Well, nobody's life is perfect," she said. "Bad things happen, you know."

"Right," I said slowly. "But this year has been really bad. I mean, first you don't talk to me for months, and then Dad quit his job. Plus, Mom sprang Grandma on us—"

"Wait a minute. I didn't talk to you for months? You never even tried to talk to me!"

"What? I did too, and you totally ignored me. You acted like I didn't exist!" I hadn't meant to shout, but how could she say that to me? How could she act like I hadn't tried to be her friend?

"I did that once, maybe twice, and maybe it was mean but so much had changed and Mom was upset that I'd been gone for so long and I—I was just trying to cope, you know?"

"But you looked happy and you . . . you said we'd talk soon

and then it was like you never knew me at all. Plus you did stuff like laugh at me when Diane talked about my dad—"

"All right, I'm not perfect," she muttered. "I get it. You and Sam can form an 'Anna Sucks' club."

"I don't think you suck, I just—are you crying?"

"No," she snapped, rubbing her eyes, and then sighed. "I'm being a total bitch, aren't I? I'm just so tired and last night Sam flirted with some stupid freshman right in front of me and—" She made a choked sound and wiped her eyes again. "Why doesn't he love me enough to be with just me? I know it's because I used to be fat. If I could just make him and everyone else forget who I used to be, then things would be perfect."

"I think—I think Sam's kind of a jerk," I said. "I mean, I know you love him, but he treats you so badly—"

"You don't understand," Anna said. "I know you're trying to be nice, but you just . . . you don't get it."

"Are you happy with him?" My throat felt tight with tears and something else, something that felt like anger.

"He's Sam."

"Yeah, but are you happy?"

"I could be," she said. "It's just—I can feel that fat girl I used to be following me around, you know? I wish I could get rid of her."

"But you have."

"No," she said, looking right at me. "I haven't. I'm still me, Kate. You know that. Deep down, I'm still me."

"But you're great."

She shook her head. "I don't want to talk about this any-more. What did you do last night?"

"I . . . I went on a date." So much for me not knowing about guys, I thought, and watched her face, unsure of what her reaction would be.

"Kate!" She grabbed my hands, beaming. "Why were we even talking about me? Tell me everything! What did you wear?"

This was the Anna I knew. I grinned back at her. "Jeans and my blue shirt."

"Oh, that's good. Hair?"

"Like this. Well, I mean I brushed it and stuff."

"Where did you go?"

"The park."

Her eyes got wide.

"Not like that," I said, and laughed as her grin got wider. "Really! We just talked, I promise. Will and I talked for hours, actually. Well, and ate tacos. And kissed some."

"Will?"

I nodded. "I know I used to say he was a jerk, and I know last year he—"

"Hooked up with just about everyone?"

"Yeah, but he—"

"It's not just last year, Kate. This year I've heard so many things—"

I shook my head. "How many girls have you actually seen him with?"

"Some," Anna said, smiling the way she did when she was angry. "Why are you trying to defend him? I get that you like him, but guys like him don't change, and everyone knows he'll mess around with anyone who has a pulse."

"Like everyone knows how perfect and happy you and Sam are?"

"Fine, be like that," Anna said, her smile fading and her expression going completely closed off, the way it did when she was really upset.

"Don't be mad. It's just that Will's actually really nice, and I think that maybe we—"

"No," she said, shaking her head. She didn't look mad anymore, just sad, like she knew something I didn't. "I know you think you went out with him, but an actual date is more than making out in the park and—"

"I know what a date is, believe it or not. We went out, Anna, and we talked. Really talked, and I like him. I was even going to call and tell him about Mom and Dad this morning but—"

"All right, stop right there. I won't argue about the date thing with you anymore, but promise me you won't do that."

"Why?"

"Because you don't go around telling guys like Will or Sam stuff like that, not ever. They don't know what to do and it makes them act weird and then they dump you for being messed up or whatever. I mean, do you think Sam knows everything about my mom? Guys can't handle hard stuff."

"So now Sam and Will are in the same category? That's a surprise, I mean, what with Will being so terrible and all. And just because Sam can't handle—" I broke off as Anna's eyes narrowed. We looked at each other for a moment, and then her phone rang.

She looked at it, and then back at me, and I knew she wouldn't answer it. Not when we were talking like this, for real. Not when we were saying things we should have said to each other ages ago.

But she did.

# thirty-four

**She answered her phone and disappeared back** toward her room, leaving our conversation behind easily. Leaving me behind easily. I sat there, shocked and hurt.

And angry.

"No, I'm not doing anything," I heard her say. "Of course I want you to come over! Didn't we talk about it already? Yeah, as soon as you can. What? No, you looked great last night. Those jeans are amazing. I wish I had a pair!"

She had to be talking to Diane, and even though I'd heard Anna make fun of how obsessive Diane was, she sounded like Diane was her best friend. And she also sounded like . . .

Well, she sounded like the kind of person she would have made fun of last year.

"Sorry about that," she said, coming back into the living room. "I've got some stuff I need to do so—"

"So you want me out of here before Diane comes over and sees me."

"You were listening to my phone conversation?" Anna looked furious.

"No. I mean, I heard stuff, but I didn't mean to."

"That's kind of creepy. No, actually, it's really creepy."

"You think I want to hear you talking to Diane?" I said. "'Oh, Diane, that sounds super great! Oh, you looked awesome! I totally agree with everything you say because I have no thoughts of my own!'"

"Wow," Anna said, crossing her arms over her chest. "Thanks for coming over and making fun of me. I wish all my friends were as nice as you."

"But you—you're not acting like the Anna I know. You talked to Diane exactly like how you used to say people always talked to her—and how you never would. Remember? You said they were so stupid, and that you never wanted to be like them."

"Right, because it was so much fun to be fat and disgusting and have no friends. Why would I want to be pretty and go to parties and have a boyfriend and hang out with people who matter? It was one thing when I was like yo—" She broke off, looking down at the phone and biting her lip.

"It was one thing when you were like me," I said quietly. "So every time you said popularity was a joke, and that you wouldn't ever want to be like Diane or worse, be her friend, you didn't mean it?"

Anna looked at me. "I meant it. I hated school, hated people like Diane, hated the idea of popularity. But I—I wanted it too. I wanted to be someone. I said I didn't, and that it didn't matter, but I never believed it. Not really."

"I did."

"Yeah, but this isn't about you. Nobody called you fat ass or wide load or laughed when you walked into a room. People came to your birthday parties and you got to go home to a normal house every day. I got to go home and take care of the person who's supposed to take care of me. You went shopping with me to all the fat girl stores, but you never had to buy the clothes, and when we went out to eat, nobody ever looked at you and shook their head like you were disgusting just for wanting food. Why would I ever want to be that girl again?"

"But I—" I paused, stunned by how angry she was. "You always seemed so happy. So sure of yourself."

"What else could I do? Be the fat girl who feels sorry for herself? I already saw what that got my mother."

"If you'd said something to me—"

"Right. Because every time I tried to talk about how I looked, you lied and said I looked fine."

"But I didn't—"

"What?" Anna said, her voice rising. "You didn't mean it? You were just being nice?"

"No, I meant it," I said. "You were my best friend and I didn't care about—"

"What, how I looked? Well, that's noble of you, but I did," Anna said. "Look, I've got to get ready because Diane's coming over, so . . ."

"So that's it? I have to go because Diane wants to hang out? I get dumped because I didn't tell you what you wanted to hear before you went away last summer, and because you think who you were before you lost the weight is worthless?"

"Right, because I'm not hanging out with you right now or anything." She shook her head, frowning. "Should I stop hanging out with everyone else and spend all my time with you? I've told you that you're the one person I count on because I know you'll always be there for me. What more do you want from me, Kate?"

"I—"

"Look, it's okay," she said. "Call me tomorrow?"

I nodded, even though things didn't seem that okay to me. But she'd just said she counted on me, I reminded myself. That meant a lot.

Right?

"Hey," she called after me as I was leaving, and I stopped in her driveway and looked back at her.

"If Sam dumped me and Diane stopped talking to me and I got fat again, you'd still be my friend, right?" she said.

"I'm always your friend," I said, and she smiled at me, then turned around and went back inside.

I started walking home. I wasn't looking forward to what-ever I'd find there, but at least I'd been able to get away for a while. I was glad I could still count on Anna.

Anna, who hadn't asked to come over or even come by work when she was at the mall after that one time. Anna, who never called me unless I called her first. Anna, who didn't want me around her new life and friends. Anna, who seemed to hate everything about her life and herself before this year, and who had forgotten me until . . . well, until she needed to know someone would be there for her.

Anna, who'd never said she was sorry for anything that had happened. For how our friendship ended before, for forgetting me. For anything.

I turned around and walked back to Anna's.

She was sitting outside when I got there, lying on one of the two lawn chairs she'd been setting up when I came over. I remembered when she got them. It was right before she'd turned eleven, and she'd talked her mom into buying them for her birthday party. She'd invited everyone in our class, but I was the only person who showed up. We'd ended up having fun though, because Anna's mom let us eat all the cupcakes she'd bought and then we sat outside on the chairs and waved sparklers around, me and Anna writing our names in the air, watching the letters flare and then disappear.

Diane was in the chair next to hers, pointing at her feet and then at a picture in some magazine. Her car was parked a few feet away from me on the street, gleaming in the sun. As I stood there, staring at them, a car drove by, the guys inside yelling hello to Diane and Anna. They didn't seem to see me even though they passed right by me.

Diane looked up, grinning, and waved at the car. She saw me and her smile faded for a moment, then sharpened into the kind of grin that makes your stomach hurt. I watched as she turned to Anna and said something.

Anna, who'd been looking at the magazine, looked up.

Looked at me. I smiled and waved, and then said, "I was just walking by," because I didn't want to embarrass her in front of Diane.

She didn't say anything. She didn't even wave. She just looked at me and then turned back to Diane, pointing at something in the magazine.

"Hey, you," Diane said, and I looked at her. "Tell your father my mom doesn't want any more Perfect You catalogs, okay? She says the notes he puts in talking about his stupid store are pathetic." She giggled, and after a moment, Anna did too.

Anna laughed at me. Again.

"Anna?" I said.

"Oh, look, Kate's upset," Diane said. "Sorry, sweetie, I didn't realize you were into vitamins too." Her voice was gleeful, pure honeyed evil. This was who Anna wanted to be with?

I looked over at her again, hoping she'd look at me. Hoping she'd say something to show she was my friend. Anything.

But she didn't, and as I stood there, I remembered something else about Anna's eleventh birthday. She'd cried. She'd cried because none of the girls everyone wanted to be friends with had come, then wiped her eyes and said she hated them before sobbing, "Why don't they like me?"

She'd always wanted to be where she was now. I just hadn't seen how much or for how long. I hadn't seen how unhappy she was. I hadn't seen her.

She wasn't going to look at me. She wasn't going to talk to me. She might say she still wanted me to be her friend, and maybe she even meant it, but she didn't really want to be mine.

I didn't think she'd say anything when I turned around and walked away, and she didn't. And that was it. Our friendship was over.

I wanted to feel free, wanted to feel proud of myself for finally seeing what had been so obvious. But I didn't feel free or proud. I wanted to go back, I wanted us to be friends the way we used to be. I wanted to know why things had to change.

I wanted to know why she didn't need me. Why I was so easy to forget.

---

# thirty-five

**I went home.**

The house was empty, but Mom had left a note. I didn't read it. I didn't care where she was. I didn't care where Dad was. I didn't care where Grandma was, where Todd was, where anyone was.

I went home and got the picture I used to have on the back of my door out of my desk and tore it into tiny pieces. I took the stuffed monkey out of my closet and threw it against the wall. It sagged limply to the ground, staring up at me with its stupid stitched-on smile.

I picked it up and yanked its arms as hard as I could, and when they popped free and I was left holding them and the monkey dropped back onto the floor, still smiling up at me, I started to cry.

I cried because Anna didn't want to be my friend. I cried for all the times I hadn't in the fall, for all the moments when I'd hoped things would change and they hadn't. I cried because I thought maybe they'd had and I was wrong.

I cried for my best friend, who I was no longer sure I'd ever known at all.

I cried because even though I hated Anna for not liking me anymore, for laughing at me, for not caring about all the memories that meant something to me, I would have given anything for her to call and say she was sorry.

I cried because I knew she wouldn't.

And when I couldn't cry anymore, when my eyes were sore and my head hurt, I picked up the monkey. I told myself to throw him away, to forget that Anna had given him to me and that I loved him.

I couldn't do it. I put him back in the closet, leaning his arms against his sides so he looked almost whole. And then I lay on my bed, looking around the room that wasn't going to be mine for much longer.

Everything was over. Anna. Mom and Dad. Our house, our family. Everything.

I was still in my room when Mom got home.

"Hello?" she called, and I managed to sit up and say, "I'm here," before I sank back into my bed, tugging my comforter up so I could tuck it around me.

"Are you all right?" Mom asked, peering into my room. Her eyes were red and swollen, like she'd been crying. I could tell from the way she looked at me that mine were the same. "Did you have a fight with Anna?"

"She doesn't like me anymore," I said. I thought I'd cried myself out but I felt my eyes sting as I spoke, and my throat felt thick, clogged.

"What happened?" Mom said, and started to come into my room, then stopped as we both heard footsteps heading toward us.

"Steve?" Mom said, a smile breaking across her face. "Steve, is that—?"

"Darling, it's me," Grandma said. She sounded worried. "I was just picking up the folder you left in the car. Remember that the papers need to be signed—"

"I remember," Mom said, staring at the folder. "I don't know why I thought you were Steve. The mall hasn't even closed yet. I should go get ready for when he gets home."

"Sharon," Grandma said, and tentatively put a hand on Mom's arm. "I think you—"

"I know what you think, Mother. You want me to decide where to live right now and then move there tomorrow. You think it's all over, but you don't know Steve like I do. He's going to come home and when he does, we'll talk and everything will be fine."

"All right, darling," Grandma said, moving her hand away. "I'll put the papers in the front hall. Why don't you go rest a little? It's been a long day."

"I'm not a child, Mother. I don't need a nap."

"Well then, at least lie down with a washcloth over your eyes for a few minutes because I'm sure that if Steve does come home, you'll want him to see you looking your best."

"First, he is coming home, and second, Steve isn't like you,

Mother. He'll care that I've been crying instead of trying to get me to cover it up."

Grandma took a deep breath, hands clenched tight around the folder she was holding. "Would he? Because from what I've seen, he's shown a singular lack of interest in anything you've had to say that requires him to think about his actions."

Mom shook her head. "It's so easy for you to judge, isn't it? But you have no idea how my marriage works. Steve isn't like Daddy. He'll always put our family first. He'll always respect me."

"Oh, Sharon, I hope he does," Grandma said, looking up toward the ceiling and blinking hard, like she was trying to fight back tears. "You have no idea how much I want that for you."

Mom sniffed twice and then let out a shaky breath. "Thank you, Mother."

She looked at me again. "Kate, honey, can we talk about what happened to you later? I need to get ready for your father."

"Sure," I said, the word coming out slowly, my mind still reeling from what had happened with Anna and from what I'd just seen.

"Well," Grandma said to me as Mom's bedroom door closed, "I think I need to sit down for a moment." Her voice was shaking a little. "Are you willing to scoot over, darling?"

I nodded, moving so Grandma could sit next to me on my bed. "Dad's really coming back?"

Grandma stared at the folder she was still holding. "Your mother thinks he will."

"You don't?"

"I think—I think I'm angry at your father, and let's just leave it at that."

"You could fix this," I said.

"What?"

"You could fix this," I said again, sitting up as the idea washed over me. "You can buy the house or give Mom and Dad money. Or both. Then we wouldn't have to move and Mom and Dad wouldn't have to worry about things so much. Everything would be fixed."

Grandma shook her head.

"You won't do it?"

"I can't."

"Why not?"

"How long?" Grandma said.

"How long what?"

"How long would things be fixed?"

"Forever," I said. "We'd have the house and Dad and Mom would be happy again. Things would go back to normal."

"That's a lot of work for money to do," Grandma said, standing up. "And Kate, you know what? It can't do it. I know that better than anyone."

"It'd be different for us. We're not you."

Grandma flinched, but didn't say anything for a moment. When she finally did speak, she simply said, "I'm sorry," and left my room, closing the door behind her. I threw a pillow at it. When Dad came home and he and Mom made up, I hoped the first thing they did was kick Grandma out.

*   *   *

Except Dad didn't come home.

Todd did, though. An hour after the mall closed, I was out in the living room, waiting for Dad and ignoring Grandma, who was sitting in the recliner, when I heard the front door open. I raced out to say hi to Dad, but saw only Todd, standing just inside the doorway flipping through the folder Grandma had left there.

"Oh, it's you," I said.

"Nice to see you too," he said, closing the folder and putting it down as we both heard Mom's bedroom door fly open, heard her call out, "Steve?"

I went into the living room and saw her standing there, a huge smile on her face.

"Steve," she breathed, and then Todd walked in behind me and her smile vanished.

"Sorry," Todd said. "I didn't think—I'm sorry, Mom."

"It's all right," she said, her voice faint. "Do you want something to eat?"

Todd shook his head. "I just came by to let you know I'm moving out. There's a girl at work who's going to let me crash at her place until I find my own. I need to grab a few things and then I'll get going, okay?"

"You need to tell your father about this," Mom said. "When he comes home, we'll talk everything out."

"So now you don't want Dad to leave?"

"I never wanted him to leave," Mom said. "I wanted him to realize that Perfect You can't be his main priority right now."

"But the mall closed a while ago, so if he's coming home, shouldn't he be—?"

"Todd," Grandma said, her voice sharp, "why don't you tell me about your day?"

"Coffee, coffee, and more coffee. Oh, and Kate, I saw Anna this afternoon. What's up with her?"

My stomach clenched. "What do you mean? Did she—did she ask you to tell me hi or something?"

Todd shook his head. "Nope. She acted like she didn't know me, which was weird, and then she seemed a little freaked out when I introduced myself to her hot friend, Diane. Is she eighteen? She said she was, but—"

"She's my age, and she's the one who made sure everyone at school found out about Dad and his stupid Perfect You party." The words came out in a rush, my throat and eyes burning. I knew what today meant—what Anna had done made that obvious—but part of me, a small stupid part, had still held onto a tiny bit of hope.

It was gone now. Anna hadn't said anything. She wasn't going to say anything. She didn't feel bad, didn't miss me, didn't ever want to be my friend again.

"Oh," Todd said. "Sorry."

I shrugged, not quite trusting myself to speak.

"Diane wasn't that pretty, actually," he said. "The coffee fumes just get to me sometimes, you know."

I smiled at him. He wasn't so bad for a brother, especially one who was moving out.

Mom made a strange keening sound, a noise that made my skin prickle with anxiety.

"Mom?" Todd and I said at the same time, and Grandma got

up and moved toward her. Mom backed away, and Grandma sat down again, her expression tense and frightened.

"He's not coming back, is he?" Mom said, and made that noise again, like a sob but deeper, more broken.

"Sharon, darling, come sit down," Grandma said, gesturing for Todd to move toward Mom. "There, why don't you let Todd take you over to the sofa? Kate, go sit next to your mother too."

I did, and so the three of us sat on the sofa. We sat there for a long time, Mom watching the door, waiting, her expression so sad it made me want to cry again.

Todd and I finally escaped to the kitchen, where we made sandwiches and wolfed them down.

"I can't believe Dad's not coming home," Todd said when he'd finished, dropping his plate in the sink. "Why can't he see how stupid those vitamins are? And how could he pick them over Mom?"

"Maybe he just needs time to think. Everything's changed so much—"

Todd snorted. "Like he hadn't known what was coming? Please. Dad's not stupid, Kate."

"Well, now what do we do?" I knew Todd was right. Dad wasn't coming home. He'd made the choice Mom had asked him to, and he hadn't picked her. Hadn't picked us.

"Remember that folder I was looking at in the hallway? There were a bunch of papers in them, and I think the house sold."

"What?"

"I know," he said. "It's . . . it's done. The house is gone. And I think Mom wants to tell us, or should tell us, and we need to go out there and get her to do it so she can get it over with, you know? I think it'd make things easier for her."

"You mean, you want her to get it over with so you can get out of here."

His expression tightened. "That's it. Turn me trying to help Mom into me being an asshole. It's no wonder you have no life, the way you automatically assume the worst about everyone and everything."

"Hey!" That hurt and worse, I couldn't help but wonder if he was right.

Maybe he was. But hadn't this year taught me that the worst was always what happened?

I glared at him. He glared right back.

"Fine," I said. "Let's go back out there and—" I took a deep breath. "You really think this will help her?"

"I think anything that will get her to stop staring at the front door would be good," Todd said. "And look, about before—"

"Me too," I told him, and we went out into the living room.

I noticed, with a great deal of surprise, that Grandma had moved over to the sofa and that she had one arm around Mom's shoulders. And that Mom wasn't trying to move away.

"So," Todd said, sitting down next to Mom on her other side as I sat in the recliner, my hands sweating as I rested them on its arms, "I should probably get going. Do you need anything?"

Mom shook her head. "Will you leave me the number where you're staying?"

"Sure. But what about here, Mom? Any news on the house?"

"Well, I was going to wait until Steve came home, but

now—" Mom said and then broke off, clearing her throat and blinking hard.

Grandma squeezed her shoulder gently and said, "It's all right, Sharon. You can do this. I know you can."

"The house has been sold," Mom said. "A family with three little boys bought it, and they're really excited about moving in. We"—she paused, and looked at me—"we'll be moving out in about a month. Maybe less. Your grandmother and I looked at some apartments today and maybe a little later this week, you and I could go and look at them."

"I can take Kate to look at them if it would help out," Todd said, pulling her into a hug. He was acting so supportive and noble I wanted to hit him.

Mom shook her head, smiling for the first time all evening, and Grandma said, "Todd, darling, how sweet of you to offer." She looked at Mom. "See, I told you the children would understand."

Naturally, that's when I started to cry. I wanted to understand, and I did see that I was going to have to move. I got that my parents had split up. I realized that my former best friend wasn't my friend again, that I'd fooled myself into thinking she was. I even saw that the guy I liked might not like me as much as I'd thought he did, that there hadn't been any phone calls wondering where I was or what had happened because what he'd said last night was just words and nothing more.

I saw what my life was. But why did it have to be like this? What was it about me that was so terrible?

"Oh, Kate," Mom said, her voice shaking and her smile fading. Grandma gave me a look.

"What?" I said to Grandma, wiping my tears away. "I'm not allowed to be sad about this? I should go outside and do cartwheels instead? My life is totally ruined."

"Don't say that," Mom said. "You still have me and your father, even if we aren't tog—" She broke off and started crying again.

"Come on, Sharon," Grandma said, clasping Mom's hands in hers and helping her up like she was too weak or sad to stand on her own. "Todd can let himself out, and we'll let Kate be by herself for a while. That's it, darling, lean on me."

# thirty-six

"Way to go," Todd said after Grandma led Mom back to her room.

"I can't be upset?"

"We're all upset, moron. But Mom's really upset, and it would have been nice if you could have thought about how she feels for a second."

"I know she's upset," I said, "but I just don't get why it's so terrible that I'm sad too. I mean, I have the worst life ever."

He shook his head. "Despite your belief that no one suffers like you do, Mom's hurting, Kate. I mean, really hurting. You think your life is bad? Try and think about what it's like for her. Also, just so you know, I'm not thrilled that sending me to college caused them to lose the house, or that I'm twenty-three, have a college degree, and can only get a job selling coffee."

"So now this is about you again. Poor, poor Todd."

"Your attitude sucks."

"Not as much as you."

The phone rang and he answered it, glaring at me as he did. "Hello? What? I can hardly hear you. Oh. Yeah, hold on a second." He held the phone out to me. "It's for you. I guess you didn't scare away that guy from last night yet."

Will? Will was calling me? He must have noticed I wasn't at work today, and now he'd called! I grabbed the phone.

"Hello?"

"Hi, Kate."

It was Dad, not Will. Disappointment washed over me so strongly I had to lean against the wall.

"Hi, Dad."

"Dad?" Todd said, his voice tight, and yanked the phone out of my hand. "Dad? It *is* you! What are you—you called and disguised your voice? What's wrong with you? Are you afraid someone might tell you that you suck for refusing to see that Perfect You is crap, or that you've made Mom cry pretty much nonstop? Or—" He paused, listening to whatever Dad had to say for a moment, and then hung up the phone.

"You hung up on him?"

"Hell, yes," Todd said. "That jackass said he can't pick you up after school tomorrow and that you don't need to come to work anymore because he doesn't want to 'burden' you. And then he swore he pretended to be the guy you went out with last night so he could get you on the phone without 'upsetting' Mom. What a liar. He's just doing everything he can to avoid her. Avoid us." He smiled at me, but it was forced. "Hey, at least you won't have to work at the mall anymore, right?"

"Do you think he'll ever come see me or you or Mom?"

"Yeah. He'll probably act like the house isn't gone and like he and Mom—well, actually, I don't know what he'll do about that. But he'll show up. If nothing else, he'll have to come by and pick up his video games. You know he can't live without them. Plus, you and me are pretty much his favorite people in the whole world. Or at least I am."

"Funny," I said, but I felt a little better.

"I'm going to take off," Todd said. He dug around in his pocket and pulled out a piece of paper with a phone number on it. "This is where I'll be. Call if anything happens or if you need anything, okay?"

"I need a ride home from school tomorrow."

"I meant something big, not driving you around," he said. "See you, Kate."

"Bye, loser."

He grinned at me. "Yeah, you definitely aren't getting a ride from me any time soon."

After he left I flopped onto the sofa, exhausted, and after a while, I heard Mom's bedroom door open, and Grandma came back out into the living room.

"Did Todd leave, darling?" she said as she sat down next to me.

"He did. Here's the phone number." I passed the piece of paper to her.

She smoothed it out and laid it face up on the coffee table. "Who was on the phone?"

I looked at Grandma, who just nodded wearily, understanding what I didn't say. "What did he want?"

"I don't have to work at the mall anymore and he can't—won't—pick me up after school tomorrow."

She sighed. "I can pick you up, darling."

Just what I needed, Grandma at school. I could see her now, rolling down her car window to offer "advice" to everyone passing by: "Darling, no one wears that color anymore," and "Darling, do you mean to look like you got dressed in the dark?"

"I'll take the bus."

"Did he ask to speak to your mother?"

"No. He actually pretended to be someone else to get me on the phone, I guess because he thought whoever answered might yell at him."

I looked over at her. She was staring straight ahead, her expression impossible to read. "It didn't work, though. Todd pulled the phone away as soon as I said, 'Dad?' and yelled at him, then hung up on him."

I thought she'd say "Good," but instead she pressed the tips of her fingers to her face, just like Mom used to do whenever she talked to Grandma on the phone.

"I guess you're pretty mad," I said.

"No, darling," she said. "I'm sad. I want your mother to be happy, and despite my reservations she seemed to be, and now—well, now she isn't happy at all. And with this move coming up . . . it's going to be very hard on her. Thank goodness I've found that I quite like shopping for apartments. We saw one today that had a terrace that would be perfect for an outdoor seating set I saw in that home decorating magazine I bought last week. You know, the one from England?"

Wait a minute. "Are you—I thought you were going home."

"Oh no, darling. I'm staying for a while longer. You know, your mother and I have never actually lived together before, at least not since she was very young. I think it will be good for us."

I stared at her, numb. This was it, then. It was really over. No more house, no more family. Now it was going to be me and Mom and Grandma, all living together in an apartment. Good-bye old, normal life. I wished I'd appreciated it more.

"Darling, you're sitting in a dreadfully slumped way," Grandma said. "I know this may sound silly, but sitting up straight is truly important. Why, posture alone can make a dreadful outfit look—well, slightly less dreadful. So why don't you sit up and—"

"I just found out I officially don't have a home anymore," I told her, sitting up straighter as I spoke, my back become more and more rigid as the words poured out of me. "My best friend not only doesn't want to talk to me, she acts like she never knew me at all. My parents aren't together because my father likes vitamins more than us. Oh, and to top it all off, the guy I went out with last night said we'd see each other at the mall today, but we didn't, and he hasn't called and I know what that means."

"What does it mean?"

I spoke slowly, and through gritted teeth. "Nothing good."

"So, when you called and asked why he hadn't called, he said something cruel? I'm sorry, darling. I thought Will seemed nice."

"Oh, right, I called him, Grandma. What a really great idea."
I pretended to pick up a phone. "Hi, Will, I didn't see you today
and I was just wondering if you noticed because I'm totally
pathetic."

She acted like she hadn't heard most of what I'd said. "Why
didn't you call him?"

"Because I don't need any more bad news. I've already got
no friends, no life, and no family, making this year officially the
worst year of my entire life. Why can't things be like they used to?
If this year had never happened, then—"

"Things change, darling. That's what life is."

"Well, I hate it. And this year, my life hasn't been change,
Grandma. It's been an end. A long, horrible end. The life I had is
gone. Over. Done."

"Darling, I'm going to tell you something important," she
said. "Things end. People leave. And you know what? Life goes
on. Besides, if bad things didn't happen, how would you be able
to feel the good ones?"

"But I've lost my parents, my best friend, my house—"

"Don't be melodramatic, darling. You haven't lost your
parents."

"Fine, they're just 'changed.' But where's the good stuff you
mentioned? Because I'm sitting here trying to think of something—anything—and I can't. In fact, whenever I think life can't
get any worse, it does."

"So, you're telling me that no matter what, you can't be
happy? Well, darling, it's no wonder you're miserable. It's what
you want."

"It's not like that," I snapped. "I want to be happy."

"So then try."

"Try? That's your advice? Try to be happy? Great, Grandma. Thanks."

"Darling, the world doesn't owe you anything."

"Wow, that so doesn't make me feel better."

"It's not supposed to," she said. "That part is up to you."

She stood up, glancing down the hall. "I'm going to check on your mother. Think about what I said, all right, darling?"

"Sure," I muttered, and when she left, I waited for a minute and then went back to my room, shutting the door firmly behind me before climbing into bed and pulling the covers up around me even though I wasn't cold and was actually still dressed. It just felt nice to be wrapped up in something safe.

I couldn't believe Grandma's idea of advice. Telling me the world didn't owe me anything and that I had to try to be happy to be happy? What kind of crap was that? I could try to be happy forever but it wouldn't change the fact that I'd been wrong about Anna wanting to be my friend again, and it definitely didn't seem like it was going to get my parents back together or even talking.

Try to be happy? Please. Wasn't that what I'd been doing ever since the disaster that was the first few days of school?

No.

The word washed over me as I lay there.

No, I hadn't tried to be happy. I'd thought about what had happened with Anna, wondered what I could have done differently, wished for things to go back to the way they were.

I hadn't tried to be happy for Dad and the changes he'd

made either. I didn't think I'd ever find any happiness in his obsession with Perfect You or what it had cost our family.

I supposed there was some happiness in not having to work at the mall anymore but, weirdly enough, that stupid job was the only thing that had actually brought me any. If it hadn't been for the mall and the hideousness of working there, plus the dismal state of my life in general, I never would have gotten up the nerve to talk to Will that first time. (All right, I basically invited him to make out with me, but it sounded better the other way.)

It was funny to realize that the stupid booth and those stupid Perfect You vitamins had helped me get to know Will. Had helped me realize how much I liked him. I'd even got up the nerve to confront him and ended up going out with him because of it.

But I'd only done that after Todd had basically told me to try living, to let people know who I was, and I'd realized Grandma had said something similar, urged me to go after what I wanted.

Try to live. Try to be happy.

I moved out of my cocoon of covers and looked at the phone. Trying to be happy sounded pretty good, but my father's attempt at happiness hadn't worked out too well for him or anyone else. And trying with Anna hadn't either.

But that's what happens, Grandma had said. Things end, people leave, and life goes on. You need the bad things to feel the good ones.

Try, she'd said.

I picked up the phone. I put it down. This was too hard. What if I'd read too much into last night? What if Will didn't want to talk to me?

Then it would be better to find out now, wouldn't it?

I picked up the phone again, and dialed.

It rang. I felt sick. What was I supposed to say? My head and heart were so full from everything that had happened today, from everything that had happened all year, that I didn't know where to start.

"Hello?" he said, and the minute I heard his voice I knew what I had to say, and it wasn't hard at all.

"Hey, it's Kate."

"I know," he said, and I could hear the smile in his voice.

THE END

# thirty-seven

**Okay, so that wasn't exactly the end. In fact, it was**
more of a beginning, and you know what? It was a good one.

Other things did end, though. I stopped looking for Anna
first thing when I got to school. I stopped looking for her in the
halls. I still see her, though. She's still dating Sam. Diane is still
her best friend. She seems happy, but I don't know if she is. We
never speak.

Mom and Dad are officially separated. Dad lost his space at
the mall when he couldn't pay next quarter's rent, and moved out
to Faron, where the big mall is. There's a woman, Gloria, who
runs a Perfect You store there, in a booth just like Dad used to
own, and he works for her. Every time I go out there, we sit in his
tiny apartment and he tells me about the displays he wants to do

and the new products he's sure will sell. Sometimes we go over to his boss's house and Gloria and her husband give me free samples to take home.

I never do.

Mom still won't let me drive by myself. I refuse to let her forget that she promised I could the moment I turn seventeen. I only have a few weeks to go now. Me and her and Grandma live in an apartment together, and it's not too bad. I have my own room, which is nice, but I still have to share a bathroom with Grandma. That's the same as it always was.

Todd wants to be a photographer now, and probably bores his coworkers at the coffee place to death talking about it. I know he bores me whenever he comes over, which is usually to mooch food. He's living with the girl he met at the movie theater back when we both worked at the mall. Her name is Wendy, and she wants to be a director. Sometimes she invites all of us over to watch her films, which usually star Todd sitting around trying to look pensive. I think they're perfect for each other.

Will and I have been dating for six months. He's still the kind of guy who will come up to me after class and say, "So, what happened in there? I lost interest as soon as the teacher started talking," but he's also the kind of guy who will decide that since it's a Wednesday, we need to go eat tacos and then drive out to the park and watch the sun set.

He's also still a really good kisser.

He makes me happy.

I still miss Anna. I still miss my old house; the front hallway, the kitchen, my room. I still miss my parents being together, and

Grandma still drives me crazy just about all the time. I even sort of miss Todd being around, though of course I'd never actually tell him that.

But things change. Stuff happens. And you know what? Life goes on. In fact, that's what life is. Who'd have thought Grandma would be right about anything, much less something so important?

I guess vitamins didn't ruin my life after all. They just changed it. Changed me.

So I can't say this is the end or even an ending because it isn't. It's just life, and you know what? I'm going to do my best to try and really live it.

BEGIN

# Like what you just read?
## Here's a sneak peek at Elizabeth Scott's next novel:

## Something, Maybe

Everyone's seen my mother naked.

Well, mostly naked. Remember that ad that ran during the Super Bowl, the one where a guy calls and orders a pizza, then opens the door to see a naked lady with an open pizza box ("The pizza that's so hot, it can't be contained!") covering the bits you still aren't allowed to see on network television?

That was her. Candy Madison, once one of Jackson James's girlfriends and star of the short-lived sitcom *Cowboy Dad*. Now she's reduced to the (rare) acting job or ad, but she was relatively famous (or infamous) for a few days after a football game with a pregame show that lasts longer than the actual game.

Whoo.

I'd love to say the ad caused me nothing but grief at school, but aside from a few snide comments from the sparkly girls (you know the type—unnaturally white teeth, shining hair, personalities of rabid dogs) and some of the jock apes (who, of course, were watching the game, and like both pizza and naked women. Not a stretch to figure they'd be interested), nobody said anything to me.

But then, nobody really talks to me. That's good, though. I've worked long and hard to be an invisible presence at Slaterville High, an anonymous student in the almost two thousand who attend, and I want it to stay that way. (The school website actually boasts that we're larger than some colleges. I guess overcrowding is a good thing now.)

However, the ad has caused me nothing but grief at home. When it aired, traffic to Mom's site, www.candymadison.net, tripled, and she worked long and hard to keep it coming back, giving free "chats" (where she sits around in lingerie and answers questions about her so-called career and Jackson) and pushing her self-published autobiography, *Candy Madison: Taking It All Off*. We actually sold ten of the twenty-five cases of the book still stacked in our garage.

And the press coverage? Mom loved it. The ad only ran once, because some senator's kid saw it and . . . you know where I'm going, right?

Of course you do, and naturally the ad became extremely popular online. *Celeb Weekly* magazine did five questions with her, and Mom pushed her website and book and then talked about how she was always looking for "interesting, quirky character roles."

The week the story ran, Mom bought ten copies of the magazine at the grocery store and wandered around the house grinning and flapping the interview at me. The phone rang almost hourly, her brand-new agent calling with other offers (mostly for work involving less clothing, which Mom turned down) and an invitation to appear on a talk show.

Not a classy talk show, mind you, but still, it was a talk show. She said yes until she found out they show was about "Moms Who Get Naked: Live! Nude! Moms!" and backed out. Not because she objected to being called a mom. Or because she knew—because I'd told her so—that I'd die if she did it.

It was the nude thing.

"I've never done any nude work!" she said to her agent. "I'm an artist, an actress—all right, yes, the ad. But I was wearing a pizza box! I want to be taken seriously. What about getting me on the talk show with the woman who says 'Wow!' all the time and gives her audience members free cars? I could talk to her."

The "Wow!" lady wasn't interested, Mom's new agent stopped calling, and today, when we go to the supermarket, *Celeb Weekly* doesn't have her picture.

"I don't understand," she tells me. "I got so much e-mail from my fans after that interview, and they all said they'd write to the magazine and ask for more. Do you think I wasn't memorable enough?"

I look at her, dressed in a tight, bright pink T-shirt with CANDYMADISON.NET in sequins along the front, and a white skirt that barely skims the top of her thighs. Her shoes have heels that could probably be used to pierce things.

"You're very memorable, Mom. Did you get the bread?"

"I don't eat bread." Is she pouting? It's hard to tell. She's had a lot of chemicals injected into her face.

"I know, but I do," I tell her, taking the *Celeb Weekly* she thrusts at me.

"Sorry," she says. "I'm just in a bad mood. They could have at least run one picture!"

"I know, but they . . . ," I say, and trail off because there's Mom, in the back of the magazine under "Fashion Disasters!" The picture they're running was taken at the premiere of a play she did way (way) off Broadway a week ago. The play ran for exactly one night. She played a nun (now you see why the play lasted one night) and wore a dress with what she called strategic cut-outs to a party afterward.

The caption under the picture reads, "Note to Candy Madison: Sometimes pizza boxes ARE more flattering!"

"What?" Mom says, trying to look at the magazine again. "Did I miss something? Is there a picture of me? Or, wait—is Jackson in there?"

"Um . . . Jackson," I tell her, and she looks at me, then pulls the magazine out of my hands and sees the picture.

And then she starts jumping up and down. Never mind that everyone in the grocery store is watching her even more than they usually do, most with resigned "Oh, why must she live *here*?" expressions on their faces, and a few "Oh, I hope she jumps higher because that skirt is covering less and less" grins.

"I'll go get the bread," I tell her, and walk away. She'll be done jumping when I get back, because she'll have seen the caption. At least this means we won't have to buy ten copies of the magazine. I would rather have food than look at pictures of celebrities. (Call me crazy, but I just think it's a better choice.)

And I would much rather look at pictures of Mom than of Jackson James, founder of www.jacksonjamesonline.com, the home of JJ's Girls, and current star of *JJ: Dreamworld*. He just turned seventy-two, acts like he's twenty-two, and once upon a time Mom had a child with him. Check out any online encyclopedia (or gossip site) if you don't believe me. The photo you see— and it's always the same photo—is of me and Jackson. It was taken when I was a baby, but still. It's out there.

When I get back, Mom has seen what they said about her, but she still wants a copy of the magazine.

"I don't think that many people look at the captions, do you?" she says as we're heading out to the parking lot, stroking the glossy cover of *Celeb Weekly*. "I can't believe I'm in here again." Her smile is so beautiful, so glowing. So happy.

Mom almost never looks happy. Not really.

"I bet plenty of people will see the picture," I say, which isn't a lie. I'm sure plenty of people will. But I bet they'll read what's under it too. She doesn't need to hear that, though. Not now.

"I'll see you after work, okay?" I say, putting the last of the groceries in her car.

She nods, and when she hugs me, I tug her shirt down.

When you're a seventeen-year-old girl living in a town famous for nothing but its proximity to the interstate and an enormous collection of strip malls and subdivisions, there aren't a lot of high-powered job opportunities.

There are, however, many, many jobs in the fast-food industry, and one of them is mine. I work for BurgerTown USA (a division of PhenRen Co., which makes fertilizer—tell me that doesn't make you think twice about your BurgerTown Big Bite) as a drive-thru order specialist.

In other words, people tell me what they want to eat; I type in the appropriate code, then read them their automated total. The catch is, I don't actually do it at the restaurant.

When you go to a BurgerTown in New York or California or Massachusetts or Wyoming or Georgia (really, anywhere except Hawaii and Alaska), your drive-thru order comes to a call center like mine, and I'm the one who takes your request for extra-large fries.

Well, me or one of my moronic co-workers (this doesn't include Josh).

BurgerTown has these call centers because of "cost efficiency," which seems to mean they want on-site BurgerTown employees—the ones stuck in the actual restaurants—to have more time to wipe off tables. Or mop floors. Or clean bathrooms. Management is very proud of the fact that they no longer need to hire outside cleaning crews for any reason.

Needless to say, on-site BurgerTown employees don't like us call-center employees much. Mom once mentioned I worked for BurgerTown when she was cheating on her diet of the moment by eating fries, but reported that "the girl who took my order made a face when I said you worked in the call center."

"Did your food taste funny?" I asked.

"Funny how?" Mom said. "Hey, have you seen my red white and blue thong?"

"Never mind," I said, but if I ever go to BurgerTown—which I won't, because I'm so sick of asking people if they want fries or pies or Big Bite combos that the thought of eating there makes me not hungry, which usually takes some serious effort—I wouldn't say I worked at the drive-thru center. Ever.

Why?

Well, you see, saying something like that is a surefire way to get the BurgerTown special—the spit meal.

We even have a secret code for it at the center. When someone's a real ass, the kind of person who says, "Now, what kind of meat do you use in your hamburgers? Will my tomato be fresh? Oh, and I want two pieces of lettuce, not one. And make it fast, 'cause I'm in a hurry!" we put in their order and then hit **.

It's one of those things you just find out after you've worked at BurgerTown for a while (all right, a day) and everyone does it.

Well, not everyone.

Josh, my co-worker and soul mate (though he doesn't know it yet), says that eating at BurgerTown is punishment enough.

"All that meat and grease and saturated fat destroys your body," he says, and I totally agree with him, really, but sometimes after I've dealt with a total ass who thinks ordering four dollars' worth of food means I owe them an ingredient reading or whatever—well, sometimes they still get the special.

Finn gives them too, which really does mean I should stop, because Finn is so—well, he's your average seventeen-year-old Slaterville male, and they can be described in one word: Blech. His interests don't include plans to help others, and as far as I can tell, his favorite thing to do is be annoying, especially to me. I'm pretty good at ignoring him.

Mostly.

"Anyone seen Polly today?" he asks. "Josh? Hannah?"

Josh and I shake our heads, and Finn grins at me. "She must be on break."

I laugh. Josh doesn't, and I sigh, wishing I could be serious like him. But the Polly thing is funny. She's always "on break" because even though she supposedly works here, she's never here. I think she's come in maybe twice the entire time I've worked here. I can understand why she doesn't come in, though. She's twenty-two, her claim to fame is that she was once homecoming queen, and now she works (well, "works") here. Some life.

She gets away with never being here because her father, Greg, is our boss, and I think he's afraid to call her out on how she doesn't work because it would mean discussing Polly's favorite activity, which is hanging out with her forty-seven-year-old married boyfriend, whose wife happens to be Greg's wife's younger sister.

It's just like a soap opera, only more boring because Polly is about as smart as a sponge and Greg spends his workday sitting in his closet of an office smoking pot.

Adults are so classy.

"That'll be $10.22," Josh says, and smiles at me as he checks to make sure the order went through. I guess he doesn't think I'm awful for laughing about Polly. Good.

I know I've already mentioned this, but Josh really is my soul mate. He's smart and kind and, best of all, isn't a complete dog like every other guy in the world.

Josh cares about things. He writes poetry (I've seen him working on it in government), is always going to coffee shop meetings for political and social discussions, and donates half of his paycheck to online social organizations.

He even reads—he's always carrying around these huge novels with tiny print and the kind of covers you only see on books you have to read for school. But he reads them because he cares about his mind. I love that.

He's also pretty cute.

Okay, he's gorgeous. Hard-not-to-stare-at gorgeous. He's got black hair and deep brown eyes and the most beautiful smile. Plus he's tall (but not too tall) and thin (but not scrawny), and just So. Out. Of. My. League.

Josh doesn't date girls like me. He dates girls with hair that's usually almost as dark as his; tall, skinny girls who care about political causes and wear short, gauzy dresses that I could never get away with. Plus, they always have cool names like Arugula or Micah.

Hannah is not a cool name. Hannah is an ordinary name.

I actually wish Hannah was my only name.

But it isn't. My mother, in all her "wisdom"—and because she was facing a paternity suit—named me Hannah Jackson James. Before I moved to Slaterville, I never thought about my name. It hadn't mattered before. Not at school, and definitely not to Mom. I even . . . well, I even sort of liked it.

I didn't like it when we moved here. Jackson was more popular back then. His website, castle, and collection of girlfriends were not quite the joke they are now, but in Slaterville, which prides itself on being a sunny, welcoming community (there are actually signs when you get off the interstate)—well, let's just say some people didn't want Jackson James's former girlfriend or his kid around.

Mom didn't care—she was dealing with other stuff then—but me? I cared. Teachers raised eyebrows. Kids in my new seventh-grade classes said—well, they said a lot of things. Mostly about Jackson, which didn't bother me because by then I hated him.

But some of the stuff was about Mom, and that did bother me.

It went away after a while. Not until I'd had a miserable time in seventh and eighth grades, not until I'd decided to become the Invisible Girl, but it did go away. And now, if someone does say something, I can handle it.

The thing is, though, I would love a normal mom. A mom with a job that doesn't involve sitting around in her underwear reminiscing about how one time she and Jackson went to a club and had sex on the dance floor, or how she got the pizza ad. (The director had a picture of her from *Cowboy Dad* as his desktop wallpaper when he was a kid.)

But I don't have a normal mom. And when we first moved to Slaterville, all Mom had was a broken heart and me, and she did what she felt like she had to. What she knew. And that involved a Web cam, underwear, and charging $24.95 per month to join The Candy Club.

I used to wish we'd move back to New York, but now I'm glad we didn't. Jackson goes there a lot more than he used to, seeking excitement and/or plotlines for his television show, and I don't want to be anywhere near him.

"Hannah, order," Finn says, and nudges me with his big horse feet.

"I know," I say, even though I'd missed the little beep that signals them, and start my spiel.

"Welcome to BurgerTown, home of the Better Burger! What can I get you today?"

When I'm done, Finn nudges my foot again.

"What are you thinking about?"

He truly is annoying. If you could put pictures in the dictionary to define words, Finn would be there. He'd also be under "jerk" and "jock," which are synonyms at Slaterville High. He's only a second-string football player, which means he sits on the bench, but still.

"You," I tell him. "You, oh glorious Finn, King of Crappy High School Football. Now stop butting your chair and your big-ass feet into my space and leave me alone."

"You know what they say about big feet," he says, and then blushes. It's the one thing he does that's almost endearing. Almost.

"Yes. No brain," I say, and he blushes more.

"I'm going to get a soda," he says. "Want one?"

"Nah," I say, even though I do, and watch him get up. Finn is barely an inch taller than I am, and on my first day, Greg said we should sit next to each other since our hair and heights almost matched.

That should give you an idea of his "management style," and explain why Polly is able to get away with . . . well, everything.

Finn and I do have similar hair, I guess. We're both blond, but Finn's hair is dark blond, and mine is the shade Jackson's used to be. (Actually, it still is, but he's seventy-two, so you know he dyes it. After all, what seventy-two-year-old man has bright blond hair?)

We also have blue eyes, although mine are dark blue, just like Jackson's again, and Finn's are light blue. They are actually not bad looking—Teagan says Finn is hot, but what does she know? She doesn't have to work with him.

"You know," Finn says, leaning over my terminal, "one day you're going to ask me out. We're meant to be together. Like peanut butter and jelly."

"Like peanut butter and jelly? What kind of line is that? When's the last time you ate?"

"I am kind of hungry," he says, blushing again. "But I'm telling you, you and me—"

"Meant to be stuck sitting next to each other. Believe me, I know that. Now go get your soda and eat something. And never mention anything involving fate and sandwiches again."

"Deal," Finn says, and ambles off to the vending machines. We have a break room, complete with a moldering sofa and matching chair, but nobody ever goes in there because you have to punch in your employee code to get in there, and however long you stay gets taken out of your pay as a break. We're all supposed to go in there if we work eight-hour shifts, but when you're getting paid crap, you don't take breaks.

Or you do, and just make sure you avoid the one place where they're monitored. Greg is actually supposed to keep an eye on us, but you can guess how often he checks in.

"Order at Finn's station," Josh says, and I let out a little sigh, letting his voice wash over me. He even sounds good. His voice is soft, and he has this way of making everything sound so meaningful. I could listen to him talk all day.

"Hannah, I'm sort of—," he says, and gestures at his own computer, and I realize he means someone needs to get the order.

"Sorry," I say, and slide into Finn's chair. Slipping on his headset, I say those magic words. "Welcome to BurgerTown, home of the Better Burger. What can I get you today?"

I switch Finn's orders over to my terminal while I'm punching in the order for three chicken sandwiches for the guy

I'm talking to, and give him his total as I'm sliding back into my own seat, my headset settling into place as the customer drives off to pick up his BurgerTown Tasty Chicken Sandwiches.

"Lull," Josh says, and I nod, tossing Finn's headset back onto his seat. I would put a knot in the cord, but the last time I did that, Finn smushed his chair right up next to mine and started making static noises every time I took an order, and all of my customers thought they weren't being heard.

It was actually sort of funny, but Josh pointed out that he'd ended up having to take most of the orders. "Some of us don't mind working," he'd said, glancing at Finn, "but it's not fair to not do anything."

"Unless you're Polly," Finn said. "Then it's fair. Which means there's a flaw in your argument. Plus someone has to do something to keep us all from dying of boredom."

Josh had just shaken his head, which I'd loved. I wish I could deal with Finn like that, but I lack Josh's ability to shrug off Finn's goading/immaturity/general annoyingness.

"I love this time of day," Josh says, and I try to think of the right thing to say.

"I love you" sounds a little intense for the conversation.

"Can we make out?" sounds like something Jackson would say, and even if I am thinking it, I never want to sound like Jackson. Ever.

"Me too" is what I come up with. And it's true—the half hour before the night crew (10 p.m.–6 a.m.) comes in is always the slowest one, when people have eaten dinner no matter how late they work (for the most part), and the late-night munchers are still doing whatever it is they do before they drive around ordering food late at night.

"I can't believe I have to meet Micah after this," Josh says. "I'm tired, and I've got a ton of homework to do."

"Me too. Not meeting Micah, I mean. But the homework thing," I babble, and Josh smiles at me.

Ahhhhhhhhhhh. It's almost enough to make me forget about Micah and how she's waiting for him.

Almost. Micah is Josh's girlfriend, and she's dark-haired and intense and plays the guitar and has political and social cause stickers plastered all over her car and can get away with wearing tiny floaty patchwork dresses. You know, the kind of thing you can only pull off if you have a certain counterculture vibe.

And I do not have it. I look like I could be a stripper, or would if I wore my hair down and didn't always make sure my shirts were big enough to hide the fact that I sprouted breasts in ninth grade. (Until then, I was like a fencepost.)

Mom says I should be proud of my body, and that when I'm her age I'll have to actually work to keep it, meaning I won't be able to eat whatever I want and will get wrinkles like normal people do.

I can't wait till then. It's not that I have abnormally enormous breasts or anything like that. (Mom's teeter on the edge of absurdity, but hers have been enhanced.) It's just that I . . . well, I have enough trouble with people looking at me and seeing Mom, or worse, Jackson. It's like they don't see me, and therefore, I see no reason to throw out there the fact that, body-wise, I look just like Mom did at my age.

Especially after she went on to use those looks to land a winner like Jackson.

That is so not what I want.

"Here," Josh says, and tosses me a small box. "I remember you said the vending machine was out of these the other day."

"Animal crackers," I say, hoping I don't sound giddy, but really, this must mean something, right? It has to.

"What are you so happy about?" Finn asks, coming back in and flopping down into his chair. "Hey, thanks for taking over my orders."

"Josh got me animal crackers," I say, and smile at Josh. "Thank you so much."

"It wasn't anything," Josh says. "I just saw them and thought of you."

"So Hannah reminds you of a zoo animal?" Finn asks.

Josh just shakes his head—so perfect! I, however, am not, and kick Finn.

"What? It was just a question."

I wonder what would have happened if Finn hadn't come back to work when Josh gave me the cookies, or better yet, if he'd gotten crushed by one of the vending machines and I never had to see him again. I also eat all the animal crackers except one. I would eat them all—I'm starving—but if I save one, then I have something to remember about Josh giving me a gift. And it is something I want to remember.

Now if only he'd like me.

I sigh. Why doesn't he like me? Besides the me not being his type thing, that is. And him being too smart to ever be interested in Jackson James's and Candy Madison's daughter. Why couldn't Mom be a social activist? And why couldn't Jackson be . . . well, how come I have to be related to him?

If Jose had been my dad, life would have been so much better.

"Good night," Josh says as we all head out into the parking lot at exactly 10:01, and I think he smiles at me again.

"Bye, and thanks again," I call out, and watch as he gets in his car.

"Careful, you're drooling," Finn says. "Is your crap bucket going to start, or do I need to hang around and jump the battery again?"

"My truck is not a crap . . . ," I say, and trail off. It *is* a crap bucket, but it was cheap, and all I could afford. "It's running fine, and I'm not drooling."

"How come you like Josh so much, anyway? All he does is sit around drinking overpriced coffee and bitching about how awful things are."

"He cares about the world."

"If he cared about the world, he'd donate the ten thousand dollars he must spend on coffee every year to charity. That would be doing something."

"And what are you doing to help people? Oh wait, I forgot. Nothing."

"Hey, I don't run around claiming I'm going to change the world or—"

"Exactly."

"Can I finish?"

"I don't know. Can you?"

Finn laughs. "I was going to say, if I want to do something, I just do it. I don't have to announce it to everyone."

"Except during football season. Oh wait, I forgot. You don't play."

"Hey, I can't control the fact that people are scared of my natural talent. Besides, I figure it's easier to let everyone else do the work."

I roll my eyes at him. "Bye, Finn."

"You're sure your truck's going to start?"

"One time it didn't, *one,* and you have to bring it up all the time?" I say, and unlock my truck door. It opens with a creaking groan, and Finn says, "Sounding good, as always," before he ambles over to his own car, which is new(ish) and has a paint job that is all one color.

"You better start, damn you," I whisper to the truck as I slide the key into the ignition, and, thankfully, it does. I head out of the parking lot, Finn behind me, and turn right, heading toward the mall, getting away from work and Finn.

I touch the animal cracker I've saved as I drive. I can't wait to see Teagan. She'll know if what happened means something.

# ABOUT THE AUTHOR

**Elizabeth Scott** grew up in a town so small it didn't even have a post office, though it did boast an impressive cattle population. She's sold hardware, pantyhose, and had a memorable three-day stint in the dot-com industry, where she learned that she really didn't want a career burning CDs. She is also the author of *bloom*; lives just outside Washington, DC, with her husband; firmly believes you can never own too many books; and would love it if you visited her website, located at www.elizabethwrites.com.